THE HERO REBELLION 1

HERO

BELINDA CRAWFORD

SECOND EDITION
Published by Hendrix & Faust, Publishers in 2026
Text copyright © Belinda Crawford 2015

ISBN: 978-0-6484881-8-7 (ebook)
ISBN: 978-0-6488745-3-9 (paperback)
ISBN: 978-0-6484881-2-5 (audiobook)

This is a work of fiction. Names, characters, businesses, places, events, locales, and incidents are either the products of the author's imagination or used in a fictitious manner. Any resemblance to actual persons, living or dead, or actual events is purely coincidental.

PRINTED AND BOUND BY INGRAMSPARK.
Australia: Ingram Content Group AU Pty Ltd, Melbourne, Victoria. US: Lightning Source LLC, La Vergne, Tennessee / Allentown, Pennsylvania / Jackson, Tennessee, United States. UK: Lightning Source UK Ltd, Milton Keynes, United Kingdom. Europe: Lightning Source UK Ltd, with facilities in Germany, France, and Spain.

The authorized representative in the European Economic Area is Lightning Source France, 1 Av. Johannes Gutenberg, 78310 Maurepas, France.
compliance@lightningsource.fr

For Mum & Chuck.
Thank you for believing.

Books by Belinda Crawford

The Hero Rebellion
(Hunter)
Hero
(Race)
Riven
Regan

The Echo
Cold Between Stars
Dark Between Oceans
Echo Between Worlds
(Brother)

Gamer

I Am Maggie Volume 1

Demons & Battleskirts
Volume 1
Volume 2
(coming late 2026)

Gods of Sundered Heaven
Through Soul to Flesh
(coming June 2026)

Short Bits
Short Bits Collected Edition 1
(collecting volumes 1–4)
Volume 5
Volume 6

www.belindacrawford.com

IN THE BEGINNING

Humans colonised Jørn; they travelled across the galaxy intent on a better way of life, away from the influence of Earth. But the drones they sent ahead, the ones that told them that Jørn was their new paradise, missed something. Something important.

The colonists arrived, settled on the surface. And started dying.

The culprit, a native spore, carried on every wind to every corner of the globe.

Genetic engineering, blending DNA from Earth and Jørn species, saved their crops and livestock, but for humans there was no cure. Instead, they took to the skies, turning their five great colony ships into cities that floated above the spore's reach.

Now, three-hundred years later, humans flourish on Jørn; their cities expanding, growing taller and wider. They have even conquered the planet's surface, building giant biodomes safe from the spore and the native wildlife.

But in this age of technological wonder, not everything is as it seems.

CHAPTER 1

It was windy on the foredeck, and cold, but the air smelled like freedom and Fink was warm against Hero's back.

The ruc-pard purred, a rumble that vibrated from his giant chest into hers, and all the way down to her toes. She snuggled deeper into the hollow between his fore and midquarters, enjoying the feel of his thick winter coat. Golden-red and silky, she sank into it, the hairs brushing her bare arms with every giant breath he took, the longer, coarser hair on his ruff tickling her cheek. Fink's black, hairless tail wrapped around them both, the heavy weight of it draped across her feet, warming her toes.

Lazy images swam through her mind, carried on the distinct pink and mawberry of Fink's thoughts – the taste of them sweet, the touch of them a soft fizz winding through her brain. She might have stopped and played for a moment in his memories, if the huge skytowers of Cumulus City weren't spread across the horizon.

She'd seen all the holotours, interrogated all of the guides, but she'd never thought the city would be so… there wasn't a word *big* enough to describe it. Surrounded by its sprawling mass of satellite 'burbs, Cumulus City rose thirty thousand feet through the atmosphere, an endless patchwork of grey and green connected by the silver threads of bridges and the restless movement of the skylanes.

Below, spires shot planetside and massive generators kept the city and its 'burbs aloft, while giant tethers prevented it from drifting with the winds.

The city was her ticket, her chance, to see Jørn, to explore the planet's surface without minders or gadgets or her mum looking over her shoulder. She rubbed the dull plasteel bracelet wrapped around her wrist. Or so she hoped.

She breathed deep and hugged her bare arms against the chill as freedom came closer and closer on the horizon.

'Hero.' The Lamb, the latest in her bevy of minders, stood in her peripheral vision clutching a heavy coat, the wind flattening her white-blonde curls against her head. Her mouth was pulled tight and her big green eyes were wide, almost swallowing her face. The way she eyed Fink looked to Hero as if she were waiting for him to flash his fangs and pounce. She held herself like one of the Old Terra creatures Hero had named her for, stiff and tense, leaning away from the 'pard as if the extra millimetre would save her if he did. A brave lamb, wary but not scared.

Hero wondered at where Tybalt – butler, tutor, substitute parent – had found someone who didn't quake before six-hundred kilograms of genetically engineered ruc-pard, bigger at the shoulder than Hero was tall, and twice as long. This woman wouldn't be as easy to get rid of as the others.

'Hero, you need to come in.' Determination gathered on the Lamb's face, in the firming of her jaw and the tiny crinkle at the corner of her eyes. When she stepped forward, Hero let herself be mildly impressed.

Fink flipped his thick, hairless tail, letting it land with a solid *thwack* on the deck not two feet from the tips of the woman's shoes.

The Lamb stopped, her gaze locked on Fink.

It was hard to tell which characteristic people found most intimidating about him. It could have been the teeth, the claws, the sheer six-legged bulk… or it could have been the reputation: the stigma of a species mixed in a lab by not just a crackpot but The Crackpot – Woolsey.

They'd all been crackpots back then, those first-gen colonists, but Woolsey had topped them all. No one else would have thought to mix a little bit of rat with a little bit of leopard and a whole lot of alien to create something big and strong and scary enough to walk the surface with impunity.

Hero wished she could be like that: big and strong and scary instead of just strange and small and *special*. Old Terra, how she hated being special.

The Lamb cleared her throat. 'Hero, come back inside, you'll catch your death out here.'

She'd catch her death in there too, swaddled in comfort and care and her own bloody good.

'Don't make me ask again.'

'Or what?' She pinned the Lamb with a look that promised trouble.

The Lamb's lips firmed. 'I'm just doing my job.'

'Get a new one.'

'And let you freeze to death?'

'I can take care of myself.'

'Is that why your lips are blue?' The Lamb took another step forward, and this time when Fink swished his tail, she barely flinched. 'You can see the city just as well from the port-side lounge.'

But she couldn't smell it there, couldn't feel it in her wind-chilled bones.

'At least take the jacket.' The woman was close enough to touch; the jacket brushed Hero's arm as she thrust it forward. 'Tybalt'll kill me if you're an icicle by the time we reach the dock.'

An unpleasant smile crossed Hero's lips.

For a moment, the Lamb said nothing, just looked at her, a stupid, stunned expression of her face, before the jacket dropped to her side. 'Really? You're going to freeze just to make trouble?'

Hero smiled wider. That hadn't been the plan, but now that she'd mentioned it...

Behind her Fink shifted, a liquid movement of muscle and tawny fur, and planted his cold, wet nose against the back of her neck.

She jerked forward and spun around. 'Fi-iink.'

He rumbled and fixed her with his black gaze, popping an image into her mind of her standing before him, lips as blue as the Lamb suggested, her dark shoulder-length hair a wind-snarled mess, and goose-pimples the size of mountains covering her bare arms. Then another image: one of him lounging inside while she shivered on the foredeck, alone.

Her expression grew dark. 'You wouldn't.'

'Wouldn't what?' A line of confusion marred the space between the Lamb's brows.

She spared the minder a look of disgust. 'I wasn't talking to you.'

'I'd forgotten Woolseys could do that.'

Just like everyone else. Most people never got past the claws or the teeth to the thing that made all of Woolsey's creations so special, and so dangerous: their ability to communicate without sound. Most companions had some sort of psionic abilities, but only Woolseys could talk to their humans.

In her mind, the image Fink projected grew. A fire and a large bowl of triple-chocolate marshmallow ice-cream appeared in the scene, held between his forepaws. Leisurely the real Fink, the one on the foredeck, rose to his feet and stretched before ambling towards the forward cabin.

'Traitor,' she said.

He barely flicked an ear.

At her side, the Lamb coughed.

She looked at the Lamb, glaring when she caught the vestiges of a smile hidden behind a politely raised hand.

'Looks like Fink agrees with me,' the Lamb said.

Hero growled and snatched the coat from the Lamb's grip before following Fink inside. The airship's sliding doors didn't slam but she'd spent a few moments fiddling with their DNA – jacking into the biological goop that was their brain and adding her own little twist to the genes that controlled the locks – and, with a twitch of her little finger and a thought to the biocomp on her wrist, they jammed beautifully.

The Lamb stared at Hero from the other side of the porthole, wide-eyed, mouth agape, the wind ripping at her thin jacket as she tugged uselessly at the door.

Shrugging her heavy coat over fading goose-pimples, Hero smiled at the woman and turned away.

Fink had her pinned with that gaze again.

'What?' she said.

He cast a look over her shoulder at the Lamb.

'You let her in then.' She brushed past him, heading for the galley. 'I'm going to find that ice-cream.'

Fink lay sprawled in front of the holofire, the flames silhouetting his ears as he twisted to lie half on his back, bathing his belly in the heat from the friction of solid light. The only sounds were the lazy swish of his tail across the carpet and his purr, the vibration filling the room. On the other side of the lounge, curled up in an enormous chair, Hero watched as the city drew closer. An empty tub, the only remnant of the ice-cream, sat on the table at her elbow.

The view from the portside lounge was as good as the Lamb had suggested, filling the floor-to-ceiling plasglas with traffic and the brown, green and grey of the satellite 'burbs.

Large and small, the 'burbs circled the city, connected by slender bridges and pipes, held together by the relays that connected them to the mag-web – the network of magnetic energy that kept the city aloft. On the web's furthest edges, the outer 'burbs, lacking the stability of their inner cousins, moved up and down in a slow-motion bob.

There were farms down there, crops and orchards and all the other things the city needed to function. They still grew food on the surface as well, in huge biodomes with filtered air and filtered water and filtered dirt, safe from the Pollen.

As they joined the skylanes, the throng of hover-sleds and barges swallowed the private airship with nary a thought and the farms below gave way to industry. After the ring of industry there were houses, single-storey at first, with yards and grass, and then double-storey and triple-storey and even larger, until the towers of the inner 'burbs – great spears of plasteel and steelcrete piercing the sky – rivalled the city itself.

The airship flirted with the edges of the metropolis, moving higher and higher, heading for the docking towers near the city's peak. After four days cooped up on her mother's airship with nothing to do but watch holos and avoid her tutors, the docking towers couldn't come fast enough.

She didn't notice when the lounge door silently slid to one side, but Fink did. The downturn of his ears and the way he curled his thick, hairless tail over his nose told her louder than words who it was. She sank low into the chair, wishing she too had a tail to flick over her nose. Tybalt had that effect.

She watched out of the corner of her eye as he set a glass on the table between them and sat, loosening his coat and flicking out the ends in one smooth movement. A point of light flashed just under the skin, where his ear met his jaw, but he didn't open his palm and answer the call. Instead, he propped his chin in one large-knuckled hand and waited like an Old Terra monk, dark and patient.

He wasn't her dad, or even an uncle, but she knew him better than either. She knew that he could sit there, as if he didn't need to blink or breathe, for the rest of his life.

Tybalt shifted, swinging his leg over his knee. 'Imogen's nice, you know. I hired her myself.'

'Who?'

His mouth firmed. 'Ms Lambert.'

'Oh right, the Lamb.' She kept her gaze on the window. 'Don't worry, I'll make her quit so you don't have to fire her.'

'Hero.' She didn't have to look at him to see the lines between his brows crinkle in a frown; she could practically hear the flesh fold together. 'We had an agreement.'

'One that didn't include the Lamb.'

'You promised to behave.'

'Who says I'm not?'

The expression on his face was more pained than angry and his eyes were tired. Unbidden came the mawberry-flavoured memory of the corners of Tybalt's black eyes crinkled in a smile instead of a frown. She glared at Fink. Sprawled before the holofire, the 'pard just flicked an ear.

'Locking your minder outside does not constitute good behaviour. Neither,' he said, 'does skipping your meds.'

'Did the Lamb tell you that?'

'No, but I did find these.' He held up two small green pills.

She stiffened, clenching her hand against the urge to check her pockets. The dreaded things must have fallen out when she palmed them at lunch.

He placed them on the table next to the glass and sat back, looking at her expectantly. 'When you're ready.'

She crossed her arms. 'I don't need them.'

He sighed, a long-suffering sound. 'It will only be worse later. If we have to give you another injection you'll be straight back to the estate and you can kiss the academy goodbye for another four years.'

The thought of the small green capsules made her shudder, but the 'stick… The memory of the cold, thumb-sized nozzle pressed against her neck, the way it hissed when it shot the meds into her bloodstream, made her stomach clench until she thought she might be sick. It was bad enough hearing voices, answering questions that no one asked, and having every friend she'd ever tried to make give her that look, the *special* look. It wasn't fair that they tried to stuff her brain with green goo as well, tried to make her stupid and numb with those tiny capsules. She crossed her arms and wished that if she threw them into the holofire, they'd burn.

'As you wish. I'll leave them here in case you change your mind,' Tybalt said. 'As for Imogen, give her a chance. The city's not like the estate; it's bigger and busier and until we know how that will affect your health your mother has insisted upon greater supervision.'

'Mother can go stuff herself,' she muttered.

'Hero.'

'What?' She whipped to face him. 'I have you, four freaking tutors and this.' She thrust out her wrist; the biocomp, a thick bracelet, gleamed dull silver in the afternoon light. 'Counting my every breath, making sure I sleep right and eat right and do my homework. What do you need another minion for? Unless you think I'm going to crack it while you're blowing your nose?'

Tybalt took the bracelet in one hand, twisting and turning her wrist as he inspected the concoction of metal and biogel. 'You've been tinkering.'

She jerked her wrist back. 'So? The stupid thing was a clunker; it couldn't even query the Library.' In fact, the only thing it had done was report her every movement and transmit enough medical data to crash an AI. Besides, she'd only made a few small modifications, it wasn't like she'd fiddled with the locator. Not after the last time; they'd been on her like fleas as soon as she'd tickled the genetic coding. 'You could have at least made it sub-dermal this time,' she said, glancing at the light dancing behind his jaw.

'You're too young,' he said. As she opened her mouth to argue, he added, 'You'd already be trying to grow an upgrade. At least this way I can slow you down long enough for your parents to change the encryption on their credit lines. They don't appreciate you spending their money.'

'Well, that makes us even then, 'cause I don't appreciate being my parents' deep, dark secret.'

He sighed. 'That's not what this is about.'

'Yeah.' She turned back to the window. 'Sure.'

'You need to trust me.'

'No,' she said, 'I don't.' Not after he'd spilled the Terra-damned beans. No one would have known she'd been hearing the voices again, that her old meds had stopped working, if he hadn't opened his big fat mouth.

At first, she hadn't noticed the meds not working. It had

happened slowly, slowly enough that the voices slipped through without her noticing, and when she did… Well, they hadn't seemed as scary as they had before.

She'd stopped taking the meds then and everything had been going well, until she slipped up and answered Tybalt's question before he'd even asked it. When he hadn't insisted she take her meds right then and there, she'd thought that he'd keep her secret. She should have known better.

That morning, she'd known something was wrong when she woke up and Fink wasn't sunning himself on the veranda outside her room. She'd learned later that they'd locked him in the stables, just in case she panicked and he ate the doctor.

She had panicked when she found the doctor sitting at the breakfast table, his big black bag beside the fruit bowl and a green-filled hypo-stick next to his plate. She would have run straight back out, except Tybalt was there, blocking the way.

He was meant to be on her side; he'd always been on her side – until that morning when he'd held her down while the doctor shot her up with green goo.

Another sigh. 'You're going to make this difficult.'

She smiled grimly. She was going to make his teeth hurt.

'Do as you like then.' Pressing his hands to his knees, Tybalt rose until he loomed, straight-backed and stiff-shouldered, over her. 'We'll be docking in half an hour. Have your bags ready.'

CHAPTER 2

The city house always reminded her of her mother, pale and tidy and perfect, with its straight lines and giant windows framed in the shiny honey-brown of carbon-wood. Even the fur-roses that lined the garden beds outside were perfect, their trumpet-shaped heads opening in unison as dusk fell and casting a pale golden glow over the hallway.

The perfection made Hero's fingers itch, made her feel small and grubby, and filled her with the urge to race through the house with mud on her feet and Fink at her back. Except Fink wasn't allowed in the mansion and Hero doubted there was any mud to be found in her mum's garden.

Her fingers itched all the more when she sat down to dinner, Tybalt at her back and two small green pills next to her water glass. He stood behind her chair, his hand firm on her shoulder, until she raised the dreaded things to her mouth. The glass came next, and she swallowed.

Tybalt's grip left her shoulder and he walked around the table to sit, with his customary coat flick, facing her.

She did her best to scowl and look sullen as she slipped the pills, nestled in the palm of her hand, into the depths of her pocket. She'd learned that trick when she was ten.

Across the table, the Lamb attempted to pierce her with a suspicious gaze.

Hero just lifted her brows and smiled.

The Lamb's gaze softened, but the suspicion didn't fade. 'Are you ready for school?' she said.

'I don't know, did you remember to pack my bag?'

Tybalt scowled. 'Hero…'

'That's her job isn't it? Bag packer.'

'Enough,' he growled.

She took a breath to argue, but the Lamb's face gave her pause. There was a hint of speculation in her eyes and a smile around her mouth. Her heart just about stopped in her chest when the Lamb's gaze dropped to the table, as if she could see through it and to the pills tucked into her pocket, and then rose back to hers. The smile around the Lamb's mouth widened, and Hero didn't have to guess what she was thinking to know she was in trouble.

A server, as tidy and perfect as the house, walked into the room, three plates stacked on his arms. Hero stared at the one set before her. Her nose curled of its own accord and she poked the steak, slightly grey with spinach-like veins of green, making it ooze on its bed of orange brussel-toes and relish. She almost gagged as she looked up at Tybalt. 'Seriously?'

'It won't kill you,' he said, the faint curl of his nose belying his distaste for the steak he was slathering in beet-mous, the purple sauce dripping over the side and pooling on his plate.

'But womba-cow?'

'I think I'd rather eat the plate,' the Lamb muttered.

'It's your mother's favourite,' Tybalt said, ignoring the Lamb as he passed Hero the sauce.

Her mother… 'She's home?'

'Yes.' The first bite went into Tybalt's mouth, and she thought she saw him shudder as he chewed then swallowed.

'Is she having dinner with us?'

'I believe Chef took a plate to her office.'

Hero slumped. 'She's working.'

'She's a busy woman.'

'Yeah, super busy.' She pushed back from the table. 'I'm not hungry.'

'Hero—'

'Give it to Fink, he's always hungry.'

Outside the dining room, the stairs curling upwards to the second floor beckoned. She took them two at a time and silently padded down the hallway, the carpet soft under her bare feet. The door was open, just a crack, and through the gap she could see her mother, standing before her desk, the womba-cow steak untouched amid a forest of holoscreens.

She had her hand on the door, ready to push it open when a voice, one that wasn't her mother's, gave her pause.

'…significant time and resources invested in this project Mrs Regan. He was hoping for a little more… progress.' The man had a voice as rough as Fink's tongue.

She crouched and tried to peer around the gap, but the door obscured all but the desk and her mum, her suit creased and wisps of blonde hair escaping her bun. Hero caught the tell-tale glow of the comm-system, staining the carpet a faint electric-blue.

'Unfortunately, Mr Meren, the site is proving to be more difficult to access than we had anticipated.' Her mum's smile was polite but meaningless, the kind Hero remembered well. 'My groundside chief assures me his recovery team is working as quickly as they can, given the constraints of the location and weather, not to mention the wildlife. I'm sure your employer appreciates the risks involved; one torn envirosuit or an overly curious avian and not only is the expedition set back, but someone could lose their life.'

'Indeed.' There was a pause before Mr Meren spoke again. 'While I applaud your regard for your employees, I hope you have had better luck with the data already recovered.'

'My technical department is working on it. The data slides the team found were badly damaged, and it's taking longer than expected to access the information. They have confirmed that the lab in which they were found belonged to Woolsey's assistant, which would explain why it wasn't packed up in the evacuation. Records suggest Dr Tymon was even more paranoid than his boss.'

'Any information regarding Ayumon?'

'None, beyond what we already know.' Her mum's voice was confident, but Hero recognised the little quirk at the end of her brow, the one she got when she was lying.

'That's… disappointing.' Silence stretched on the other side of the comm, broken only by the murmur of more whispers. 'Perhaps we should consider hiring another firm to handle the matter.'

Her mum's spine straightened until it was as rigid as plasteel. 'If you wish, but in such a case, I will be obliged to inform the relevant government authorities of our find.'

'I must wonder at your insistence on such outmoded obligations. Your company has never bothered with such before.'

'Times change, Mr Meren, as do obligations.'

'So we see, a side-effect of motherhood no doubt. Tell me, how is your daughter? I hear she's set to start at Morague Academy.'

Her mother's knuckles whitened where they gripped her arms. 'Forgive me, Mr Meren, but I prefer to keep my family life out of my business dealings.'

'Really? But isn't Bayard Explorations a family business, Mrs Regan? Or did you not take over as CEO when your aunt passed away?'

Hero's mother didn't answer, but now her smile wasn't just tight, it was brittle.

The man sighed. 'Continue your investigations, Mrs Regan. We will remain with Bayard for now.'

The holocall ended with the soft fuzz of the comm-system powering down, and Hero watched her mum's shoulders slump as she uncrossed her arms and rubbed at her mouth. Hero frowned. She'd never seen her mum look worried before. Angry, frustrated, even sad, but never worried.

Something tart, sweet and the bright shiny green of a strapple tickled at the back of Hero's mind. Something that reminded her of the Lamb. She scanned the room, her eyes catching on a shadow and the tip of a shiny black shoe, hidden behind the crack of another door. Her gaze travelled up until she caught a glimpse of tight white curls. But if the Lamb had followed her up the stairs, why hadn't Hero heard her? And why was she spying on her mum instead of hauling Hero back to the dinner table?

Hero leaned forward to catch a better glimpse, but her foot had gone to sleep while she crouched there. She fell against the door, nudging it just enough for the hinges to groan.

For a second, maybe two, there was silence on the other side of the door, and she let herself hope her mother had missed the tell-tale sound. But her mother had ears like a lethyt, and the soft hush of footsteps crossing the carpet was all the warning Hero had before the door was yanked open.

'Hero.' For a moment, her mum looked worried and then her mouth turned down into a familiar look of disapproval. 'Eavesdropping is not an acceptable pastime.'

'Then maybe you should encourage me to take up a hobby,' she said as she picked herself up, hopping a little at the pins and needles shooting up her leg and doing her best not to wince. 'Like barrier racing.'

Her mum's mouth flattened like it'd been crushed by an airship and the tiny lines between her brows deepened into caverns. 'We've had this discussion. Be glad you're even in the city.' She turned on her heel, leaving the door open, and walked to her desk.

Hero followed. Her mum's study was a square room, with a wall of steelglas overlooking the huge lawn, lit for the night by the endless lines of fur-roses. Another wall held her mum's collection of Old Terra books – with actual Terra-made paper between their covers – as smelly as they were crumbly.

She plonked herself into one of the soft, cherry-red chairs, as old as the shaggy rug was new, in front of the desk. 'You were happy enough for me to be here two months ago, but now you're too "busy" for me? It's not like you actually do any parenting, you know.'

'I do more for you than you realise or, apparently, are capable of appreciating,' her mum said as she shuffled the screens above her desk.

'Like what? Hiring tutors who force me to take meds?'

'Everything I do, and everyone I hire, is to keep you safe.'

'Sure, if safe means shut up and bored so your friends can't see your embarrassing little secret.'

Her mum sighed and her hands stilled. 'That's not what this is.'

'No? Then let me race.'

'No.'

'But Mum—'

Her mother swung around and the look in her eyes made Hero shrink back into her seat. 'I said no.'

Stubbornly, Hero crossed her arms and prepared to argue.

'No,' her mother said again, pinning her with that stare. 'I know you, Hero, so don't think I don't know what this is about. You've never so much as given a toss about barrier racing as a sport; you want to go groundside and you think that being a racer will get you there, but it won't, not while I have anything to say about it.

'Working groundside is hard, dangerous work – nothing like those documentaries or that *Zebra Fry* show you're always watching. People get killed. I lose eight to ten riders a year to predators and accidents, not to mention the injuries and people who live the rest of their lives disfigured. I am not letting you subject yourself to that.'

Hero held her mum's gaze, eyes as brown as her own, but darker somehow – meaner perhaps, more determined – trying to ignore the muscles in her back that wanted to squirm. She finally looked away. 'You used to do it.'

'I used to do a lot of things, and I lost people dear to me because I did.'

She looked back. 'Like who?'

'That's not your concern.' There was that little quirk at the end of her brow, and Hero wondered what her mum was lying about this time. 'The point is, I am not losing you too, so forget about racing.'

'You can't stop me.'

'Oh,' she said, 'but I can.' The look in her eyes caused a neutron bomb to go off in Hero's stomach, exploding nerves all over the place.

The last time her mum had looked at her like that, she'd sent Fink to the Farm for two of the longest weeks of Hero's life and this time… The look in her mum's eyes promised something much worse; she wasn't sure what would be worse than having Fink sent to the Farm, but she was sure her mum would find a way to do it.

Desperate to get away from that gaze, she shoved herself to her feet and wandered over to the holographic bust on the other side of the study. The holoemitter showed an older woman, her hair gone to silver and a gleam of amusement in her eyes. Ursula Bayard, her great-great-grand aunt. A former rider herself, Ursula had founded Bayard Explorations when the cities decided that the men, women and companions who had kept them safe during those first perilous generations were no longer needed. Now the company provided security and resources to all manner of people headed for Jørn's surface. It also produced some of the best tech this side of the equator. Tech she could use.

Hero cleared her throat. 'Who were you talking to?'

Her mum crossed her arms. 'How much did you hear?'

'Enough.'

She sighed. 'He's a client, an important client, and that's all you need to know.'

'What are you doing for him?'

She shoved away from the desk. 'Don't you have to get ready for school tomorrow?'

'No.' Her eyebrow didn't twitch like her mum's; she'd spent a long time in front of the mirror making sure. 'What's Ayumon?'

'It's none of your business.'

'What if I want to make it my business?'

'Hero…' her mother warned.

Time to try another tack. 'What if I want to know about Bayard?'

'Bayard?'

She shrugged. 'It's the family business, and it has the best technical department in the city. If you won't let me race, you could at least let me build stuff.' Stuff she could use to ditch the tracker in her bracelet, among other things.

Her mum's eyes narrowed, suspicion in their depths. 'Why do I feel like this is a ploy?'

'You're paranoid?'

'Or,' she said as she walked back around her desk and sat, 'maybe I just know my daughter too well.'

Maybe she did, but that wasn't going to stop Hero from trying. She followed her mum across the room and sat in the armchair before the desk. 'So?'

Her mum looked at her for several more moments, and Hero barely resisted the urge to squirm. 'I'll think about it.'

The workstation, a shiny black semicircle, illuminated the room. Hero sat surrounded by screens, elbow-deep in holos of her mum: at expensive restaurants, getting out of hovers, smiling and laughing with people in expensive clothes with perfectly poised expressions. Her dad was there, in a few of the holos, without his moustache, a lock of hair sticking up and his tie pulled loose.

She'd pushed those holos aside. They were too perfect, too easily found. She'd wanted the things her mum didn't want her to know, the things her mum's personal AI hadn't managed to scrub from the nets.

With a few adjustments, and the addition of a little program she'd grown just for the occasion, she'd set the house's AI to scouring not just the scattered sub-nets, but the prime-net as well. She didn't expect it to find anything on the prime, not with all of the personal and social AIs sanitising the data.

It may not have been very bright but after six hours of searching, the house AI struck platinum, or at least a tiny bit of it.

The report was old and brief, and in its single paragraph it didn't mention her mother's name, but there, in a holo helpfully enlarged by the AI, was her mum. She was young, with a flurry-thyt on her shoulder, the flyer's delicate front paws buried in her hair, its paper-thin wings spread behind her head, the light shimmering green, purple and blue over its pale skin. Her mum was dressed in a slim-fitting jacket with the Morague Academy logo on the breast, and trousers the same blue and gold as the boy by her side wore. Looming behind them, its short, spiky coat and frills the same colour as their uniforms, stood a pea-dragon, one giant golden eye twinkling at the holocam. Over the holo ran the caption, 'Racers gather for annual Cumulous City Race finals'.

Her mum hadn't just spent time on the surface, she'd been a racer too – a scout, or so she guessed from the 'thyt perched on her mum's shoulder. Had something happened to her? But what, and who was the boy standing next to her?

She enlarged the holo again, focusing on the boy's face. There was something about him, something familiar about his perfectly parted blonde hair and brown eyes, about the way he smiled that reminded her of… She zoomed the holo out again, until she could see her mum standing shoulder-to-shoulder with the boy who could have been her twin. Except…

'I don't have an uncle.'

CHAPTER 3

The next morning, the Lamb was waiting by the front doors, a satchel in one hand. Hero breezed past her, ignoring the outstretched bag, and climbed into the black behemoth waiting on the hover pad.

Inside the hover, the leather seats faced each other over an ocean of carpet beneath a transparent domed roof. Despite the space, there was barely enough room for Fink to curl up at Hero's feet, his large black-flecked muzzle in her lap. When the Lamb climbed in she looked for a moment at Fink, sprawled across two-thirds of the vehicle, before taking a seat facing Hero across the 'pard's great bulk.

Tybalt followed the Lamb, settling in the second before the hover's magnetic levitation device hummed, the generators raising them above the perfectly cultivated circle of lawn and through the mansion's privacy barrier, slipping into the traffic already streaming overhead.

All around them, skytowers shot spacewards, sparkling in the lights of passing hovers and holoboards projecting their messages into the crowded lines of traffic. Skybridges – enclosed walkways, some three or four hovers wide and several storeys deep, others as delicate as a spideruck's web – criss-crossed the spaces between buildings, forming narrow channels through which the traffic flowed.

The hover descended into the oldest part of the Core; what little natural light there had been was quickly eaten by the skytowers and endless traffic, but Hero didn't notice. She'd been up all night, her mind wrapped up in the uncle she'd never known she had and in trying to find a way around her mother's racing restriction. It was the latter that occupied Hero's mind now. She doubted she could convince the academy tutors it was all a mistake, and there was no way she could hide being on the barrier team if she did. No, if she wanted to race she was going to have to get creative. But how?

Around them the skylanes slowed and then stopped. Something flashed under a streetlight and then another something and then another until it seemed like a stream of shadows passed her vision. Hero plastered her hands and nose to the plasglas, straining for a better glimpse of the fleeting shapes as the hover began to move again. She lost them under an archway but found them again racing along an overpass, still covered in shadows, but the forms of legs and tails and riders were easy to make out in the half-gloom.

The breath left her body and she pressed tighter against the dome, wishing she could be through it and down on that bridge, watching all those wondrous shapes flash by. Deep in his throat, Fink warbled and his muscles quivered.

Street racers, they were street racers. Pedestrians scrambled out of their way as they ducked and weaved through the city. Drones, oad-hawks – all mottled green feathers and blunt heads – and other small flyers scooted along ahead of them, relaying information to the riders' scouts, hidden away in some deserted arcade, who in turn relayed directions and warnings to their riders.

She remained glued to the glass, admiring the shapes of the riders' steeds: the bounding lope and scaled spine of a sterdane, the sleek hide and sinuous tail of a toa-mare, and wondered at the taste of such freedom. How it would feel to ride like that, without walls to block her in, the breadth of the city her playground and the smell of it in her nose.

Her fingers curled against the glass, wishing she could claw her way through. Street racing – that was their ticket to the freedom they'd always dreamed of.

In the back of her mind Fink all but danced on his toes.

Soon, she sent back, *soon*.

'What is it?'

Nose a bare inch from the glass, Hero shot Tybalt a quick glance. He leaned forward with his elbows on his knees and a small frown between his brows as he peered out the window.

She sat back and turned to the view on the other side of the hover. 'Nothing,' she said.

His eyes narrowed. 'Nothing?'

'That's what I said, isn't it?'

'Hmm.'

Hero watched out of the corner of her eye as Tybalt continued to peer out the window, and knew when he caught sight of the racers by the flattening of his mouth. 'Don't even think about it,' he said.

'Think about what?'

'Those street races are illegal for a reason, Hero.'

'And?'

'Don't push it.'

She smiled at him.

Tybalt crossed his arms.

Next to him, the Lamb sighed and covered her eyes.

Morague Academy rose from the depths of the city, its base lost in the shadows of skytowers and lanes, its top covered in the shadows of towering neighbours.

The hover flew closer, circling the building as it prepared to land. As thick as a city block, the tower's sides were blackened by the soot of generations of traffic and covered in a changing patchwork of holoscreens. Some projected faces, holograms the size of a barge, into the traffic, shouting slogans at drivers and passengers alike, while others enticed hovers to enter auto-washes and boutiques. A few were small, flat vids with 'breaking news' scrolling across footage of the outer 'burbs and an angry woman shoving her face into a holorecorder.

With a gentle hum, the hover closed in on a semicircle of hover pads a hundred metres below, settling onto a pad next to other sleek hovers. A handful of black-suited men and women, chauffeurs and chaperones, she guessed, clustered around the vehicles, but the platform was empty of all other life.

'No welcoming party?' she asked.

Tybalt's face was tight, his brows as dark as his eyes and just as displeased. 'We're late,' he said as the hover's door hissed open. 'I imagine everyone is in class, where you're supposed to be.'

The entranceway was huge, large enough to accommodate three Finks side-by-side. The hall beyond was a large, double-storey cavity, with passing hovers visible through a steelglas wall to the right and two large lifts standing like columns at the back. The Morague Academy logo, a rearing 'pard before a shield, rotated between them, projected three metres above the plas-marble floor. The hall was deserted but for a girl with a linch-adder wrapped around her neck.

The 'adder was easily the length of Hero's arm, its breast covered in purple feathers that tapered into the yellow scales of its belly and a long, sinuous tail. It mantled its green wings and hissed at the sight of Fink.

The girl scowled, her eyes as dark as her hair, and caught Hero's gaze. A touch of lavender, tainted by the unpleasant taste of menthol, pushed at the edges of Hero's mind and, startled, she pushed back. The girl's eyes widened, her pale golden skin turning a shade whiter, before she hurried away.

'Ms Lambert,' Tybalt said, his eyebrows meeting in a single line above his nose. 'You have Hero's class schedule?'

The Lamb nodded.

'I have it too, you know,' Hero said.

Tybalt barely spared her a glance. 'Make sure she gets there,' was all he said.

CHAPTER 4

A low, flat tone echoed through the classroom, interrupting the hum of the holoscreens and the tutor's firm, precise voice. Hero looked about in confusion as students rose from their workstations and left the classroom in twos and threes.

'Lunch, Ms Regan.' The tutor tapped her workstation when she didn't rise with the others.

Behind her Fink's stomach rumbled, and he projected an image of a thick slab of womba-cow – grey-red, bleeding and still warm enough for steam to rise in the cold air.

She grimaced. 'Really?' she said with a backwards glance as she scooted towards the door.

In her mind, she saw him shrug, the impression of mawberry-flavoured words forming along with it. *He was hungry and sometimes a muffin didn't cut it.*

The Lamb was waiting for them outside the classroom, frowning at a biocomp embedded in her palm.

Hero frowned as well; how come she hadn't noticed that before?

'The dining hall is just down this corridor.' The Lamb gestured over her shoulder. 'I'll meet you there,' she said.

Hero's frown didn't budge as she watched the Lamb hurry away, her short white-blonde curls bouncing with each step. Never before had one of her minders left her alone in a public place – they barely left her alone at home – and that was twice now the Lamb had abandoned her post. What was she up to?

Fink nudged her back, projecting another image of a very large, raw steak. *Besides*, he thought at her, *wasn't she always complaining about never being left alone? Why look a gift puff-cat in the mouth?* The image that appeared in her mind, of a sleek orange head, its cheeks puffed out so that its spines formed a halo around the 'cat's jaw, and a bright blue bow atop its head, almost made her smile.

'Because it's strange.'

What was strange was her insistence on standing here when there was food to be eaten. He gave her another nudge and she reluctantly started forward.

The academy's holotour had been thorough, and she'd been expecting the dining hall to be large, with plush seats clustered around small tables and an entire wall made of steelglas. She'd even expected the view, the tiny figures of people moving in the arcades opposite and across the skybridges, lit by the headlights of the hundreds of hovers dashing past, while everything between the towers fell away into the black of the city below.

What she hadn't expected were the students – more people than she'd ever seen in one place. She'd seen crowds on the holoscreens, but she'd never been part of one, never experienced the noise or the constant flurry of motion that pulled her gaze first one way and then another. There were people piling plates with food from a large central table, and others lounging in chairs or wandering around. There were the companions – big, small and others in between. They hovered above heads or lounged by their people; in one corner a badger-zyl – a long, squat explosion of black and white scales – and a puff-cat rolled about, play fighting with mock growls and snorts.

Her heart was beating too fast and she thought she might have forgotten to breathe. It was, was…

Fink nudged her shoulder.

'Brilliant,' she whispered. And scary.

This time, when Fink gave her a nudge, he pushed her towards the buffet with its swarm of people, sneaking in a lick behind her ear as he did so.

'Fi-iink,' she said, wiping the wet spot with a sleeve.

He pruckled, a strange purring cough, like a chuckle, as he wandered away. She watched as he ambled over to a sterdane, greeting the huge, grey-speckled companion with its short frilled ears and scaled spine, with a flick of his hairless tail and a politely extended nose. It didn't matter how many claws he had, or how big or how scary he was, Fink never seemed to have a problem making friends.

With a deep breath to gather her courage, she headed for the throng of students around the buffet table, mentally practising 'hello' with every step.

She was just two moments from where the smiling boy from class and his blonde companion waited in the buffet line, and he was starting to smile at her again and she was trying to smile back, when someone clasped her shoulder.

The assault on her brain, in crisp green shades, was instant and overwhelming. *Can't believe the lieutenant thought this was a good cov—*

She jerked away from the Lamb's grip. 'Must you always touch me?' From the corner of her eye, she saw the boy and his friend turn and stare. She thought she even heard the blonde giggle.

'I'm sorry, I didn't realise there was an issue...' The Lamb frowned, like she was piecing something together in her mind, followed by a gleam in her eye. 'Are you all right?' She reached into the satchel slung across her chest.

The spit dried in Hero's mouth and her thoughts went straight to the tube of pills she just knew was in there. 'I'm fine!' she snapped and started back towards the buffet.

The Lamb cleared her throat. 'Your meal has already been prepared.'

'What?'

'Your mother thought the academy's menu might be lacking, and she arranged for Chef to prepare something else.' The Lamb gestured towards a table in the corner of the hall, where someone in the white apron and black uniform of the academy's kitchen staff was laying out plates.

There was another giggle and a snort from the pair at her back. The blonde, a round-faced girl with large eyes, did a poor job of concealing her grin, while the boy pinned her with a speculative green-eyed stare.

She raised her chin and strode to the table. The tension and excitement of new friends turned into a deep, ugly curl of humili-ation that crawled around her side and sunk its claws into her belly. When the Lamb moved to sit across from her, she glared.

'Do you have to sit with me as well?'

'Well, no, but…' She looked around the room, at the gazes turned their way, and sighed. 'I'll be over there if you need me,' she said and plucked a plate from the table.

Need her? Yeah, like she needed Pollen poisoning. At least, once the Pollen finished turning her brain into a mould factory, they'd fit her out with greyware. There'd be no stopping her then, not with her brain wired into the nets, no matter how many bracelets or minders they saddled her with.

She picked at a strapple-cherry tart, usually one of her favourites, but her appetite had left with the boy's welcoming smile. She watched Fink roughhouse with the 'dane instead. At least one of them was making friends.

'Is that a strapple and cherry tart?'

Startled, Hero looked up and met the smiling boy's gaze. 'What?'

'The tart,' he said as he slid his tray onto the table. 'It's strapple and cherry, isn't it? I could smell it all the way over there.' He gestured to the buffet.

'You smelled it?'

'Of course.'

The blonde slid her tray onto the table and sat in a single sinuous movement.

'It's strapple and cherry,' he told the girl.

'My granddaddy makes that.' The blonde, her eyes a blue so pale they were almost white, propped her chin on her hand and smiled. 'Yours smells better.'

'I'm Dorian,' the boy said. 'This is Tis. We were wondering,' Dorian said as he leaned across the table, his eyes wide, 'what's it like having a ruc-pard for a companion? I mean, we've heard the stories, like the boy who was mauled to death by his own kitten, but is it true they can read your mind?'

Hero pondered Dorian for a moment. There was something in his eyes, a canny glint that weighed and measured everything it saw. 'Yes,' she said, cautiously.

'Could he read my mind?'

At the back of her mind, suspicion raised its head, and her eyes narrowed in response. 'If he wanted to.'

Dorian barely seemed to notice her sudden tension. 'Could he read my mind and then tell you what I was thinking so you could cheat on a test?'

Outrage hit her instantly and she pulled back, as if he'd tried to slap her in the face. 'What? No.'

'Why not?' Dorian's eyes were wide and curious, but the glint in their depths was cold.

'He doesn't do things like that.'

'I'd do that. I'm horrible at math,' Tis said around a mouthful of noodles. 'What about hairballs? I bet he gets those.'

'Sometimes.'

The girl shuddered. 'Disgusting.'

'You know,' Dorian said as he looked over his shoulder to where Fink was greeting an oad-hawk perched on his rump, 'he doesn't look that scary. I don't know what everyone was making so much fuss about.'

'Fuss... about what?'

'Well Angus is on the junior race team – that's his oad-hawk sitting on your 'pard's rump – and he was saying, more like whining actually, that you shouldn't be allowed on the team because 'pards are so dangerous and yours might hurt someone. I think he was just worried you'd beat one of us.' He shrugged and smiled like the thought didn't bother him.

'You're on the barrier team?'

'Oh sure.' Dorian's smile grew coquettish and he looked at her from the corner of his eye. 'That's my 'dane over there.' He pointed to where Fink still sat with the oad-hawk on his rump and the grey-speckled sterdane at his side. 'He has the best racing pedigree in the western hemisphere.'

'Mmm-hmm,' Tis said around another mouthful. 'Dorian hasn't lost a single race since his parents bought Grey for him two years ago. They're the academy's star team.'

'Are you joining the barrier team?' Dorian asked, a challenge in the lift of his brow.

She tilted her chin and met him stare for stare. 'No,' she said.

'Really?' Tis's eyes widened. 'Why?'

Hero felt her cheeks redden, her tongue caught in her mouth. She didn't know what to say. She wasn't going to tell them the truth, that her mum thought she was a fragile little freak. But she had to say something; the curiosity in Tis's eyes was turning to suspicion. So Hero opened her mouth but before she could decide what to say, Dorian interrupted.

'Everyone wants to be on the team. You see that girl over there?' He pointed to a noisy table where the girl with the linch-adder sat. 'That's Norah Joshi. She's tried to get on the team three times, but nobody wants to be her partner. They'd rather use a drone than have her scout for them.'

'Why?'

Tis spoke. 'She scouted for her older sister in one of the street races down in the Twilight, and they were caught. Her parents hushed it all up so she didn't get expelled but her sister wasn't so lucky. They shipped her off to a reform school or something. I heard it was that one over the New Gobi ice desert.' Tis shuddered, but the look in her eyes was avid. 'Can you just imagine? They say it floats so low you have to wear one of those masks that filter out the Pollen and there's meant to be snow everywhere.'

'Anyway,' Dorian said, waving a hand in the air, 'the only thing that matters is that Norah was caught, and no one wants to partner with a scout who let that happen. I mean, how good could you possibly be if you can't dodge the police?'

Fink stuck his head between Tis and Dorian. The girl squealed.

He cocked his head and purred, gently butting Tis's shoulder.

Tis laughed, a small nervous sound, as she tentatively reached out to scratch him between the ears.

Grey loomed behind Dorian; the scales that covered his snout and ran all the way down his spine gleamed in the overhead light.

The boy's comm-unit chimed. 'There's a barrier team meeting in a few minutes. You should come,' he said as he rose. 'Not that you'll understand anything of course, but afterwards I can probably convince coach to let you on the team.'

Hero felt her face tighten as she thought of what the coach would say to that request. Would it be a simple *no*, or would they actually explain why, telling everyone that she was *special* and *fragile* and *ill*? Whatever it was, she didn't want any of the students hearing it, so she smiled and shook her head. 'Thanks, but if I move from this chair the Lamb will kill me.'

'The Lamb?'

She gestured towards where the Lamb sat, eyes intent on the readout from her palm-unit.

Dorian's gaze, shadowed by the flop of his fringe, followed her finger, the corner of his mouth curling in a barely-concealed sneer when it lighted on her minder.

'Well, if you can't evade *her*…' he said, letting the thought dangle. 'It's probably just as well.'

Tis giggled, her hand covering her mouth.

'Come on Tis,' Dorian said.

With another giggle, Tis rose and followed him and Grey out of the dining hall.

CHAPTER 5

The next day, Hero stood in the archway to the cafeteria long enough to spy the Lamb standing next to a table covered in carefully prepared plates, before she turned on her heel and marched the other way. Fink grumbled as he followed in her wake, projecting images of steaming haunches of meat and piles of muffins into her head until she spun around and glared at him.

'*You* go get lunch then.'

By himself?

'Yes!'

His ears twitched back and forth as he thought about it, before he leaned forward and touched his nose to hers. *Did she want anything?* he thought at her.

Hero wrinkled her nose at his fish-breath. 'Surprise me.'

That had been a while ago. Now she sat cross-legged in the middle of a corridor, a strapple half-eaten and half-forgotten in one hand, while she used the wall interface to browse the Morague archives with the other. Fink sprawled at her back, scoffing the cake he gripped lovingly in one forepaw.

Before her, in overlapping squares and rectangles projected outward from the wall, were holos of her mum. Except the girl in the holos didn't look like her mum, not exactly. Surrounded by friends, she was laughing, talking and smiling, her flurry-thyt either perched on her shoulder or cradled in her arms, the flyer's pearlescent skin and long, delicate feathers a perfect complement to her mum's blonde perfection. She looked happy and fun and all of the things Hero had never thought her mum could be.

Without a name, it took her longer to find her uncle, but she eventually did. There he was, standing in several images beside her mum, wearing the same racing uniforms with the pea-dragon – long and lean, its scales rippling blue and gold – and flurry-thyt at their backs and a trophy flickering in their hands.

She touched his face.

'Paris Regan,' said the Morague AI.

A name – her uncle had a name. 'My mum and uncle were really on the Morague race team?'

'Correct.'

She spun the holo, looking at it from all angles. What had happened then? Where was her uncle? Why didn't her mum ever talk about him, and for that matter, why hadn't her dad? She leaned in close, seeking some clue, some hint in the blue uniforms and beaming faces.

'What are you doing?'

She jumped, the strapple falling from careless fingers and rolling across the carpet.

Fink pruckled and snatched up the fruit, demolishing it in one bite.

Hero glared at him, before turning her gaze to the intruder.

Norah Joshi didn't notice, but the 'adder half-buried in her hair did and hissed. Norah absently scratched his head – the flyer's inner eyelids closing in bliss – as she focused intently on the holo. She pointed to the trophy in Hero's uncle's hands. 'That's the Junior Intercity Cup.' She pointed to Hero's uncle next. 'Is that your dad?'

When Hero didn't answer right away, Fink stuck his nose in her neck.

'No,' she said.

Fink nudged her again.

She grimaced. 'He's my uncle.' Fink's nose was barely halfway to her neck when she continued. 'I think he died.'

'Oh.' Norah shifted, her expression uncomfortable. 'Sorry.'

Hero shrugged, her gaze on the 'adder as it slithered into the other girl's lap. 'What's his name?'

'Harish.' Norah ran her fingers down the 'adder's green-feathered back, causing the little flyer to stretch his neck and croon. 'Where's your nanny?'

'The Lamb's not a nanny,' Hero snapped.

'Oh,' Norah said again, her fingers pausing on Harish's back and a blush staining her cheeks a darker shade of gold. 'What is she then?'

Suspicion made her study the other girl's face, but she only saw genuine interest. 'She's a minder.'

'Is that like a bodyguard? Because I would have thought that your 'pard made that redundant.' She gestured over Hero's shoulder to where Fink was now cleaning his paws.

'He does,' was all she said.

Turning back to the holoscreen, Hero took a snapshot of her uncle's face and set the AI to searching its databanks, hypercon-scious of Norah looking over her shoulder.

'What are you looking for?'

Fink twitched his tail against her ankle. *Be nice,* he thought at her.

'My uncle,' she said.

'But you said he died.'

'I said that I *think* he died.'

Fink's tail twitched again.

She sighed. 'Something nasty happened to my family. Something to do with the races, which is why my mum won't let me race. I think it has to do with my uncle, who I didn't even know I had, and if I can find out what it is…'

'Your mum will let you race?' Norah looked doubtful.

'Probably not, but it's a start.'

'You know,' Norah said as she reached for the wall, 'if your uncle was on the race team, you should try the Intercity Barrier League. They keep bios on everyone who's ever raced, right back to the first Riders who went down to explore the planet.' A new screen appeared, and Norah's fingers flew. 'It's not connected to the prime-net, so it's a little hard to find but…' She shrugged.

'How do you know how to find it then?'

'My sister was on the team. She won the Intercity Cup too.'

Hero frowned as a memory from the day before tickled her mind. 'Wasn't your sister expelled?'

Still in Norah's lap, Harish rustled his wings and hissed.

Norah's mouth tightened, but she nodded. 'My dads – they're both lawyers – convinced the judge not to charge her, but as part of the deal they had to send her to that boarding school over the New Gobi ice forest. It's not as awful as they say, but my sister says they're really strict. At least she was able to take Golem, her slale-bear, with her. My dads could have sent him to the Farm.'

Hero shuddered.

'Anyway,' Norah said as she flicked her screen towards Hero, 'here's your uncle's bio.'

Paris Regan stared out at her, blonde and perfect, just like her mum, but with a cocky twist to his lips and a gleam in his eye, as if he knew something – a joke or a secret, something he was sure she wanted to know. Like where he was and what had happened to him.

There were more images in the bio, and she scrolled through them, coming to rest on one of her mum and uncle shaking hands with an older woman in black.

Norah leaned closer. 'Looks like your uncle and… ah… that's your mum, right?'

Hero nodded.

'Well, it looks like they were recruited by the Streakers.'

'The Streakers?'

Norah blinked. 'You don't know who the Streakers are?'

She shook her head.

'But, I thought you wanted to race?'

She crossed her arms. 'I do.'

The other girl stared at her for another few moments, searching her face for something – Hero couldn't tell what. Finally, with a look in her eye like she thought Hero might be a little stupid, Norah spoke.

'The Streakers,' she began, 'are one of the best professional race teams in the League. They've won the Intercity Pro Cup three years running. Everyone who signs up with them becomes a superstar.' Norah looked at her closely. 'You've *never* heard of them?'

She frowned. 'I don't like sport.'

'Then why do you want to race?'

'I want to go to the surface.'

Norah didn't say anything, but her mouth opened and closed a few times, until she sat back and looked confused.

Hero turned back to her uncle's bio. Paris Regan's official biography was a collection of vids and news articles with titles like 'Shiny new additions to Streakers' lineup', 'Regan twins do it again' and 'Paris Regan, racing's baddest bad boy?'. It was the one at the very bottom of his file, though, that caught her attention. She touched it and the headline expanded, the vid playing almost instantly.

'Streakers fans were reeling in shock today, after the horrifying accident that almost claimed Paris Regan's life. Onlookers—'

She paused the vid. On the screen, her uncle was enclosed in a stretcher, grim-faced paramedics at his side, while his pea-dragon tried to limp after, broken leg tucked against its side, feathers twisted and crumpled.

Fink looked over her shoulder and whined.

Norah leaned back in. 'Did your uncle recover?'

She closed the vid and scanned the titles for more. There was only one – more a notification than an article, a few lines of text without vid or holos. She skimmed over the words, picking out the ones that mattered, like 'coma', 'life support' and 'brain damage'.

'No,' she said. 'I don't think he did.'

'So, he died…?'

Hero shook her head. 'It didn't say that.' In fact, it didn't say much of anything, and not one thing at all of—

A giggle interrupted her thoughts, just before the wall exploded with images of Norah. The puppet-like caricatures sang in high-pitched voices, snorting and dancing while chasing each other around a mock race track, banging into walls and running into police.

Hero looked at Norah. The girl's eyes were wide and her cheeks pale. For a moment, she looked frozen to the spot and then her cheeks flushed and she reached for the wall, her fingers scrambling over the screens.

The moment Norah touched the animation, it exploded again, growing until it filled the hallway and twisted around the corner. Norah raced after it, Harish riding her shoulder, as laughter erupted from the other hallway.

Hero followed, her puzzled frown turning to a glare when she rounded the corner.

Tis stood there, her biocomp – a fancy sub-dermal model – aglow under the skin of her forearm, and a gaggle of classmates at her back, all of them giggling and pointing.

One boy spotted Norah standing in the middle of the hall, arms limp at her sides, and nudged his friend, who snorted, almost choking, as he turned and laughed harder.

Norah looked ready to cry.

Hero pushed through the crowd surrounding Tis and grabbed the girl's wrist.

'Hey,' Tis said, trying to pull her hand free. 'Let go.'

She gripped tighter and set her fingers to work on the screens floating above Tis's forearm. It only took a few moments. The Morague AI was similar to the one at the mansion, with the same overactive immune system, and a brief foray into its secondary core had it sending a pulse that made Tis squeal and her arm jump.

The wall animations died with Tis's biocomp.

The laughter stopped.

Tis gaped at her.

Norah's mouth hung open, while Fink stood behind her, his mid-shoulders shaking as he pruckled.

Glad you found it funny, Hero thought as she marched past them both and headed back to her spot by the wall.

Norah sat down beside her. 'Thank you,' she said.

Hero shrugged and enlarged one of the articles attached to her uncle's bio. 'You're welcome.' For several long seconds she stared at the articles, something about her uncle being arrested, then she frowned. 'Why does Tis hate you?'

'She doesn't, she just needs someone to pick on. She chose me.'

'Because of your sister?'

Norah shook her head. 'She did it before that.' She pulled a candy dispenser from her pocket and rolled it about in her hands. 'Something… happened my first year here. It wasn't so bad when my sister was here too, on the race team, but when she got expelled… They all think I'm a freak.'

'Why?'

She shrugged and slipped a small pink candy between her teeth. 'They just do.'

That wasn't all of it, Hero felt it in her bones, but before she could open her mouth to ask Fink stuck his nose against her neck.

Don't, was all he thought at her.

So, she didn't.

Whispers and nudges flowed around the classroom, bouncing from station to station, visible only in the sideways glances of the students behind them. Nothing though, disturbed the surface of her station, or, she thought, Norah's.

Pacing around the central holo, the snow-covered mountains of the southern continent floating above it, Mrs Rahm cast her sharp-eyed gaze around as if she could sense the gossip.

Across the classroom, Tis avoided eye contact, keeping her head down, her eyes firmly on her screens, while everyone else stole sideways glances at Hero, like they couldn't quite believe what she'd done.

Hero frowned and turned back to the continent above her own station. Hovering over the plains was Thoh City and, three hundred kilometres south, a tiny dot in comparison, the boarding school Norah's sister had been sent to. It looked cold, tethered above the ice forest, rendered in shades of white, blue and grey.

A bubble popped into being above the forest. Small and discrete enough to avoid Mrs Rahm's gaze, it pulsated.

Frowning, she touched it.

Like the hallway during lunch, her workstation exploded. A parade of ruc-pards chased jerky little animations of herself around a ring of clowns with drums and trumpets, while old-fashioned fireworks lit the air, making enough noise to turn her ears numb.

'Enough.' Mrs Rahm slammed her hand down on the workstation and the carnival winked out as if it had never been. 'Ms Regan, from the expression on your face, I am willing to believe that this disruption is not your doing. However, I will tolerate no more, is that clear?'

She nodded.

'Excellent.' Mrs Rahm swiped her hand over the station and the southern continent sprung back to life. 'Now, as I was saying…'

A muffled giggle made Hero raise her head. From the other side of the classroom, Tis smiled.

CHAPTER 6

The fur-roses cast a deep blue-tinged glow across the room, with Fink a large, shadowy mass sprawled between the door and the bed. In the half-light, only long practice and the half-seen swish of his tail prevented Hero from tripping over his bulk.

She was reaching for her pyjamas, neatly folded and tucked under a pillow by one of the maids – Hero usually left them wherever they fell, which was usually the floor – when another light washed the room in pale blue.

Fink flicked his tail over his snout and grumbled as he rolled away from the light.

On the other side of the room her workstation glowed, the central holoscreen lit up and the icon of a red-breasted bird pulsed in its centre. She frowned. A bug in the system? Finding a diagnostic amongst the collection of slides on her desk, she touched the icon.

It spiralled out, bringing the other two holoscreens to life along with a score of smaller ones she hadn't even been aware of. The recordings and data files were nothing but a messy, colourful jumble of shapes and half-muted sounds, until she spotted someone – a familiar someone, with tight white-blonde curls and sharp green eyes – and realised not what, but who she was looking at.

'The Lamb.' The name was barely a whisper on her lips.

The Lamb's life was spread across the screens. She peered closer, shuffling through the files as she pulled her chair in under her, pyjama bottoms forgotten on the floor.

Her parents, early life, friends, awards, school. It was all there. But who had sent it and why? She couldn't see the Lamb doing it, and there was no name or return address, just the icon of the bird still pulsating in its own little screen.

She reached for the box of data slides. If this was Tis sending her another cruel joke then the diagnostic wasn't going to find it – but the Rabbit would.

The workstation hummed as she pushed the slide into the input gel.

She'd grown the program herself – carefully replicating and rearranging the genes of a digital template – when her first workstation caught the same flu that took down half the systems in the western hemisphere. Most of those had needed replacing when the biogel that supported their operating systems had turned to lumpy mush, but not hers. The Rabbit did its work well.

One by one the files disappeared from her desktop, the program chewing through them as it hunted for anything that would give her workstation a serious cold. When it was done, the station flashed green – the diagnostics all clear – and the Lamb's files reappeared, once more spread across her screens.

Hero frowned and hunted through her slides again, pulling out the Coyote and slipping it in next to the Rabbit. If there wasn't anything nasty in the data, where had it come from?

The workstation hummed, the central screen scrolling numbers and chemical markers as the Coyote tracked the sender. When a minute passed, her frown deepened, and by the time two minutes and then three had slipped by, she was tapping her fingers against the desktop and her feet against the floor. The Coyote *never* took this long.

The station flashed white, 'no sender' appearing in the air an inch from her nose.

A few screens later, and she was elbow-deep in the Coyote's logs. There couldn't not be a sender – everything came from somewhere. But there was no mistake, no overlooked chemical marker or strand of DNA. It was as if the message had been born out of the planetary net itself, rising from the electrons like that Old Terra goddess out of the sea. She didn't think even an AI could make that happen.

Her eyes flicked to the robin symbol, a signature hovering in its own little screen. This Robin was good, scary good.

If there weren't any viruses in the files, then maybe there was something in them that the sender wanted her to see. She scrolled back through the data. She saw the Lamb in pre-school, her hair a white ball of fuzz, and she saw her standing next to a woman in a police uniform, both of them with the same pale blonde hair. There were academic transcripts from schools in the Grip and a scholarship to a university in the Horizon, where she majored in bioscience.

It was the perfect qualification for a scientist, or a naturalist or any one of a hundred other jobs that had to be better than looking after Hero. So why was she?

The files stopped after the Lamb finished university, except for a note at the end of her transcripts. It simply said, 'Recruited.'

CHAPTER 7

'Doctor Woolsey's proposal split the governing council. Does anyone recall why?'

Almost the entire class raised their hands and Mr Lee, the tutor, selected Tis as if he were handing her a medal.

'Doctor Woolsey wanted to turn us all into freaks.' Tis smiled wide, her eyes glittering with glee as the class tittered.

Mr Lee cleared his throat. 'Not quite,' he said.

Hero hadn't been able to decide if, with his skinny frame, big eyes and equally big ears, Mr Lee was old enough to teach, but no one had arrived to drag him away. She was almost disappointed; the way he bounced around the class, his face animated to the point of being comical, gave her a headache.

'Mr Alexander.' He singled out Dorian. 'Can you give us another answer?'

'Woolsey wanted to mix human DNA with Jøran, like we did with the companions, but no one knew how that would affect us. It was safer to build the cities.'

'Correct, Mr Alexander. The changes to our DNA could have killed us as easily as the Pollen itself. Now, does anyone know—'

Angus, the boy on the other side of Hero, interrupted. 'How did the colonists know the cities would be safe?'

'They performed tests, which showed that the Pollen was confined to the lower levels of the atmosphere.' Mr Lee's brows rose and fell with each word and his grin almost split his face when he pointed to

Tis. 'Yes, Ms Wolfe?'

'Is it true that it rots your brain?'

'Not exactly. The Pollen *colonises* the brain and corrupts it; to what end our scientists haven't been able to tell, but they suspect that it is what gives the native wildlife their telepathic abilities.'

Hero tuned the tutor out, although the others hung on his every word, their hands flying up and down in an endless stream of questions. As if they couldn't all recite Jørn's history in their sleep. Across from her even Dorian, behind his customary cool, looked animated.

She'd rather have been learning biology, even if it meant studying the roaches that infested the city's lower levels. How the only pure-blooded Terra species to survive the Pollen became a hover-sized behemoth had to be more interesting than some ancient argument. She could use that information if she ever lost her mind long enough to take a run through the Street level. It might even be fun to put her feet on the city's actual streets, if the roaches didn't outnumber the garbage piles. Even the maintenance bugs were armed and armoured. No, the information she wanted, the information she could use, was how to trace a message that came from nowhere.

It had been a week since the Robin, as she'd taken to thinking of the mysterious sender, had gifted her with the Lamb's past. Though she tried every trick she knew, and a few she'd newly gleaned from the sub-nets, the Robin remained as much of a mystery now as then.

As for the Lamb… Hero resisted the urge to peer into all of the classroom's dark corners. The woman was a ghost, the way she blended into the background, always somewhere out of sight, yet with her eyes fixed firmly on Hero's skull. It was unnerving, but not as much as the half-heard voices in her head.

She'd never gone without her meds for so long, and could have had a nice little pile of them by now, but she enjoyed the zapping sound when the flash-trash incinerated them. If only the mental whispers were as easy to get rid of; instead they built in her ears, coming in fits and starts that grew worse as the week progressed. At times, she could barely control the urge to cover her ears. Fink helped then, wrapping his tail around her wrist or purring in her ear, enveloping her in a mawberry-scented cocoon.

Despite that, she'd slipped up a few times, answering questions that weren't asked, and though she'd scored a few puzzled looks, no one had called her freak yet, at least not to her face. People – students and tutors alike – still skittered out of Fink's way though, whispering *Woolsey* like a profanity.

The scent of lavender brushed her mind. Through her screens she saw Norah, the 'adder draped over her shoulders, her mouth white and pinched as she popped another one of her ever-present pink candies. She did that a lot, and Hero wondered at the significance of it as the scent of lavender became tinged with menthol and faded from her mind.

Her workstation beeped, a small screen to her left flashing a warning. She frowned and glanced up, her eyes catching Tis's. The girl chewed on her lip and there was a gleam in her eye, like she was waiting for something exciting to happen.

Hero's cheeks still burned with the humiliation of the scene in the classroom on her first day.

After that, she'd brought in the Rabbit and none of the other bugs Tis sent got through. For the past week Hero had watched as the gleam in the other girl's eye faded in frustration.

The small screen flashed again, the Rabbit finishing its work, and a big red button with 'Return to Sender' appeared on the screen. Hero smiled across the classroom, and it was Tis's turn to frown.

Fink's cold, wet whuff against the back of her neck just about made her jump. He didn't like what she was thinking. He flashed her a memory of her own humiliation before projecting it onto Tis's face.

It served the other girl right, Hero thought as she hit the button.

Tis's workstation exploded with song, her screens dissolving into a menagerie of tutors and students, with all sorts of wings and fins and tails parading across its surface. Above them stood The Crackpot in a white lab coat and a brightly-coloured top hat, twirling an oversized 'stick around her head like a baton.

The lunch bell was almost lost amid the laughter that followed.

She slipped out of the class as Mr Lee cornered Tis, her cheeks as red as Hero's had been. The look Tis shot her over the tutor's shoulder promised retribution.

Fink grumbled, butting her with his head. *That hadn't been nice.*

'That…' Hero just about jumped out of her skin as Dorian linked his arm through hers, '…was brilliant. You have to show me how you did it.'

As soon as Dorian's skin touched hers, she could feel him, sharp and sweet and yellow-blue in her mind. Grey sidled up on her other side, stymying Fink, who for a second looked as confused as she felt, before shrugging his mid-shoulders and ambling along behind.

Unease slithered through her gut. Since that first day, Dorian had been friendly enough, though distant, his smiles tight at the edges and barely reaching his eyes. The arm through hers and the sparkle in his eye made her suspicious, but in her mind, Fink was unconcerned.

'I didn't do anything,' she said as they walked down the corridor to the dining hall.

Dorian didn't say anything, but next to her Grey whuffed, as if in laughter.

Tis squeezed past Grey, pinning Hero with a look that burned all the way down her spine, before stalking towards the dining hall, her shoulders hunched.

Fink nudged her in the back. *Trouble*, he thought at her, flashing her an image of Tis's glare. *And soon.*

Dorian chuckled. 'Mr Lee will have her doing extra history homework for a week.' Pulling on Hero's elbow, he steered them towards a turbo lift. 'Best to avoid her for now.'

'Where are we going?' She thought about digging in her heels, but the thought of putting up with Tis staring at her while she ate curdled her stomach.

Dorian smiled. 'It's a surprise.'

Fink grumbled. *Wherever it is, it had better have lunch.*

The lift opened onto an auditorium only slightly larger than her mother's ballroom. Padded benches in long tiers of tiny alcoves faced a plasglas wall two storeys tall.

On the other side, a spideruck dashed by. Its feathers gleamed pink and green in the light, its eight many-jointed legs a blur of motion. Hero was too far away to see the student crouched over its back, but she could imagine the look of concentration as the curtain of energy chasing them grew closer.

Dorian wound his arm through hers and tugged her to the right. 'The race track,' he said. 'You should see it on a race day. Madhouse.' He grinned. 'Of course, all the really interesting stuff happens here.' They'd reached a door on the far end of the auditorium, and Dorian opened it with a flourish.

A fraction of the auditorium's size, its view unobstructed by any kind of wall, the room was full of workstations and benches, and a handful of students. As Dorian guided her first through the benches then past the stations, none of the students looked up, too engrossed in the images displayed on their screens. She saw the spideruck on one student's screens, and a pea-dragon on another's. It wasn't until she heard them talking into small comm-units attached to their collars that she realised that they were scouts, guiding riders around the race track.

'The senior barrier team,' Dorian said, gesturing to the scouts and the racers still on the track. 'They get the morning off every Wednesday to train. Sometimes they practise right through lunch, but it looks like they're stopping today,' he said, indicating the students coming in off the course.

The course was a white gleaming expanse of plasteel that spanned the breadth of the level, dissected by shifting walls of plasglas and the faint shimmer of the barriers. In the distance, she could make out the shapes of other students in other trackside lounges and tack rooms on the far side.

As the last of the students left the course its walls settled, no longer moving, and the barriers stopped shimmering.

'The teachers deactivate the course except for races and practice sessions,' Dorian said. 'If they didn't, who knows how many kids they'd have to rescue from the traps. Especially them,' he said, jerking his chin towards the lounge on the other side of the course. 'Only the try-hards and wannabes, like Norah Joshi, hang out over there. It's practically a museum.

'I have to talk to Coach Roan,' he said with a lazy wave of his hand. 'If you want to check out the course or anything, you can.' He smiled as he walked away, but there was a look in his eyes, something cold, something sly, that sent a shiver down her spine.

Fink's whine distracted her. She looked at him to see his ears pricked forward, his gaze intent on the track and his tail twitching with a life of its own.

She bumped his shoulder. 'Want to go out?'

He bumped back. *Yes.*

She swung onto his back with a grin.

As Fink all but pranced towards the course, she saw the lift open out of the corner of her eye and turned her head to catch Tis's glare. Hero couldn't say why but it raised the hairs on the back of her neck. But then Fink's claws were click-clacking on the shiny white track, and thoughts of the other girl fled her mind.

This was the first barrier course ever built. Before the barrier races, Riders had trod here, trained here, sweated and hurt here. She could almost see them thundering down the straight and around the corner, wiping past her on slale-bears and toa-mares and ruc-pards. It made her heart race and her breath come short. She wanted to do that, be that, down on the surface, where the real adventure was.

Between her knees, Fink rumbled, sharing her sentiment.

She leaned forward, ruffling the fur between his ears. 'We'll get there,' she said. 'I promise.'

With a barely perceptible wriggle, Fink leapt forward. She barely had time to clamp knees to his sides and grab a handful of ruff before he skidded around a corner. Leaning low over his forequarters, she laughed as they barrelled down the straight, the wind of their passing sweeping her hair aside and filling her nose with freedom.

She'd missed this.

They'd missed this, Fink corrected as he skidded around another corner. *The city had too many walls.*

She hunched lower over his neck, feeling the *tha-thump* of his hearts between her knees and revelling in the bunch and release of his muscles. If she reached out with her mind she could feel the coarse, sandpaper texture of the track under Fink's paws, the weight of her on his back and the slight hum of electricity…

Ahead, the floor began to move, a section the length of her forearm rising until it was level with Fink's chest. He jumped, clearing the hurdle with millimetres to spare.

Something fizzed, and she whipped her head around in time to see a curtain of gold shimmer into existence behind them. Her eyes widened and her heart tapped out a double-time in her chest. Dorian had said that the track wasn't active.

She swallowed and leaned further over Fink's forequarters. 'Don't stop,' she said as the shock skin rushed towards them.

As the barrier gained speed, nipping at Fink's tail and lifting the hairs on the back of her neck, the walls started to move. One popped up ahead of them, and Fink barely managed to turn, slamming them sideways into the plasglas. The impact stung, but not as much as the shock skin would if it caught them. They kept moving.

A heartbeat ahead, the floor fell away, creating a gap too big to leap and walls too high to climb on either side. Across the gap, floating at what would have been the perfect height for a scout if they had one, was a holographic ring, the key to reactivating the floor. Her stomach fell with the floor and she gripped Fink with her knees, curling her fingers as tight as she could in his ruff.

Beneath her, Fink gathered himself to make the impossible leap.

He jumped, and she looked down into the yawning blackness. Just how deep did it really go?

A streak of yellow and purple flashed past her ear and through the ring. The light flashed once, and the floor reassembled itself beneath them. The streak, a familiar-looking linch-adder, made a loop and raced back towards them. There was a harness strapped between its wings and something clutched in one of its talons, which it flung towards her as it arched back around.

Instinctively, she caught it – an earpiece the size of her thumbnail – and slipped it into her ear.

'Take the next right,' Norah's voice commanded. 'That shock skin will dissipate as soon as you hit the slip field.'

The intersection loomed, with three corridors branching off the main one. She nudged Fink to the right.

'Okay,' said Norah. 'The next bit is tricky. Follow Harish and don't touch the floor.'

The track opened up, sections of the floor rising like stepping stones, the slip field flooding the rest with an oily green glow.

They bounded from step to step, no sooner leaping from one to the next before it crumbled beneath them. The 'adder flew ahead, guiding them through the maze.

Wasp-bots came next. Barely the size of her thumb, the drones swarmed them as soon as the last stepping stone crumbled, shocking them with their stingers and clouding the air until it was almost impossible to see. They were in her face, stingers jabbing at her cheeks, her eyes, the back of her neck, each thrust setting off another little explosion under her skin. She buried her face in Fink's ruff and covered her head with her hands, but the little bots just moved to attack her arms and her ribs. Each new shock rode in the wake of the last, stabbing at her bones.

Beneath her, Fink growled and snapped, but she felt each twitch of his skin, every flinch as the wasp-bots stung him again and again and again.

'Hero,' Norah's voice rang in her ear. 'Hero! You have to get to the edge of the swarm, just a few metres, before they increase the strength of the shocks.'

'Increase—?' Hero yelped, electricity lancing through her side, shuddering along her ribs and squeezing her lungs, even as Fink jolted and whined.

Lifting her head, just a little, Hero dug her hands into Fink's ruff and urged him forward.

Somewhere above them, out of the bots' reach, Harish flew, giving eyes to Norah's voice in her ear as she guided them through.

They stumbled out of the swarm and skidded to a halt in a clear-sided cell. A wall thumped into place behind them, cutting off their escape.

'That doesn't look good,' Hero said.

Fink rumbled agreement.

'It isn't.' Norah sounded strained. 'The box was permanently deacti-vated last week. Someone's messing with the course controls.'

Harish, resting on Fink's rump, squawked and took flight as the box's walls began to move inwards.

Hero's heart stopped, and then started up again in a painful rhythm. 'Where's the off switch?'

'I don't know. Whoever reactivated the box has changed its protocols.'

Frantically, Hero cast her gaze around the rapidly shrinking space, looking for a switch or button or anything to get them out. But there was nothing, just white floors and walls too high and smooth to scramble over.

Fink shifted, curling his tail in close and rearing on his haunches as the walls squeezed in closer. She saw it then, a glowing circle of orange light that had been hidden beneath his paws.

'There,' she said, half-hanging off his back.

Fink hit the switch with a paw and the box fell away, leaving a clear run to the finish line. He didn't hesitate, stretching out into a gallop the 'adder was hard-pressed to keep pace with.

Norah didn't even have time to yell a warning before Fink's feet went out from under him. She felt the impact squash the air from his lungs as he hit the track on his belly, the slick green light of a slip field glowing around them as together they slid, spinning rapidly until they came to rest on the finish line.

Hero slid off, the lactic acid in her legs making them wobble. She knelt by Fink's side and put a hand on his shoulder as he wheezed the air back into his lungs, until he gradually stood.

Something fluttered above her head – the 'adder coming to rest on Fink's shoulder.

'Thanks,' she said to Harish, as much as to Norah.

'You're welcome,' Norah said into her ear.

Harish took off and the device in her ear went dead. Slowly she and Fink made it to the tack room.

With adrenalin coursing through their veins and her heart pounding in time with Fink's, it took a moment for the scene before her to arrange itself in her mind.

Dorian smiled at them from behind the barrier course's controls. 'Well,' he said, 'it looks like you can race. It's really too bad Mummy won't let you join the team.'

Behind him, Tis giggled, and the rabid mix of glee and anticipation in her eyes sent a shiver down Hero's spine.

'Is it because you're crazy,' Dorian continued, 'or are you just scared?'

Fink's already stiff ruff rose further, his throat vibrating with the beginnings of a growl.

Lying next to Dorian, Grey raised his head, his frilled ears flattening in response.

The tension just about made Hero's skin crawl. 'I'm not scared,' she said, stalking forward even as Grey flashed his teeth. 'And I'm not crazy.'

Tis giggled again. 'That's not what your records say.'

'But don't worry, you don't have to hide it anymore,' Dorian said. 'We told everyone.' He gestured to the large screens and the strips along the walls, and there, on every surface were her school records with the word she despised above all others stamped over the top: SPECIAL.

It felt like the planet had stopped, everything on it pausing for one perfect moment while she stared at that word plastered across her face, and imagined it in every hallway and every classroom.

Her insides shrivelled. She took two steps towards the nearest wall, her feet numb, toes dragging on the ground, and her insides, already scrunched into tight ball, froze.

Hero's breath hitched. Shuddered in. Shuddered out.

Behind her, Fink whined and nudged her back.

Dorian had done more than just publish her school records. Beneath the dreaded word 'special' scrolled others; schizophrenic, paranoid, medication. A flicker of movement caught her eye, a tiny screen inset into the poster. Her hand trembled when she reached for it.

It exploded at her touch, zooming out until it was twice as big as the poster itself, forcing Hero back a step. On it played out the scene from the morning Tybalt had held her while the doctor shoved the 'stick full of green goo into her neck. The Hero on the screen thrashed and yelled, her eyes so big they almost swallowed her face, except she didn't look desperate or scared or any of the other things that were even now crawling up her throat. She just looked crazy.

Tis giggled in her ear. 'Do you like it? I had to hack the headmaster's personal files to get that vid. It was tricky, but worth it.'

Hero stared at Tis, her blood pulsing loud in her ears before it rushed to her feet, and she almost stumbled as she spun on her heel and hurried towards the lift. If she could get back to the classroom, she could get rid of the vid – she was sure she could – and maybe, if she were quick enough, no one would see it.

With her head down, she almost ran into the girl standing beside the lift. The girl had her back to her, eyes glued to Dorian's public service announcement, but the linch-adder peering out of her dark curtain of hair confirmed it was Norah.

Indecision rooted her feet to the floor. The lift was right there, but her gut shrivelled at the thought of meeting someone's eyes, of that look… She backed up, but Fink was there, warm and solid. Harish trilled at him, and Norah turned in response, just as the lift doors whooshed open. She barely met Norah's gaze, but she saw enough to know her eyes were wide and there might have been sympathy in them, but then there might have been disgust too. It was easier to stick her chin in the air and brush past the other girl than to find out.

CHAPTER 8

The next morning, whispers followed her all the way to class, accompanied by sideways glances and fingers pointed at her back. She felt them everywhere, felt them sliding not just over her but the Lamb as well. All of them, talking and laughing behind their hands.

In class, she hid behind a curtain of holoscreens, but they couldn't block out the words, spoken just a little too loud for secrecy. The dreaded words. *Special Girl*. Dorian even said it right to her face, while Tis giggled.

By the time lunch came around, the skin on her back crawled and she waited until everyone left before coming out from behind her station. The hallway outside was deserted. She turned away from the dining hall and headed for a lift up to one of the trackside lounges that Dorian had reviled the day before.

She found a lounge deserted by all but a pair of older students and their companions. Only the companions – a bager-zyl, with its pointed black and white face and short, stubby body, and a dober-shepherd, lean and almost as tall as Fink, the deep red and gold of its fur shining in the overhead lights – looked up, and they were more interested in Fink than her.

Leaving Fink to his new friends, she wandered over to one end of the lounge. Two alcoves faced each other across the carpet. They were shadowy, lit only by the glow of the holos within. She moved towards one. The holograms themselves stood in a semicircle. Larger than life, four of Jørn's greatest Riders flickered on their dust-covered plinths. Before the mag-web, they had braved the planet's surface to scout for food, water and other supplies.

They wore skin-tight envirosuits under the tough, bulky overalls and boots that had been the Rider's uniform, their helmets tucked under their arms, their companions behind them. The roomal was a golden behemoth, towering above them all with its upright posture and a neck almost as long as its body. Its muscular tail was longer than its neck and body combined, and thick enough at the base that Hero would have had needed a second pair of hands to encircle it. That didn't make the slale-ram standing next to it look any smaller, not with its huge shoulders and large, scaly head, horns curling around blunt ears to end in sharp points either side of its snout. Its black scales drank in the light and spat it out again in iridescent ripples that changed colour with each new angle. Hero doubted that even Fink would roll about with one of those, not that he'd ever get the chance.

The roomal and the slale-ram weren't seen in the cities anymore. The roomal wasn't even in the Farm's breeding program, extinct but for a few samples stored in the gene-banks, right next to those for Old Terra dogs, horses and wombats, probably never to be seen again.

The Farm was like that, or so her mother said, always making things bigger and better but never looking backwards.

The Lamb spoke from behind her, making her jump. 'Reminders of the people who made all of this possible, not that many remember.' She started to point the holos out. 'Lau—'

'Launce Misra, Julia Yi, Suk Song and Beatrice Shrew.' Hero knew them all, knew their companions, their missions, how they had died. Beatrice was her favourite, and not just because of the grey-speckled ruc-pard at her side. 'That's Puca,' she said as the holos flickered. 'A second-gen 'pard. The geneticists spliced more rucnart DNA into them then.' It had made the 'pards stronger but the extra helping of genes from Jørn's largest land-based predator had made them more dangerous too.

The Lamb was silent for a moment, studying the holos with her. 'I didn't realise you wanted to be a Rider.'

Hero shuffled her feet. 'There are no more Riders.'

'Of course there are.' The Lamb smiled. 'They're just not called Riders anymore.'

'You mean like the people who work for my mum.' Hero shook her head. 'They're not Riders. Not really. They have drones and hovers and envirodomes. All *they* had,' she said, pointing to the holos, 'were their companions.'

'And a shorter life expectancy.' The Lamb shook her head. 'It was a hard life.'

'But it was free.'

'Nothing's free from the inside of an envirosuit.'

Hero paused at that, her head snapping around. 'You've been groundside?'

'Just once, during training.'

Hero's gaze narrowed. Not just anyone was allowed to go to the surface. 'What sort of training sends a nanny groundside?'

The Lamb froze, and Hero thought she saw panic in her gaze but it was gone an instant later. 'I wasn't always a nanny,' she said.

'What were you?'

The Lamb smiled but didn't answer.

As the Lamb turned back to study the holos, Hero studied her. There was something in the way the woman stood, in the way the light shadowed the planes of her face and muscles of her arms that made her look less like a lamb and more like a shunk-wolf, all lean strength and wicked teeth hidden under a fluffy white coat.

What had that note at the end of the Robin's files meant? Who, or what, had recruited Imogen Lambert, and why?

The Lamb raised a brow when she caught her staring. 'I'll see you at the end of the day.' She turned to walk away.

'You're the only minder who's ever left me alone outside of the house, you know,' she said to her back.

'You're a big girl,' the Lamb said over her shoulder.

Hero watched as the Lamb walked away, carefully avoiding Fink and the dober-shepherd as they wrestled on the floor. When she had disappeared into the lift, Hero turned back to Beatrice Shrew and Puca. 'I'm going to be just like you,' she said. 'One day.'

Both Rider and 'pard gazed into the distance but, as their holos flickered again, it seemed that something else stared out at her.

She felt the shock like a jolt to her heart. She scurried forward, peering at the holo, but the white, formless shape that had been there before was gone, leaving only Beatrice and Puca behind.

She blinked and almost turned away until something fluttered on Puca's harness. She leaned close to the chest piece, staring hard at the faded blue bird with its red breast, engraved in the holographic leather, its wings extended in flight. For several heartbeats, nothing happened and the tension in her spine built, a tight coil of nerves wrapped around the bone and creeping, vertebra-by-vertebra, upwards. The bird moved.

She jumped. Holostatues didn't move, and most definitely did not flutter in the manner the bird just moved its wings.

She looked closer and then, as suspicion darkened her mind, whipped around, but the alcove was clear. There was no one there but her, no one to point or laugh or giggle and say 'Gotcha!'.

She turned back to the holo. The robin still fluttered its wings. If it wasn't a trick, then what was it? Some sort of glitch in the emitter? A virus? It didn't look like any virus she'd ever seen, or programmed. In fact, it didn't look much like an engraving anymore either. Where before there had just been an outline, now she could make out eyes and feathers and the pointy tips of its feet.

Slowly she reached out, expecting her hand to pass through the beam of light; instead she felt the silky softness of feathers and the gentle prick of talons as the bird hopped onto her hand.

Startled, she jerked her hand back. The bird disappeared. Curious, she again reached her hand towards the holostatue. The bird reappeared, ruffling its feathers as if it had never left her fingers. It obviously couldn't exist outside the statue's projection field, no matter how real it felt. 'Still a hologram then,' she said to herself.

A hologram that would have taken the programming skills of a genius. But why here, in this forgotten alcove of equally forgotten heroes, where almost no one would see? It didn't make sense. Unless someone really was messing with her.

As she pondered that, the bird hopped towards her wrist and pecked at her bracelet, its beak making a fizzing sound when it hit the metal. She wondered how she could get her hands on its DNA, until the bird's pecks made the bracelet spit and spark, the shock slithering through her skin.

She yanked her hand back with a hiss.

Fink stuck his head over her shoulder.

She just about jumped out of her skin.

He rumbled in concern.

'I would be okay, if people would stop sneaking up on me.'

He didn't sneak, she just wasn't paying attention.

'Whatever. Weren't you wrestling with the dober-shepherd?'

He was, but she wasn't very good, not enough legs. Besides, it was almost time to go.

'Go where?'

The lunch bell rang.

Back to class.

'You can tell the time now?'

No, but the dober-shepherd could.

'Sure she can.' Hero straightened, rubbing her wrist and taking a last look at the holostatue to see the robin back in its place on Puca's chest guard.

CHAPTER 9

Hero had barely settled back into her workstation after lunch when her bracelet sparked again. It didn't shock her, but a line of light leapt to the smooth, black surface of her workstation and disappeared.

Fink peered over her shoulder, his ears and whiskers pricked forward in interest. *That was strange*, he thought at her. *How did she do that?*

'I didn't,' she said.

Oh, well okay then. He sighed miserably, sending her a final thought as he settled into a comfortable spot behind her. *He'd missed lunch again, and now she owed him something tasty.*

'I'll have Chef make you a spice cake.'

With icing, and extra chocolate.

'Fine,' she said, only half-listening as, amid the forest of physics exercises and tutorials, a new holoscreen sprung to life. There were just two words on it, "Meet Me", with a timestamp underneath and a red-breasted robin in the corner. Her mysterious messenger wanted to meet her tomorrow during lunch, but where and why?

The message vanished, erasing itself from her station like it had never existed, but it left something behind. She leaned in close, peering intently at the square of criss-crossing lines with a pulsing dot at its centre. It looked like a map, but of what?

'How did you get a schematic of a sealed level?'

This time, she nearly leapt right out of her seat.

Norah smiled. 'Jumpy?'

'Snoopy?'

'At least I'm not breaking any laws, even if it is only a minor one.' She shrugged and reached up to scratch Harish's head. Looped around her neck, Harish cracked an eyelid as he shifted in his sleep. 'Not that that will stop you from getting expelled.'

'They can't expel me for looking at something.'

'But they can if you break into a secure database to get it.'

'I didn't break into anything.' This morning at least.

'Then how come the schematic is on your screen?'

'I don't know. And what makes you such an expert anyway?'

Norah's nose rose in the air. 'My dads are lawyers.'

'Is that why *you* weren't expelled?'

'*I* wasn't expelled because I didn't do anything illegal.'

'That's not what everyone else says.'

'Like the way everyone else says you're loopy?' Norah raised her brow. 'Just because they say it, doesn't mean you have to believe it.'

Fink nudged her mind, sending her an image of Mrs Rahm's stern, freckled face just in time for her to hide the map before the tutor walked past.

'Enough socialising ladies, physics waits for no one. Go on,' she said, pinning Norah with her stare. 'Back to your workstation.'

As Norah dutifully retreated to the other side of the classroom, Hero pretended to work on the equation before her, waiting until Mrs Rahm had walked away before she called up the map again. It had to belong to the academy – given the midday meeting time it was the only place that made sense – but the tower had over three-hundred levels and the map gave no indication of which one.

Fink whuffed in her ear, his whiskers tickling her neck. *What was she doing?*

'What do you think I'm doing?' she whispered.

He sent her a memory of the last time Tybalt had caught her hacking her mum's credit line, and the look on his face, part disappointment and part anger, while he lectured her. Fink twitched his nose, his whiskers dragging along her cheek. *He wasn't quite sure what expelled was, but he was pretty sure it was worse than that.*

'I'm not getting expelled.'

Was she sure?

'Yes,' she said, catching a boy staring at her, a look of embarrassment mixed with horror on his face.

She jutted her chin out and raised her voice a little. 'Do you mind?'

He turned back to his workstation, his hands flying over his keyboard. She caught the faint ding of messages sent and received.

Across from her, Tis giggled and next to her, Dorian barely tried to hide a loudly muttered 'Freak' behind a cough.

She glared at him and went back to studying the map behind her curtain of holoscreens.

CHAPTER 10

By lunchtime the next day, she had the map figured out. It showed the layout of level two hundred and forty-eight, one of over two hundred that had been sealed and abandoned decades ago. As Norah had warned, access was restricted and Hero had spent several hours planning a way to reach it.

They couldn't use the main lift; it was too easy to notice it going where it shouldn't. Instead she found a disused service lift, squished behind the academy's kitchen. Getting it to take her so far below wasn't very difficult once she popped the maintenance panel; the tricky part had been masking the tracker in her bracelet. There had been no way to disable it without bringing an army or worse down upon her head. But with a little tweaking and a minor cold, she'd managed to fool it into thinking she was in the classroom. But that wouldn't last long, a half-hour, if she was lucky.

Whatever the Robin had to say, she hoped it was quick.

Fink shifted nervously as the lift whisked them downwards. *Couldn't they have done this after lunch?*

'No,' she said as the doors opened.

Beyond the small semicircle of light cast by the lift, level two-forty-eight was dark and quiet, heavy with dust and stale air. She shivered from the cold. No one wasted power where it wasn't needed, but there must have been some, because as she stepped out of the lift, emergency lighting began to glow in dim, yellow lines along the walls, disappearing into the darkness.

She shivered again. The click of Fink's claws against the floor echoed in the void, sending prickles rippling under her skin.

The lift doors closed behind them. Without the lift's light, the yellow-tinted gloom grew heavy and the shadows, as thick on the ground as the dust, grew with it.

Maybe this hadn't been such a good idea.

Fink shifted against her, sending her images of a plate full of food and his hopeful face.

Pursing her lips, she pushed the thought of ghosts and lunch out of her mind and swung onto Fink's back. The Robin knew things, things about the Lamb, and Hero suspected even more. If she wanted to know what it knew, then they had to meet.

She activated the Robin's map and the small screen above her bracelet added its own blue tinge to the gloom. Two tiny figures, one of a girl and the other a ruc-pard, showed their position, while their destination was a dot somewhere in the far south corner. Between them lay a maze of corridors.

With a slight squeeze of her knees and a half-thought, Fink started walking into the darkness. The light along the walls was broken in places, leaving gaps where she could just make out doors. She wondered about the people who had lived behind them. Maybe if she dragged her hand along the walls, she'd pick up their memories as easily as she would the dust. The thought sent a shiver down her spine. If she could, would they stampede through her mind, fading as quickly as they came, or would they linger, haunting her until she died?

Beneath her, Fink stopped and rumbled, his chest vibrating between her knees. He twisted his head around to look at her out of one black eye. *Would she stop? She was giving him the willies too.*

She sunk both her hands into his ruff. 'Sorry.'

That was okay. Besides, he didn't blame her, it smelled funny down here.

'Like how?'

Like dust and old things. He lifted his nose, making it flare and twitch as he took another breath. *And roaches, he definitely caught the scent of roaches.*

'Roaches?'

Mmm-hmm. There is an intersection up here. Which way where they going?

'Ugh.' She glanced down at the map. 'Right. There aren't meant to be any roaches up this high, the maintenance crews are meant to keep them out.' But then, they were also meant to dust.

He shrugged and started down the next corridor. *He didn't think there'd been anyone down here in a while, not that he could smell.*

'Great.'

Don't worry, he had teeth and claws. He could take a roach, no problem.

'Ugh-huh. The biggest thing you've ever taken down is one of Mum's sparkle fish.'

It was a pity she'd stopped stocking them.

'Only because you ate them all.'

The map took them deep into the maze, twisting and turning down what seemed like an endless series of hallways, until they turned one more and found themselves at a dead end. In front of them was a door, just like all of the others.

She glanced down at the map. 'This is it,' she said as she slid from Fink's back. 'The map leads here.'

With no emergency lights along the walls, the gloom was deeper here and neither she nor Fink could see clearly, but she could see enough to know there was no one waiting for them.

'Hello?' Her voice echoed eerily in the dark.

Nothing.

Fink moved close behind her hand made an enquiring cough.

Still nothing.

Hero bit her lip and studied the map. 'We're in the right place. Maybe the Robin is late?'

A point of blue-white light suddenly glimmered in the centre of the door. Curious, she reached out to touch it, but before she did the glow expanded, forming a robin-shaped hologram. It hovered in the air before her, as it had in the alcove of Riders, perched on an imaginary branch, its wings tucked neatly against its sides as it cocked its head and chirped.

Fink stuck his head under her arm and straight through the holo, dissipating it in a cloud of static.

'Fi-iink,' she complained, but before the last syllable left her tongue the bird had reappeared on the tip of his nose.

It ruffled its feathers and opened its beak, but instead of chirping, it spoke. 'Welcome.' Behind it, the door started to open.

Fink yowled in pain.

Hero spun. In the gloom she could make out a linch-adder, half-wrapped around Fink's neck, its fangs sunk into his ear as he reared on his hind legs and batted at it with his other four paws. She made a lunge for the 'adder, grabbing its scaly half-feathered tail before she had to leap out of the way of Fink's thrashing.

'Harish!' The girl's voice startled the 'adder into flight.

She didn't need to see the girl's face to recognise her, not when lavender and menthol brushed the edges of her mind. 'You need a leash on that thing.'

'He's not a thing,' Norah shot back, 'and you were glad enough he didn't have a leash when we got you out of that mess on the track.'

'He didn't attack us then.'

'Yeah, well your *Woolsey* hadn't tried to eat him then either, so we're square.'

Hero glanced sideways at Fink, letting the statement hang in her mind.

He rolled his lip, flashing a hint of fang, as he replayed a memory from that morning. In it, Harish dived at the 'pard's head, trilling war cries, until he snagged one of Fink's ears in his claws, causing the 'pard to snap. *It wasn't his fault that the 'adder was bite-sized.*

'Fine,' Hero said, even as a glare settled over her brow. 'We're even. What are you doing down here?'

'What does it look like I'm doing?' Norah put her hands to her hips, and in the darkness, Hero could feel her glare right back. 'I'm following you.'

'Why?'

'Because you're up to something, and it's going to get you in trouble.'

Hero narrowed her eyes, but before she could open her mouth to ask why the other girl would care, something skittered in the darkness.

Fink's head shot up and his ears pricked forward, his huge body tensing. He growled.

'What was that?' Norah said.

At the other end of the hallway, something big blocked the emergency lights.

Hero swallowed. 'I think it's a roach.'

'What?' Norah squawked in much the same way Hero imagined her 'adder did.

'A roach,' she repeated, pointing towards the advancing shadow.

'Oh.' Norah's eyes went wide as she turned to look. 'But, the maintenance crews—'

'Have you noticed the dust?'

At her side, Fink crouched. *It wasn't very big, he could take it.*

More sharp, pointy feet than could possibly belong to a single roach skittered in the darkness.

'But you can't take a swarm,' she said as she swung onto his back. She held out her hand to Norah. 'Get on Fink.'

'Huh?'

'Get on.'

'But—'

'Just hurry up,' she said. The skittering came closer. 'Unless you want to be roach food.'

For a moment the other girl just stood there, and Hero thought she was going to refuse, until the long swaying ends of the roach's antenna caught the light. Norah slapped her hand into Hero's, who pulled her up just as Harish launched into the air.

'Hold on tight,' she said.

Fink leapt forward.

They pounded down the hallway, the roach looming larger and larger, until they were close enough to see the hard, shiny curve of its exoskeleton and the drool glistening on the serrated edge of its mandibles.

Beneath them, Fink bunched his muscles and Hero gripped him tighter as Norah's arms squeezed her waist. Two strides from the roach and Fink jumped, almost flattening the insect as he spring-boarded off its back, twisting in mid-air to bounce off the adjacent wall and around the corner. He hit the ground and barely slowed as they raced for the lift and safety.

Ahead of them, Hero could see Harish streaking through the air, his wings and tail pumping. She wondered how he could possibly know what he was doing – or where he was going – without Norah to guide him, until he came whipping back around a corner, his beak open in a screech that just about pierced her ears.

'Stop!' Norah yelled. 'There's a whole swarm around there.'

Fink skidded to a halt.

'How'd you—?'

'Harish,' she said. 'He's a scout, remember?'

'But how—?'

'There's no time, just turn around!'

Antenna waved around the corner, and Fink didn't need to be told twice, spinning on his hindquarters and barrelling back the way they'd come.

'Go right,' Norah said as they approached another intersection.

'The map says left.'

'Just do it.'

Harish banked right and Fink followed. Hero twisted to look over Norah's shoulder, seeing another mass of antenna-waving shadows down the corridor they would have taken. Swallowing, she twisted back.

She lost count of the twists and turns they took, but Fink was breathing hard and the air behind them was heavy with the skittering of pointy feet, when the lift came into sight. Its doors were closed, but Harish dived at it, clinging to the control panel and pounding it with his beak, until, with a ding, it opened.

With the roaches almost nipping at his heels, Fink didn't slow down. Instead, just a handful of strides from the lift, he sat back on his hindlegs, his claws screeching along the floor as they skidded into the lift.

Twisting about, she reached for the control panel, to find Harish already there and the doors closing. With another ding, the lift started to move.

Fink sagged to the floor, panting. Hero slithered off his back and joined him, followed a moment later by Norah. Harish glided from the control panel to perch on her shoulder.

'So, why did you follow me?' Hero asked.

'I told you, you're going to get yourself into trouble.'

'Why do you care?'

'Why wouldn't I?'

'Because no one else does.'

Norah pinned her with a look. 'You need better friends.'

Fink raised his head and grunted.

'Human friends,' Norah amended as she stood, offering her hand.

Hero studied it for moment, wondering what the other girl wanted. Was it just friendship, or was there something else? Maybe the whole thing was a trick and—

Fink gave her a nudge.

She put her hand in Norah's and let the other girl pull her to her feet, just as the lift reached its destination.

The doors dinged open. The Lamb stood on the other side, her arms crossed and her comm-unit flashing an angry red.

Hero felt her face go white. The cold she gave the tracker on her bracelet must have worn off.

'You're late for class, and your mother wants to see you after school,' was all she said.

CHAPTER 11

In the hover, the Lamb didn't say anything, but there was a kink to her lips and a gleam in her eye that gave her the look of an emgator, smiling from beneath the water.

It made Hero nervous. If her mother found out she'd bypassed her tracker and gone where she'd gone, she could kiss the academy, the city and any hope of freedom goodbye. She could only cling to the fact that the Lamb had lied to the headmaster when he stopped them in the corridor to admonish Hero and Norah for being tardy.

'My fault,' the Lamb had said, smiling her emgator smile, and the headmaster had let them go without another word.

Hero should have felt relief at the Lamb's lie, but that smile… What was she waiting for? What did she want? The questions churned in her stomach as they skirted the city's core and headed for its outskirts.

Gradually, through the patchwork of holoboards and holoscreens, the towers they passed began to look newer and less stained with dust and dirt. The closer to the outskirts they went, the more the buildings were faced with steelglas and the more sunlight shone off their surfaces. The outermost towers gleamed orange in the light of the setting sun.

High on the city's edge, where the air was thin and stray thermals caused the hover to dip and shudder, Bayard Explorations occupied the top one hundred and twenty-seven floors of one such tower.

Still buffeted by the wind, the hover slid through an opening in a steelglas dome and settled on the floor of a large hover bay. Judging from the activity, it wasn't the visitors' pad. Around them, people in uniforms emblazoned with the Bayard logo were loading shuttles with crates and boxes while others were under vehicles or pulling them apart.

A few companions, great hulking sternards, that were a bigger and shaggier version of sterdanes like Dorian's Grey, barked greetings at Fink as they walked past. Most were loaded up with tech harnesses and survival gear, standing next to humans in heavy pants and boots with equipment belts slung around their waists. From the bulky packs at the riders' feet and the enviromasks at their sides, she guessed it was an expedition heading groundside and briefly wondered what their mission was. She didn't see any science or survey equipment, although that could have been packed in the crates being loaded aboard the shuttle. But then, neither did she see any rich clients dressed to go on a hunt, carefully controlled and managed by Bayard scouts, just so they could hang a new rucnart pelt on their wall.

At another time, she would have stopped and talked to the people just to find out, but the Lamb kept her moving.

The Bayard AI accosted them almost as soon as they crossed the threshold. Its avatar, another featureless humanoid, shimmered to life directly in their path.

'Greetings. Please identify.'

'Imogen Lambert and Hero Regan. We have an appointment.'

'Of course. Please follow the green line.' At mid-height along the wall, a line of green light streaked away from the avatar. It stopped at the junction of three corridors and pulsed gently, waiting for them to catch up.

The Lamb marched after it, leaving Hero to hurry along in her wake and forcing Fink out of his lazy amble.

Inside, Bayard bustled with people and companions, all of them with the white and gold Bayard logo on their chest and somewhere to go. Some followed their own holographic lines, in reds and blues and yellows, down the corridors, but most hurried about with their heads bent over personal readouts.

A lift whisked them upwards, the floors ticking over and over. She fidgeted. Imogen smiled, and Fink sighed against the back of her neck. *He hoped this didn't take long, they'd missed lunch again.*

The lift deposited them at the very top of the tower. The green line streaked ahead, down a wide corridor with cream-coloured walls lined with actual paintings, to pulse before the desk of a middle-aged man behind a workstation the size of Hero's bed.

'Ms Lambert. Ms Regan.' The receptionist smiled as he nodded to them both, although it seemed to grow wider when he inclined his head towards Hero. 'Your mother is just finishing a call, but she said to show you in immediately.' He stood and gestured for them to follow.

Her mum's office reminded her of home. It had the same soft wool carpet, the same lighting and knick-knacks, and the same piles of work covering the desk. The only difference was the window: a huge pane of plasglas stretching the width of the office, looking out over the tops of the surrounding buildings and to the patchwork of 'burbs beyond.

'I've sent the information to your workstation.' On one of the holoscreens on her mum's desk, a man in a lab coat looked apologetic. 'I'm not sure what more we can do. There are only a few records of Ayumon's mission prior to colonisation and none after Doctor Woolsey's outpost was officially evacuated.'

Ayumon. The name rang a bell in her memory and she recalled crouching outside her mum's study, eavesdropping on the argument between her and the faceless man.

Next to her, Imogen stiffened, like a skunk-wolf sighting prey, and Hero remembered something else: the tips of two shiny black shoes peeking out from behind another door.

She looked to Fink, but he shrugged his mid-quarters. *He hadn't even been there.*

'What about the Planetary Librarian?' her mum asked.

The man in the lab coat shook his head. 'I had it run a thorough search of the archives and...' He raised his palms. 'As far as the Library is concerned, the Ayumon AI no longer exists.'

She thought she heard her mum curse under her breath. 'Thank you, doctor. Tell me if you find anything else,' she said and ended the call. Sighing, her mum rubbed at the crease between her brows as she turned to Hero. 'How was school?'

She raised her chin. 'It was okay.'

'Hmm.' Rising like her bones ached, her mum came around the front of the desk and took a seat in one of the lounge chairs before it.

Without a word, Imogen took a chair opposite, her smile dislodged by the faint line of tension running through her body.

Hero remained standing, her arms crossed, as she waited for the lecture.

'I've spoken to the school.' Hero's spine stiffened. 'As well as your tutors, everyone seems to think you're doing well. So I've arranged for you to spend some time here, in the tech division.'

Her jaw might have been hanging open, but Hero wasn't quite sure. She'd been expecting to be bundled into the nearest airship and sent back to the estate. Instead... The Bayard tech division produced the best equipment this side of the New Gobi. If she could get her hands on it—

A memory, tinged mawberry, exploded behind her eyes. In it, she was eight years old and stood before a large hole in her bedroom wall, with the other half of the device she'd filched from her mum's study in her hands. Her mum had stopped bringing devices home after that.

'Doctor Tachi, the division's head, has agreed to an informal internship, which will be worked around school and study, and...' her mum continued, pinning Hero with a look that promised dire things if she stepped out of line, 'contingent upon your continued good behaviour.'

The sideways slide of her eyes towards the Lamb was reflex. The woman just raised her brows and smiled. Hero narrowed her gaze; there was a catch here, wasn't there?

'It's not racing, and it won't get you groundside, but it won't get you killed either.' Her mum paused, as if expecting something from her.

Hero just looked at her, her mind racing as she tried to put together the Lamb's silence with this newfound boon.

Her mum's lips came together, compressing into a thin line as she got to her feet. 'It's as much as I'm willing to comprise. Take it or leave it.'

'Thanks, Mum,' she said.

Her mother's shoulders and lips relaxed. 'You're welcome.' She smiled, the expression making her eyes sparkle. 'You should also thank Ms Lambert. It was her recommendation that swayed me.'

The smile on Imogen's face grew, but there was something calculating behind her eyes that rang alarm bells in Hero's mind.

'Thank you,' she said.

The holoterminal beeped with an incoming call.

The Lamb rose. 'I'll escort Hero to the tech lab.'

With three floors of labs filled with gadgets, the tech division was a playground made up of racing harnesses, biocomps, drones, probes and micro hovers. The thoughts that had been racing around her head, of Ayumon and Imogen's strange behaviour, were forgotten the moment they stepped out of the lift.

The same man in the lab coat she'd seen on her mother's holoterminal waited for them inside. In person, he was tall, with a pudgy belly and a lined but serious face. Hero wondered whether it was his work, or the prospect of having his boss's daughter as an intern that caused the bags under his eyes. He had a data sheet in one hand, holoscreen aglow above it, and a lab-coated assistant at his side. He looked up when they approached.

'Doctor Tachi,' the Lamb said, making introductions. 'Hero Regan.'

'Yes, thank you.' Doctor Tachi's smile was distracted, but his eyes were sharp.

'I'll leave you to it.' With another smile, the Lamb departed.

Fink trailed the Lamb, thoughts of womba-cow steak firm in his mind.

Hero watched them go, and wondered what the Lamb did when she wasn't following her around.

The click of a stylus brought her attention back to the doctor.

'Right, follow me,' he said, and marched into the maze of labs.

Hero had to trot to keep up. They passed clear-sided lab after clear-sided lab, all with something on the workbenches or holoscreens that made her fingers itch to touch.

'You're starting out in inventory,' Doctor Tachi said. 'Mr Peare is the overseer and will be your supervisor while you're there. You will also need this.' He handed her a data slide. 'All staff are required to pass this certification before they can assist in the labs, most especially our very junior staff.' He pinned her with a look. 'Which would be you. Understood?'

She nodded.

'Excellent.' He came to a halt before a workstation large enough to require its own room, behind which sat a large man with a crinkly face and no hair. 'Mr Peare, this is Ms Regan, your new assistant. Try not to lose her in the warehouse.' With a smile and a clasp of her shoulder, the doctor left.

Peare waved her over, barely looking up from the workstation. 'Right, well Regan, here's how things work.'

The inventory system was huge, a smorgasbord of drones and biocomps and a gazillion other things she'd only ever dreamed of. If her fingers had itched before, now they practically burned. But with Peare looking over her shoulder, the most she could do was make a mental shopping list.

When a lab technician called Peare away, she dived into the database, rummaging through her mental shopping list. One record immediately caught her eye, distracting her from her list: Ayumon.

Casting a glance around to make sure Peare was still absent, she brought it up on screen.

There wasn't much to see, just a list of artefacts brought back from a groundside expedition and a link to a report she couldn't access without a few hours alone or a more sophisticated bracelet.

She wasn't the only one trying to take an unauthorised peek. A brief pause was all the warning she had before she was dumped out of the record with a large 'unauthorised access' notice stamped on the screen.

'Someone's tickled network security,' Peare said over her shoulder. 'You?'

She shook her head. 'No.'

He gave her a hard look and nodded. 'Let's see if we can find out who it was then, shall we?' he said, bringing up a holorecording with a few flicks of his fingers. If Peare had had eyebrows they'd have met over his nose as he scowled.

Hero peered closer at the holovid. Whoever had tried to access the report had covered the security-holo first; all that was left to see was the edge of a workstation and a familiar pair of shiny black shoes.

'Damn,' he muttered, reaching for a comm-unit. 'Get me security. I think we have a problem.'

Dinner was as silent as the ride home had been, where Imogen's shoes had gleamed in every passing light. To Hero, it had seemed as if there was a disco going off in the corner of her eye, one that not even the novel presence of her mother on the seat next to her could distract her from. Even with no lights to dance off Imogen's shoes, she still couldn't take her mind off them. When Imogen left the table, she followed.

Near the garage, she hid behind a sideboard and when Imogen slipped inside, she rushed the door, catching it a second before it closed. On the other side came the sound of a comm-unit, and a man's voice answering.

'I have something,' Imogen said.

'Is it any good?'

'Maybe. I'll meet you at the usual place.'

'Give me fifteen minutes.'

The comm-unit beeped as the call ended.

The sound of an engine starting had her peeking around the door just in time to see a mini-hover shoot out of the garage door, Imogen in the driver's seat.

Hero's heart beat faster and her knees were jelly-like as the full realisation hit. Imogen was a spy, she had to be, and now she was going to take whatever she'd stolen today to… to whom? Whom was she going to meet, and whom did she work for? There was only one way to find out.

She ran back to her bedroom.

Fink lay in his usual position in front of the holofire, half-twisted on his back with his fore and midlegs in the air, but he raised his head and chortled when Hero scrambled in.

'Imogen's a spy,' she burst out. 'And we're going to search her room.'

He sat up abruptly. *They were what?*

'Searching Imogen's room,' she said as she rummaged through her collection of data slides, grabbing the one she wanted.

He shot her an image of a very angry Imogen, his ears twitching in discomfort.

'She's gone to meet her handler… or whatever – she'll never know. Now come on, you're my lookout,' she said before heading out the door.

Imogen's suite wasn't locked. Hero would have locked her door if she was spying on the people she lived with, but apparently Imogen didn't live by the same rules. Perhaps she'd thought a locked door would raise suspicion. Beyond the door the room was neat, tidy and devoid of personal belongings or any sort of personality beyond that of her mother's decorator.

She started with the workstation, a tiny black desk that was hardly more than a comm-unit, pressing the data slide into the input. The program went to work, blurring the desktop in a tornado of tiny screens that popped up and then away, but there was no password for it to hack and nothing of interest for it to stir up in its search.

For a moment, disappointment settled in her stomach, but then she narrowed her eyes and looked around. If she were a spy, she probably wouldn't hide anything in her workstation either.

She searched the bed then, but there was nothing in it, under it, stashed in the wardrobe or in the underwear drawer. Searching behind the sofa failed to reveal so much as a hairball, nor did the desk or the ensuite. She looked around the room, cushions and sheets thrown about in her search, drawers and cupboards all standing open.

Fink grumbled. *So much for the Lamb never knowing someone had been there.*

She frowned at him and thought. If she were a spy, where would she hide her kit? If she even had a kit. Maybe Imogen kept everything in her head; greywork wasn't that uncommon. She could have had anything implanted in her skull.

Fink chortled. *He'd found something.*

In the darkness of the wardrobe, a small package was attached to the ceiling, out of Hero's reach, but not Fink's. She took it from his forepaws and opened the pouch, uncovering a data slide and a slick-looking biocomp, the kind that wrapped around the user's forearm like a second skin.

'A bracer,' she said, her eyes lighting up. 'What kind of nanny needs one this fancy?'

Fink just flicked his ears and looked nervously towards the door, sending her an image of a herd of angry Imogens, all larger-than-life as they charged through the door.

She rolled her eyes. 'Worrywart.' But he had a point. Spy or not, when Imogen found her room trashed and her stash gone, she was going to come looking for someone. Hero just had to make sure it wasn't her.

A quick circuit of the room and she had the cushions back in place, bed sheets straightened and drawers closed. It might not have been as neat as before but at least it wasn't a bomb site.

Fink was already waiting for her in the hallway, his ears twitching madly.

'You worry too much.' She gave him a rub under the chin as she passed and led the way down the stairs. The slide was all but burning a hole in her pocket, and the bracer... She couldn't help the slight skip in her step as she thought of it.

Halfway to her room, she rebounded off Tybalt's chest. She stumbled, but he caught her elbows before she crashed to the floor and stood her upright. When she looked up, the surprise on his face was quickly replaced by a forehead-wrinkling frown.

'Fink,' he said as he looked over her head. 'Out.'

With a small whine, Fink disappeared out the balcony door.

Tybalt shifted his gaze from the departing ruc-pard to Hero. 'What are you up to?'

'Nothing.'

He crossed his arms and stared at her.

She stared back.

Long, silent seconds clicked by and the stolen package, tucked under her arm, gained a weight beyond its size.

Tybalt blinked first. 'What is that?' He gestured to the package.

'A surprise.'

'May I see it?' He held out a hand.

'No, it's a *surprise*,' she said with a roll of her eyes.

'Will I regret letting you keep it?'

'No.'

'Will there be any unexpected purchases on your parents' credit lines?'

'No.'

'Will there be any unexpected purchases on *my* credit line?'

'No,' she said again, drawing the word out to three syllables in exasperation.

Tybalt's gaze narrowed, his eyes shadowed by the drawn line of his brows, and he considered her in silence.

She tried not to squirm.

He sighed and something unwound in the line of his shoulders, the suspicion drained from his expression and it left him looking tired. 'Fine. Off with you,' he said, with a tilt of his head towards her room. 'Tomorrow's a school day.'

Back in her room, the workstation hummed as soon as she put her hands to the black surface. It was the work of a few moments to access the house's many security-holos and alter the recordings, substituting the image of her and Fink entering Imogen's room for Tybalt. It wasn't her most masterful work but it would create enough suspicion to keep Imogen off her back for a while.

That done, she dug the data slide out of Imogen's package and pressed it into the input gel. Data, scrambled worse than that time she'd tried to make eggs for breakfast, filled the holoscreen.

'Damn.' It was encrypted. She sorted through her slide collection before finding the one she wanted and pressing it into the gel beside the first.

It hummed for several long minutes, during which Fink scratched at the balcony door and she let him in to lounge before the holofire, before it beeped and another screen popped to life.

She swore, a word that made Fink raise his head and tilt his ears sideways in surprise. The data slide wasn't just encrypted, it was DNA-locked. She swore again.

Fink whined.

'If it were any other type of encryption…' she began. But it wasn't, and without the correct DNA sample there was no way she was cracking it, and if the slide was locked, then the bracer… She dug it out and put it on.

Studded with holotransmitters and biocircuitry, the bracer was a thin sheet of transparent biogel. It wrapped around her forearm like a cool cloth and came to life with a shiver, like a rush of goosebumps, before it turned translucent and glowed with blue-white veins of electricity.

Nothing happened for a heartbeat, and then a small holoscreen appeared above her wrist. *Unauthorised user. Emergency functions only.*

'Damn,' she muttered, and cast a glance at her workstation. Not only was she going to need that DNA sample, she needed better equipment too.

CHAPTER 12

The next morning over breakfast, Imogen's resemblance to an Old Terra lamb had faded. Her green eyes were narrow and her brows were a stern line as she stared at Hero across the table. She looked more like a shunk-wolf more than ever, bright green eyes locked on her prey. Hero could almost picture the sharp white muzzle and the black feathers running in parallel lines down her back.

Hero calmly poured syrup over her pancakes and concentrated on cutting them into bite-sized pieces. Her ears were buzzing, a high-pitched squeal that was close to driving her insane, and Imogen's stare was a strapple-flavoured laser that only made it worse. At least she wasn't hearing voices, yet.

Her trick with the holocams obviously hadn't worked – either that, or Imogen had confronted Tybalt.

He sat at the other end of the table, and although the frown across his forehead almost made his brows touch, it was being directed at his palm-unit and he looked more distracted than angry.

Getting up from the table was a relief, but not as much as climbing into the hover and having Fink settle at her feet. The buzzing faded from her ears, and not even Imogen's stare, Tybalt's distracted frown or the stolen data slide tucked in her sleeve could disturb the peace she felt.

The sense of peace followed her, a comfortable bubble that floated her out of the hover and into the academy, so that she almost missed Norah waiting for her in the foyer.

The purple flash of Harish's tail was the first notion she had that the other girl was beside her, and if it hadn't been for Fink's mental nudge, she might have jumped out of her skin. Again.

'Are you grounded?' Norah asked.

'No.'

'But your minder caught us red-handed.'

'She kept her mouth shut.'

'Why?'

'She's got secrets of her own.'

'Like?'

Hero stopped in the middle of the corridor, Norah stopping beside her. For a moment, she eyed the other girl as she considered how much to tell her. She hardly knew Norah, but there was something about her… Lavender and menthol brushed the edges of Hero's mind, and she made her decision. 'She's a spy,' she said and continued walking.

'A spy?' Norah walked several steps in silence. 'Isn't that a little… paranoid?'

'Believe me or not, but I caught her.' She stopped outside the classroom and looked around, but Imogen was nowhere in sight. 'And I need your help at lunch.'

In the back of her mind, Fink let loose a mental sigh. *Not lunch again.*

Norah narrowed her gaze. 'Why?'

'To figure out what she wants, and who she works for.'

She crossed her arms over her chest. 'Will we get into trouble?'

'No.'

Harish hissed from Norah's shoulder. Hero glared at the bird.

'Okay,' she said. 'Maybe.'

'Regular trouble or we're-going-to-get-expelled trouble?'

'Regular.'

'Are you sure?'

'Positive.'

A glazed look crossed Norah's expression, and her lips moved, just slightly, as if she was talking to someone. The bell rang, and her eyes refocused. 'Okay. You can tell me about it during class.'

'You ready?' Norah said when the lunch bell rang.

Fink grumbled, projecting an image of a plate piled high with raw womba-cow and the sensation of an empty belly.

'I saw that.' Norah's eyes were wide as she rubbed her stomach. 'And felt it.'

Harish ruffled his feathers.

'I think we all did.' Hero slapped Fink's shoulder. 'Go get something to eat, I'll be fine.'

Was she sure?

'Yes.'

With a gentle head butt, he trotted down the corridor, tail held high.

Norah gave Hero a nudge and gestured behind her. 'There's your minder.'

Imogen's face held a look of determination, one Hero hadn't seen before, and it felt like it was all settled on her.

Norah grabbed her arm. 'Come on.'

Together, they ran for the nearest lift, piling in before the doors closed and just in time for Hero to catch Imogen scowling at her.

Something breathed against the back of Hero's neck. When she turned, she was face-to-snout with Grey, with a close-up view of the scales that covered his big black nose. He huffed, bathing her in the scent of day-old womba-cow.

She gagged and sidled sideways, coming shoulder to shoulder with Norah.

On the other side of the lift, Tis giggled. Dorian stood next to her, his arms crossed across his skinny chest as he leaned against the wall. He smiled.

Hero narrowed her eyes.

Dorian's smile widened.

At her side, Norah shifted, her expression tense as she slipped a small pink candy between her lips.

The soft chime of the lift came just before the doors opened at her back, and Norah again grabbed Hero's elbow and tugged her out of the lift. Hero kept her eyes fixed on Dorian's, her own lips curling as his smile wobbled and the lift doors closed.

'You're asking for trouble with Dorian, you know.'

She turned to Norah. 'I'm good at trouble.'

'Yeah, I noticed.' The other girl looked around before heading left down the empty corridor. 'That doesn't mean you have to chase it.'

Hero kept silent, her forehead creased in thought as Norah slipped into a large, empty room and headed straight for the door on the other side.

Harish leapt from Norah's shoulder and took perch on a ledge half-hidden in the room's shadows.

'This is the secondary tack room,' Norah said, her fingers dashing over a keypad. The door slid open, lights flipping on inside to reveal the workbenches and empty racks of the disused room. 'My sister and I used it to work on our race tack. It's a little out of date, but it works fine.'

'We're not meant to be in here, are we?'

Norah shook her head. 'But Harish will keep watch.'

Slipping the data slide from its hiding place under her bracelet, Hero placed it on the workbench. The moment the slide touched the shiny black surface, the bench's diagnostic systems hummed and a larger-than-life holographic model appeared above.

On the other side, Norah's hands stilled. 'A slide? I thought you said you found a bracer.'

'It was too big to fit up my sleeve.'

'Then why did we sneak into the tack room? You can just stick that in a workstation.'

Hero shook her head as she dug a small packet out of her pocket. 'It's DNA-locked.'

Norah's jaw dropping was almost audible. 'You're not kidding, are you?'

Hero shook her head.

'And you think I can crack that?'

'No,' she said as she took over the bench's controls and set to work. 'But I can.'

That morning, Hero had swiped Imogen's fork, hoping that her DNA was the key. It could have been anything – a fur-rose, a fly, Imogen's long lost aunt – but she hadn't had time to search Imogen's room again, and she probably kept the sample on her anyway. Now, Hero carefully took the fork and laid it next to the slide. Used by the academy's race team to check over their gear, the workbench wasn't made for cracking encryption algorithms, but with a little fiddling its diagnostic systems were soon turned to the task.

Hero carefully manipulated the controls and watched as the bench sampled Imogen's saliva and the holograph above it morphed into a strand of DNA.

'How do you even know what you're doing?' Norah asked.

'Practice.' Next to the DNA strand, she brought up a spiral-like model of the encryption algorithm.

'On what?'

'Mum's credit lines.' The two models spun slowly in the air above the workbench. Just as slowly, she rearranged the DNA model, removing the small, coloured nodules until the gaps in the nucleotides fit the encryption model like a key in a lock.

A screen replaced the models above the workbench. On it was a thin-faced man, visible from the shoulders up. His hair was greying and his face deeply lined.

'It looks like a holovid,' Norah said as she reached for it.

The thin-faced man's brow wrinkled as he talked. 'We've identified Patricia Regan's contact as Benedict Meren, confirming our suspicions that she's working with the Klaude. We're still trying to confirm what this has to do with the Ayumon AI. None of us can quite figure out what Regan or the Klaude would want with an old weather satellite. Records suggest it was scrapped during the Construction.

'The usual data is attached. You'll want to take a closer look at Meren's known associates. Research dug up a nice little surprise.' The man's screen disappeared, replaced by another showing a light-haired man in a suit, the filename identifying him as Benedict Meren.

Hero leaned closer to the screen. There was something wrong with his eyes: they were black, shiny and mechanical. 'Are they …?'

'Cybernetic,' Norah said from the other side of the workbench, her eyes glued to another screen full of data. 'And they're not the only greywork he has. If you plugged him into the planetary net, he could double as an AI.' She frowned as she continued reading. 'Says here that he caught a bad case of Pollen poisoning and it damaged a large chunk of his brain. Without the greywork, he'd have the IQ of a two-year-old.'

Hero nodded, but her attention was on another screen, displaying a gallery of Meren's known associates. The face in the third row from the bottom made her stomach sink. He was younger, his hair shorter and he wasn't wearing a suit, but he had the same line between his brows and the same dark eyes as the Tybalt she knew today.

Outside the tack room, Harish squawked a warning.

'We have to go,' Norah said as she switched off the bench and snatched the data slide from its surface.

Hero's gut tightened as the screens winked out. She needed to know more, had to know how Tybalt was connected with Meren, *why* he was connected. 'I wasn't finished with that.'

'Read it later.'

'I can't, it's still locked. It'll only work on the bench.'

Norah threw her the slide. 'Then stay, but I'm not getting caught sneaking around.'

From outside the tack room came another squawk, and Norah hurried out. With a last look at the workbench, Hero followed.

Grey almost blocked out the entire doorway.

Carefully, Hero squeezed past his huge grey-speckled bulk,

sucking in her stomach to avoid touching him. There was something about the sterdane that made her nervous. His size and the upwards curve of his ears made her stomach curdle and she wished that Fink was there.

On the other side of Grey, Norah stood, her hands on her hips and Harish perched on her shoulder. 'Why don't you mind your own business, Dorian?'

'The Twilight race is our business,' Tis said, stepping in past Dorian and poking Norah in the chest. 'And you're not welcome.'

'What makes you think we're even interested in it?'

'It's the biggest street race in the city, everyone's interested. Besides, why else would you be sneaking into a tack room?'

'Homework.'

Dorian scoffed. 'Whatever. Just stay out of the Twilight this weekend.'

'Why?' Norah cocked a hip. 'You scared we might beat you?'

Dorian's lips twisted into a smirk as he caught Hero's gaze, but his eyes belied the expression. 'Not with the Special Girl on your team.'

Hero crossed her arms and glared back. 'Then what are you worried about?'

'Nothing.'

'Doesn't sound like nothing.'

'Just stay out of it, Special Girl, or you might get hurt.' He cast a glance over her shoulder.

Her spine tingled and she turned in time to see Grey leap.

A paw, the width of her chest, drove her to the ground. The wind left her lungs as her back hit the floor, and her head echoed with the impact that followed. Between the spots that sparkled across her vision, she thought she saw Norah dash forward and Tis grab at her arm, and then there was nothing but Grey. All she could see were his teeth, stark white against the red of his tongue. He could swallow her head with that mouth, snap her neck, or do one of a billion other things she'd seen Jørn wildlife do on the holodocs. She remembered the blood, the carefully edited gore, and bit her tongue against the small, frightened sound that fought to pass her lips.

With the one part of her brain that wasn't swimming with fear, she wondered if 'danes killed their prey before they ate it.

Fink's snarl ripped through the air.

Above her, Grey crouched, the tendons in his forelegs and neck tensing. An answering sound rippled from his throat.

Her blood curdled. She half-twisted to follow the 'dane's gaze. Fink stood half in, half out of the doorway, his ruff a dark halo about his head. His lips were drawn back from teeth and gums. A strapple rolled out of a bag and stopped between his paws.

For several long moments she didn't breathe. She didn't think anyone else did either.

'Holy Terra.' The words sounded like Norah's.

Somewhere on the other side of Grey, Tis giggled, the sound small and nervous.

In the periphery of her vision, Hero could see Dorian pale under his tan. He took a hesitant step forward.

This time, when Fink snarled, it was with the promise of blood.

Dorian stopped, and went whiter still.

Grey moved then, taking a slow, cautious step that put him between Fink and Dorian, the rumble in his chest growing louder.

Fink unsheathed his claws in response, all twenty-eight of them gleaming black in the light.

Hero saw the bunching of Grey's muscles a split second before he leapt. He barrelled into Fink with his lips back and his own claws forward.

'Fink, no!' She scrambled to her feet and reached for Fink with her mind. All she found there was rage and something deeper, something darker that scared her even more than Grey.

As the two huge animals rolled across the floor, she took a deep breath and dived deeper into his consciousness, looking for the Fink she knew, the one who brought her strapples. She had to stop the fight before Fink hurt Grey, or worse. It wouldn't matter that Grey had started it, Fink would finish it and then... She shuddered. The

Farm didn't give ruc-pards second chances. She stretched her mind and tried to reach Fink again, but his mind was closed to her, hidden behind a shiny wall of anger and fear. This was bad.

A whistle, like wind between buildings only louder, pierced the air. Fink and Grey broke apart and cringed, their ears flat to their heads. Hero slapped her hands over her ears. Out of the corner of her eye, she saw Tis and Dorian do the same.

Norah stood in the doorway to the tack room, a small black sphere in her outstretched fist. A circle on the front of the sphere glowed red and then winked out, taking the noise along with it. She tucked the controller into her pocket.

On her shoulder, Harish rearranged his feathers and squawked.

For a moment, no one said anything. Fink and Grey still crouched, every muscle tense as they stared each other down.

Norah moved first, marching over to Hero and hauling her to her feet. 'Come on,' she said. 'We need to go.'

Hero nodded, but stood her ground as Norah tried to pull her away. She swallowed, and did her best to steady the wobble in her voice before speaking. 'Fink,' she said.

He flicked an ear in her direction and she thought he wasn't going to come, but then he rose and inched his way towards her, never taking his eyes from Grey.

They walked out with Fink shepherding them towards the lift, Hero stopping only long enough to scoop up the strapple as they left the others behind.

The lift ride was silent, as was the slow walk to the dining hall where they sat in an empty cluster of chairs by the large plasglas wall. Lunch was only half over. It felt longer. Fink's ruff slowly settled, but his claws were barely sheathed and he growled at anyone who came too close.

Hero twisted the strapple in her hands. The smell of Grey's breath was still in her nostrils, but it was the memory of Fink's snarl, his bared teeth, and the way he and Grey had slashed and rolled their way over the floor that stuck with her.

'So,' Norah said. 'You have racing tack, right?'

She looked up. 'What?'

'Racing tack. You know, saddle, tech harness,' Norah said, and nodded towards Fink. 'For him?'

'Why?'

'Because we're crashing the Twilight race.'

The strapple stilled in her hands.

'You do have the gear, don't you?'

'Yes.'

'Good. So, we go to your place after school and practise.'

'You want to compete in a street race?'

Norah smiled. 'Who doesn't?' she said. 'But I want to wipe the smile off Dorian's perfectly pouty lips even more.'

'And beating him in the Twilight race would do that?'

Norah's smile turned into a grin. 'Yes.'

Hero bit her lip, remembering Dorian's smug smile, Tis's giggle, and her image plastered all over the school with SPECIAL stamped on top. Her fingers clenched in Fink's ruff.

His thoughts roiled against hers, more red now than mawberry, as images of Grey pinning her to the ground twisted through his mind.

'Okay,' she said. 'Let's do it.'

CHAPTER 13

It wasn't as simple as a few stolen hours on the race track. There were logistics to work out, like how to slip the tracker in her bracelet. It took her awhile, several sleepless nights and as many afternoons in the Bayard tech department, in any spare moment she could steal from under the inventory master's eyes.

She couldn't disable or fool the tracker, like when they had gone to meet the Robin, and she couldn't just leave it behind. If it stopped reporting her biorhythms for more than a moment… she shuddered to think of the consequences.

She found the solution in the nightly bin of parts destined for the recycler. She didn't notice the arm until she walked under it and its cold, gel-like fingers dragged through her hair.

She squeaked and ducked sideways.

Fink pruckled.

She spared him a glare, before turning her gaze to the arm hanging, limp and scorched, out the top of the bin. Made of the clear, synthetic gel the lab techs used to simulate human flesh, it was just what she needed. With a quick glance around, she snatched it out of the bin.

Once she reprogrammed the biorhythms to match her own, it would no longer matter where she went, so long as she left the bracelet and its hunk of fake-Hero somewhere it wouldn't be disturbed. The tracker would tell her minders she was right where she was meant to be, while the arm reassured them of her continued health.

Of course, that left her without a bracer, but she figured the one she'd taken from Imogen would do – after she'd bleached it. This might have proved tricky, if the bracer hadn't been developed by Bayard. With the right admin codes all she needed was a workbench and a little time, both of which she found at the academy. It was just too bad that Dorian and Grey were there too.

Outside of the mansion, Fink refused to leave her alone. This was fine as the stench of Grey's breath was still in her nose, and the weight of his paw was a ghost against her chest. She felt safer with Fink beside her, but it made going to the bathroom awkward.

'Fink,' she said, pushing his nose away as he tried to follow her into the stall. 'Not here.'

He grumbled, but stepped back so that the door could slide closed. When he sat, she could see the silhouette of his fur squished up against the frosted plasglas, and hear the flick of his tail against the tiles. There may have been a few startled gasps from other students, but she didn't pay much attention, not until she was coming out and caught the sharp edge of a nervous giggle.

Tis cast one quick glance at Hero as she backed out of the bathroom, but the bulk of her wide-eyed, slightly sick expression was reserved for Fink.

He puffed his ruff, just a little, and she scampered.

It would have been funny, if Hero hadn't known how the other girl felt. She rubbed at her chest, where the memory of Grey's paw still pressed.

The corridor outside was full of students and companions heading to lunch. With Fink almost stepping on her heels, she turned against the tide and headed towards the nearest turbolift. There hadn't been any mental sighs or forlorn looks when he found out they'd be spending another lunch hour in the tack room, but his ears had pricked up when Norah had offered to go the dining hall and bring them food.

They passed Dorian, surrounded by a clump of pretty-faced supplicants.

Hero could feel the hate coming off him, and the fear, but it didn't do her any good. Right behind Dorian was Grey, with his lips starting to curl and his ears pushed right back.

Fink puffed out his ruff and growled in return. It was a sound almost too low for humans, but that didn't stop them scattering just as fast as their companions. She didn't know how many people Dorian had told about the fight, but from the number of students hurrying for an exit it looked like enough. Maybe even enough to get Fink in trouble.

Grey's eyes were just as wide as Dorian's, and his tail looked like it wanted to curl under his belly, but she didn't wait to see. She just grabbed a handful of Fink's ruff and pulled him towards the nearest lift.

There were spider-frogs jumping in her stomach as the doors closed behind them. Fink bumped up against her side to offer reassurance, but his muscles were still tense and there was an edge to his thoughts, a mental growl that turned her spine cold.

It was okay, Grey had surely followed Dorian to the dining hall, and well… She took a deep breath and started walking as soon as the lift doors opened.

They didn't see anyone. The route to the tack room and the foyer before it were as deserted as the room itself, but even though the spider-frogs subsided, she could still feel them in her stomach.

Bleaching Imogen's bracer was easy, once she'd bypassed the locks preventing access. It didn't take much, just a strand of hair pilfered from Imogen's jacket, and the mechanism that restricted it to a single user was wiped clean, along with any data it might have held.

It would have been nice to get a peek at whatever it was that Imogen was doing, but she needed the bracer more than she needed answers.

Locking it to her own DNA was just as easy, although it took a little longer, and as she waited she rubbed her arms and wondered what was taking Norah so long. Working on the bracer had taken her mind off her stomach, but now, in the silence broken only by the click of Fink's claws as he paced, she could feel the spider-frogs again, hopping about.

A tickle at the back of her mind made her frown. Fink looked towards the door as she turned, his ears pricked forwards. He stalked out, his head low and a rumble vibrating his chest.

She hesitated a second, but only a second, before she lifted her chin and followed. The space outside the tack room was empty, but the mental tickle grew stronger and she followed it out into the hallway and around the corner.

Tis was beside the lift, back to the hall. Hero couldn't see what she was doing, but her giggle made Hero's skin crawl.

Something thumped on the inside of the lift. The tickle against her thoughts was taking on a flavour, a soft lavender tinged with menthol.

Norah.

Tis must have trapped her inside.

Hero was going to yell, but Fink was already creeping up behind the girl, his steps silent, without even the faint click of his nails to give him away. His nose an inch from her neck, he growled, very, very softly.

Tis froze. She turned, and even from where she stood Hero could see her blanch before she scrambled at the lift controls. She was through the doors almost before they fully opened, pushing Norah out as she stabbed at the close button.

They watched silently as the lift closed and the numbers on the control panel rose.

With a harrumph, Fink turned and padded back towards the tack room.

Harish launched himself from Norah's shoulder and joined him.

Hero looked at Norah – they laughed at the same time.

The day before the Twilight race, they finalised the last of their plans. They'd use Norah's place as their base camp. Her dads would be out of the city, visiting her older sister at the New Gobi boarding school where she'd been exiled – after earning herself a criminal record for the same thing they were about to do. All Hero had to do was convince her mother and Tybalt to let her sleep over at Norah's. She already knew how to get Imogen off her back, which was handy, since Imogen started in on her almost before the hover lifted off the academy's pad.

'That was a nice job you did with the security vid.' Imogen held out her hand. 'I want the items you took. If you give them back now, that will be the end of it.'

Hero raised a brow. 'Or?'

'I don't think you want to go there.'

She dug in her bag, pulling Imogen's data slide from the hidden compartment she'd been carrying it around in all week. 'You know, if you don't want people to read your stuff, you shouldn't encrypt it with your own DNA.'

Imogen froze, resembling a lamb again as Hero could see her wracking her brains. Just as quickly, she relaxed. 'You need more than a saliva sample to break a DNA lock.'

Hero smiled widely.

At her feet, Fink grunted. *She looked like a 'pard when she did that, all teeth.*

Mentally, she stuck her tongue out at him, and spoke to the Lamb. 'You mean, like the workbenches in the academy's tack rooms?'

'You can't...' The Lamb trailed off, her eyes widening for a split-second before they narrowed to slits. 'Of course you can.' She leaned back in the seat. 'So, can I have my items back now?'

'Sure.' She tossed the data slide across the hover.

The Lamb snatched it out of the air. 'And the other thing?'

'Sorry,' Hero said, and pushed up her sleeve to reveal the bracer, now locked around her forearm. 'Bleached it already.'

'You—' The Lamb's lips became a thin, hard line and Hero

wondered whether the veins in her forehead would actually burst. 'Do you know what you've done?'

She tilted her head to the side, the smile slipping from her face. 'Yes,' she said. 'Are you going to tell me why you're spying on my mother?'

'No.'

'Are you sure?'

'Yes.' Imogen leaned forward, her elbows on her knees, and pinned Hero with her gaze. 'Have you told anyone about me?'

There was something in Imogen's eyes that made Hero uncomfortable, made her want to squirm. It was like being pinned under a laser, a very serious laser that added another three gravities to her personal part of the universe. Her plan wasn't quite so much fun anymore. 'Maybe.'

'I need better than "maybe". It's important, Hero.'

'Why?'

'It just is. Have you told anyone?'

Fink shifted and ever-so-gently touched his snout to Imogen's hand. He flashed her a strapple-flavoured memory lifted from Imogen's mind of people in purple uniforms with palm-units and bracers just like the one now clamped around Hero's forearm.

Her eyes widened. 'You're a police officer?'

It shouldn't have been possible, but Imogen's lips tightened further as she jerked her hands out of Fink's reach. 'What do you want, Hero?'

'What makes you think I want anything?'

Imogen just looked at her.

She shifted on the seat and crossed her arms. This wasn't going the way she had planned. There was a leaden feeling in her gut as if she were the bad guy, or maybe, just a spoiled, petulant brat. 'I'm spending the weekend at a friend's.'

'Does Tybalt know?'

'Not yet, but when he says yes, you'll offer to mind me. Only you won't, you'll be somewhere else, somewhere far away from me.'

'And what are you going to do while I'm not there?'

'That,' Hero said with a smile, 'is none of your business.'

'I can't just let you run around the city.'

'What makes you think that's what I'm going to do?'

'Why else would you need to ditch me?'

'You're annoying.'

'Who's your friend?'

'Does it matter?'

'It does.'

'Norah Joshi.'

'Norah…' The frown between Imogen's brows changed, became considering. Her eyes flicked from Hero to Fink and then the bracer. Some light must have gone off in her brain, because the frown cleared and her lips softened enough to form a smile of their own, one that made Hero nervous. 'Fine,' she said. 'We have a deal.'

CHAPTER 14

The taxi descended deeper into the Twilight, past old holoboards through thinning streams of traffic, to where the lights weren't as bright and the hovers not as new.

'That should do it,' Hero said as she entered one last command on her bracer's holoscreen.

Across from her, Norah concentrated on her own holoscreen. With a deft movement of her fingers, she spun it around to face Hero. 'I have you: location, vital stats and encrypted comms. You?'

She nodded. 'Same.'

The orange veins of energy that ran under the bracer's surface dimmed to a soft blue-white glow as she powered it down. Imogen's smile was stuck in her mind: the way her lips had curved just so and how she'd looked at Hero like she could see right through her skull. She rubbed her hand over the bracer before zipping the left sleeve of her coat, hiding it. That smile still made her nervous.

It had been a strange feeling, that morning, standing on the pad outside Norah's house and watching Imogen's hover rise into the traffic. She'd never been without supervision before and there had been a hole in her chest, a great big empty place, where excitement had battled the fear at its edges.

If Fink hadn't been there, warm and solid, she might have called Imogen back. She pressed the chime on Norah's front door instead.

Norah's dads had been welcoming, if somewhat distracted as they rushed out the door, overnight bags and a large box in hand.

She'd barely had time to glance around the apartment – a large, open space with square-shaped furniture and holopaintings lining the walls – before Norah hustled them out the door and into a waiting taxi. She'd had just enough time to set up her old bracer with its fake Hero mould to transmit her pre-recorded biodata but not enough to tell Norah about Imogen being a cop.

The taxi landed. Outside the viewport, the pad was dark, lit only by a few flickering lights and the head-beams of other hovers. Other taxis touched down just long enough to disgorge their passengers before taking off again. She'd heard tales about the Twilight, about the things that went on, particularly this far down. She could understand why the hovers didn't hang around, as anxiety joined with the mess of emotions already curling in her chest.

The door opened and Harish swooped past her ear.

'Come on.' Norah jumped down and headed into the gloom. 'We'll be late.'

'You know where we're going, right?'

'Yes.' She reached back and grabbed Hero's arm. 'Come *on*, we have to get to the next checkpoint before it expires. Without the next piece of the map, we'll never find the starting line.'

Fink nudged her in the back and purred.

Taking a deep breath, she scooped up the bulky tack bag at her feet and followed Norah. The warren of arcades was as dark as the landing pad and echoed with the sounds of people. Most carried holocams or had their eyes glued to their cuffs or bracers, like Norah. Others carried bags out of which poked the necks of bottles or came the sharp crinkle of food packets.

Fink raised his nose to the air, and in Hero's mind she smelled what he smelled. There was the salty-sweet tang of strapple fries, the cheesy scent of instant-heat burgers, the sweaty musk of people and companions and underlying it, the dusty, mildewy scent of the generations gone before.

More people joined the stream weaving their way through the arcades and over skybridges, eyes on their bracers or palm-units, all seeking the next checkpoint with the next piece of the map. The checkpoints and map fragments had been a precaution at first, an elaborate ruse to stop the police from showing up at the starting line and arresting them all. Now it was as much a part of the race as the race itself, or so Norah had tried to convince Hero. Personally, she could have thought of better ways.

It was a slow journey, but as they drew closer to the race, the stream of people thickened until the sound of the crowd rivalled the gales of the upper city. She began to see the companions then. There were small flyers, like the wasp-keies, barely the size of her hand, and larger striders, like the badger-zyl and the turt-sheep, no taller than her chest. It wasn't until the map on Norah's bracer told them they were just a skybridge away from the race that she saw another racer.

The toa-mare wound its way through the crowd, a sleek line of darkness. Its thick, hairless hide gleamed purple in the broken lighting. A boy walked at its side, tall and thin, with skin as dark as the 'mare's.

Fink chortled a greeting, barely loud enough to cut through the noise of the crowd.

The boy didn't turn his head, but the 'mare did. It looked over its shoulder and when it saw Fink, it flashed its tail, almost knocking out the other boy walking behind with an oad-hawk perched on his shoulder.

Fink stopped in the middle of the arcade, his ears twisting sideways and his head up, like he'd just been slapped in the snout. She felt the bewilderment spread across his mind like a yellow-green stain before he shook his head and continued walking.

She stared at the toa-mare's back and nudged Norah's shoulder. 'Who's that?'

Norah leaned in close. 'Timon Dane, his 'mare is Phara and that's Henry behind them, their scout. They're one of the best teams on the street circuit.'

'Better than Dorian?'

She shrugged. 'Maybe. They'll probably go pro one of these days, if the police don't catch them first.'

The crowd thickened again. A few weeks ago, she had thought the academy's dining hall was crowded, but this... She felt small. Moving closer to Fink, she urged him to walk faster so as not to lose Norah, who was now marching ahead of them.

The skybridge seemed too narrow, or maybe the number of people in it grew. The spot in her chest, which just a few hours ago had been a hole, churned as she lost sight of Norah. Once, twice, a third time, her friend disappeared amongst the bags and jackets ahead. Standing on her toes, Hero could barely see over the shoulders in front of her. She thought she caught sight of Harish's distinctive yellow and green tail, and pressed forward.

The skybridge opened out into a square as she edged past a woman whose dark clothes and the comm-unit attached to her ear might have made her look out of place were it not for her green hair.

A flash of green and yellow in the crowd drew her gaze upwards to where Harish circled overhead, before Norah reappeared next to her.

She grabbed Hero's wrist, just below the cuff. 'Come on, the racers are gearing up over here.'

Norah pushed through the crowd ahead of her, still gripping Hero's arm. Lavender, with the faintest hint of menthol, brushed up against her mind. She stumbled, breaking Norah's grip, and the sensation vanished.

Norah looked back only long enough to grab Hero's arm again, above the cuff this time, before she continued to push forward.

A line of holotape marked the racers' area, and a scrawny guy in a too-tight shirt held out his hand to stop them crossing. 'Creds?' He had a voice too deep for the size of his chest, its rumble no doubt aided by the metallic biocomp wrapped around his throat.

The screen over Norah's bracer morphed into a holo of a linch-adder hovering over a slale-bear.

The guy waved his hand over the holo. He frowned at the screen that flicked to life over his palm before jerking his chin towards Hero. 'When'd you get a new partner?'

'When the cops caught my sister.'

'Huh, yeah.' His other hand flew over the screen above his palm and the holo above Norah's bracer changed, a 'pard replacing the slale-bear. 'All right, you're good.'

'Thanks Rom,' Norah said as a section of the holotape winked out and they walked through.

The racers' area was a sea of fur, scales and feathers among which riders dipped and ducked, securing saddles on companions the size of Fink, while around them, scouts checked the harnesses on their flyers.

Norah let the bag she was carrying slide from her shoulder, Harish coming down to land as she knelt beside it. 'We'll gear up here.'

Hero swung the bulky bag off her own back and knelt to pull out Fink's tack.

The saddle was compact and light, with a collection of straps and pads designed to keep her on Fink's back during the leaps and sudden turns of the race. She'd put it on a million times, sometimes in the first light of dawn, when shadows made it impossible to see and all she had was practice and the feel of the leather beneath her fingers. Now, her hands fumbled with the straps that secured it across Fink's chest, the vacuum seals defeating her as the nerves in her stomach found their way to her fingers.

Calm, like a warm, furry hug crept into her mind as Fink curled his tail around her ankle.

She smiled and buried her face in his ruff. 'Thank you.'

He whuffed against her neck. *She was welcome.*

The chest strap hissed into place, and he reared up on his hind legs so she could secure the straps that slipped between his fore and midlegs and under his belly.

Last out of the bag came her helmet. As she fitted the plasglas skull cap, its biocircuits came to life, forming an intricate pattern of light in the otherwise transparent surface.

'Is that a…' Norah's eyes were wide.

Hero nodded.

'And does it have the…' She made a large circle in front of her face.

Unzipping the left sleeve of her coat, she pressed her thumb to the bracer and a holoscreen instantly encompassed her head.

Norah stared at it in silence, then shook her head and turned back to the readout on her bracer. 'I'll send Harish's vid feed to your helmet.'

With a hand on Fink's shoulder, she swung onto his back and settled in the saddle.

The square looked different from Fink's back. With the extra height, she could see past the press of fur and scales to catch her first real glimpse of the square. It was packed. People crowded around the edges of the racers' area and took up whatever space they could find, seeking a view of the large holoscreen overhead. Among the racers was a restless shuffle of hooves and paws as riders finished checking saddles and scouts made last-minute adjustments to the harnesses that allowed them to communicate with their companions.

Static buzzed across the inside of her helmet's holoscreen, before a spiralling image of the central holoscreen made her sway in the saddle. Instinctively, she clutched at Fink's ruff even as the straps tightened over her legs, preventing her from slipping off his back.

'You getting that?' Norah stood at Fink's side as another aerial loop-de-loop played across the holoscreen.

Hero nodded. 'Mmm-hmm.'

'You have it on full-screen, don't you?'

'Mmm-hmm.' The vision cut out and she relaxed her grip on Fink's ruff.

'You might want to change that. Harish likes to cut things close.'

Norah's bracer beeped, and she turned her attention to her holoscreen. Her smile almost split her face as she looked up at Hero.

'They've released the course map. It's starting.'

A hush came over the crowd and a new image covered the inside of Hero's holoscreen. Through it, she could see the same bright red numbers projected on the screen above.

The scrawny guy's overly deep voice boomed over the hubbub of voices. 'Riders and scouts, take your positions.'

'Keep your comms open,' Norah said.

Harish swooped past her shoulder to perch on Fink's neck, crooning as he stretched out his head to Norah.

Norah smiled and reached up to scratch him at the base of his long neck. 'And trust Harish, he knows what he's doing,' she said, before rushing off to the sidelines with the other scouts.

A flash of green drew Hero's gaze to the crowd forming behind the scouts, and her eyes caught those of the green-haired woman she'd edged past in the square. The woman looked more out of place now, muttering into her comm-unit, her eyes glued on Hero. A little bit of ice mixed with the adrenalin in her blood.

Harish flapped his wings, nearly hitting her in the face, and squawked.

'What are you waiting for?' Norah spoke in her ear. 'Get to the starting line.'

Strung across the square, a thick ribbon of green and blue holotape marked the starting line. Settling between a slale-bear and a spideruck, she looked around and tried to quell the nerves blooming in her gut. Some of the faces around her were excited, others grim; eyes narrowed, gazes straight ahead. The girl on the spideruck grinned at her, the expression almost reaching her eyes, while the boy beyond – Timon Dane, she recalled – was as inscrutable as his toa-mare.

Fink spotted Grey before she spotted Dorian, on the other side of Timon Dane, his ruff puffing out about his ears as he growled.

The 'ruck sidled sideways with a nervous quack, bumping into the 'mare who in turn sidestepped into Grey.

There was a drone hovering next to Dorian's head, and it turned as he did. He caught her eyes and smiled, a tight twist of his lips. He said something into his helmet and over the hum of the crowd, she could almost hear Tis giggle.

A soft *bong, bong, bong* echoed inside her helmet, bringing her attention to the holoscreen as the countdown began. At five, the mawberry flavour of Fink's mind touched hers, or maybe she touched his – their thoughts were so mingled it was impossible to tell.

At three, Harish launched himself skyward, pumping his wings hard as he streaked ahead with the other flyers.

At two, Fink crouched, muscles tense.

At one, they leapt forward.

For a moment, it was just her and Fink, the breadth of the square open before them, but 'pards had been engineered for their ferocity, not their speed, and the pack overtook them in heartbeats. Bodies pressed against them from either side, a slale-bear on one, the spideruck on the other, as the pack bunched to fit through the skybridge's narrow opening. Timon Dane and his toa-mare led the pack; the familiar blue-speckled shape of Grey, with Dorian crouched over his back, were not far behind.

'Watch out,' Norah yelled in her ear just as Harish screeched past, dive-bombing the racer on her left.

The racer, an older girl on a slale-bear, ducked and the object she'd been about to throw at Hero went wild, exploding in an electric-blue mist as it hit someone else.

Her heart thumped and her fingers itched for something to throw back, but she and Norah had not had the time to find or make the kind of bombs street racers used.

She narrowed her gaze at the girl.

The girl smirked back, reaching into one of the pouches slung across her chest.

The mawberry-tinged image of a vacuum seal beside the girl's knee appeared in her mind.

Hero smiled.

The girl's smirk turned to a puzzled frown.

Fink slammed into the slale-bear's side, and as the girl grabbed at her saddle's pommel, Hero leaned down and hit the vacuum seal by her knee.

With a hiss, the girl's saddle slipped sideways and whatever it was she'd been reaching for went off in a puff of violet smoke.

'Zorina's always liked her potions a little too much,' Norah said in her ear.

'What was that last one?'

'I don't know, but from the way she's staggering around, it was probably a Violet Night,' Norah said. 'Yeah, definitely a Violet Night.'

The pack tightened as it thundered onto the skybridge.

The spideruck slammed into Fink, throwing them against the bridge's tubular sides. The steelglas was cold and hard, and in the brief second it took Fink to regain his footing, Hero had a geagle-eyed view of the endless drop beneath.

They were off again, the bulk of the pack stretched out before them, scouts dodging the bots and bombs being hurled through the air as the racers jostled for position. Twice they watched riders and companions fall, incapacitated by a puff of coloured smoke or a flash of light.

'The first barrier is coming up.'

On the inside of her helmet, the view changed. A diagram of a semi-transparent wall with a round hole in its centre appeared on the skybridge.

'What is it?'

'A modified shock skin. You have to jump through the hole.'

'I thought this was meant to be hard?'

'It is.' The feed from Harish's harness grew large on her holoscreen, and she saw a flurry-thyt – its iridescent hide shimmering pale orange, yellow and red – hunched over a switch. 'Unless the switch is down, there is no hole.' An oad-hawk knocked the 'thyt from its perch, and a doe-oc slammed, horns first, into the space where the hole had been. Blue sparks rippled over its hide, the girl on its back barely jumping free before the animal crashed to the ground in a bundle of delicate legs and twitching hooves. 'But don't worry, Harish knows what he's doing.'

She could see the barrier now, a wall of glowing blue less than a dozen strides away. The oad-hawk was on the switch; the spideruck that had thrown them into the wall passed through the barrier. The oad-hawk rose, flapping its wings and the hole flickered.

Just a few strides to go, but she didn't see Harish. 'Where is he?'

'He's coming.'

The barrier loomed large, the hole growing smaller and smaller until she doubted even Harish could slip through. Three strides to go, two—

Fink sat back on his haunches and started to skid.

Harish didn't bother knocking the oad-hawk aside; he dove into it, wrapping his tail around its wings and squeezing so that they hit the switch together.

Fink slid through the hole.

'I told you, he likes to cut things close,' Norah said in her ear.

Beyond the barrier were arcades, and boardwalks and endless corridors through towers both residential and commercial. Twice, they leapt over startled pedestrians and once skidded under a landing hover, Fink sliding on his belly while Hero flattened herself against his back. Harish was everywhere, shrieking warnings and dive-bombing the other flyers as he raced ahead, scouting the track. All the while, Norah was in her ear telling her to turn left or right or even, on occasion, had them scrambling up narrow staircases and down lifts.

As the barriers became more difficult, the pack thinned and she and Fink made ground, until she could see Dorian and Timon Dane battling it out ahead.

The 'mare flicked its tail towards Dorian, aiming for his head, but Grey sidestepped, slamming his weight back into the 'mare. At the same time, Dorian grabbed Timon and yanked him sideways, trying to topple him from the saddle. They struggled. Timon broke loose and tried to grab at Dorian, but became too busy trying to pull his 'mare up as Grey used his weight to drive her into a wall.

They were close enough that Hero caught the echo of Dorian's laugh as he lobbed something at the pair. Whatever it was exploded in a mess of white, spreading until it covered not just them, but a good portion of the narrow walkway.

'It's a spider-bomb!' Norah yelled in her ear. 'Take the crates! Take the crates!'

With a slight nudge, Fink veered towards the boxes, bounding up them like a monstrous set of stairs. He leapt up the last step and the boxes fell away, the saddle's straps biting into her legs as he scrambled to keep them from going over the edge. Together, they peered into the three-storey drop below.

She swallowed. 'This is a shortcut?'

In the darkness ahead, Harish squawked.

'I'm the scout, remember? Trust me. There's a beam two metres in front of you. Jump to it.'

Her holoscreen shifted, peeling back the gloom. There *was* a beam ahead, barely wide enough for Fink and surrounded on either side by nothing. She clenched her hands in his ruff. 'Can you see it?'

The scent of mawberries filled her nose as Fink shared her sight. She felt him nod and gather himself, his muscles were hers, and together they leapt.

The beam swayed as they raced along it, held aloft only by what looked like portable anti-grav units stuck to the walls of the towers on either side. There were two more gaps to leap, and after looking down once to see only darkness below, she kept her eyes on Harish as they followed him through the twists and turns. The last beam tilted down, and Fink was barely able to hold on with his forepaws as they skidded its length.

They thundered out of the alley just in time to see Dorian and Grey flash past, hurling a silver object at them.

Hero barely managed to duck and a white, gooey thread plastered itself to her cheek as the spider bomb exploded.

Fink's breath came hard, his hearts thumping, as they raced after Dorian and Grey. They dodged another bomb as Harish harried Tis's drone, and were gaining when Hero heard the sound of hooves coming up behind. She looked over her shoulder.

Timon Dane leaned over his 'mare's neck, his scout's oad-hawk streaking ahead with something shiny in its claws.

Hero ducked, but the 'hawk whistled past and dropped the object on Dorian's head. There was a flash and Grey's legs went out from under him.

She turned to smile at the other rider as they drew shoulder-to-shoulder, just in time to see another shiny object flying through the air. It impacted ahead of them. Fink squeaked as his paws skidded in the sickly green glow. She could hear the scrape of all twenty-eight claws against the plascrete, but the slip field was strong and she only just managed to hit the saddle's quick-release before they crashed, Fink landing hard on his side. Together, they slid the length of the slip field, before thudding up against a wall.

Heart pounding, she looked up at the sky, feeling Fink's chest rise and fall against her back.

Harish screeched overhead just as Norah yelled in her ear. 'Get up, get up! Dorian's out of the shock trap. You can't beat Dane, but you can still beat Dorian!'

With a lurch, Fink got to his feet and she scrambled into the saddle.

Up ahead, Dorian was barely clinging to Grey's back as the sterdane bounded off the wall at the end of the T-junction and streaked left towards the finish line.

'Go right! Go right!' Norah yelled in Hero's ear.

'What—'

'Do it!'

They went right, Fink's claws leaving marks in the plascrete as they slid around the corner.

Hero looked over her shoulder as they raced away from the finish line, and could just make out Dorian, a silhouette against the bright, flashing lights. 'The finish line is the other way.'

'So are the police.' Norah's voice was strained.

Her hands clenched in Fink's ruff. Her knees must have tightened against his sides, because he slowed to a halt in the middle of the dark arcade and twisted his head around, looking at her out of one black eye.

Getting arrested would mean a one-way ticket back to the estate.

'Harish caught sight of them just a second ago. They haven't made a move yet; it looks like they're waiting for the race to finish so they can arrest everyone. If we move now, before they jam the comms, they might not catch us.'

'They jam the comms to stop the racers getting away?'

'Yeah. When they do, I'll meet you here.' The map on the inside of her helmet shifted, the yellow line twisting away from the finish line in a convoluted path around and back the way she and Fink had come. 'I'll be there in ten—'

Silence filled her ears and a red light flashed in the corner of her holoscreen. 'Norah?'

A siren whined through the arcade, and she twisted in the saddle, looking once more towards the finish line. The lights were just as bright as before, but now they flashed red and blue. She narrowed her eyes and the holoscreen zoomed in, magnifying the darting silhouettes until she could just make out faces, including Dorian's as a purple-clad officer gripped his shoulder.

Beneath her, Fink tensed. Hero whipped her gaze back, her helmet automatically adjusting to the gloom as she scoured the arcade. There was nothing to see, but as the mawberry flavour of Fink's thoughts crept into hers, she heard the soft echo of boots.

Norah's yellow line went forward, further into the arcade and towards whomever waited for them, but a glance at the map showed a corridor somewhere behind them. Shifting the map to a corner of the screen, she kept her gaze peeled on the darkness ahead and nudged Fink with her knee.

He crept backwards, moving slowly.

On her screen, a shadow began to move, another close behind. She zoomed in as they moved through the faint orange glow of a holosign. The image was grainy, pixelated by the gloom and the distance, but their uniforms were black and they each had something round and stubby in their hands.

As Fink continued to ease his way backwards, she zoomed in closer on their hands, switching the holoscreen to infra-red and the round stubby things came into focus. Stunners. Unease trickled down her spine.

Fink moved faster.

The shadows halted in the shifting light of a sign and her gaze caught on the familiar green hair of the woman she'd seen lurking around the starting line. She didn't look like a police officer.

Through the gloom and distance, she saw the woman raise her stunner.

Hero barely had time to respond before Fink leapt backwards, twisting in the air, just as a bright bolt of light whizzed past her arm.

They made the last few metres to the service corridor in record time.

The woman had tried to shoot her. She looked over her shoulder. Was she following? She didn't know and couldn't hear anything over the mad pounding of her heart and Fink's paws thumping against the floor.

He slid to a halt and coughed. *There's a door.*

She looked at it stupidly.

Fink poked her leg with his nose. An image of her opening the door popped into her head.

She was out of the saddle and hooking her bracer into the security panel before she had time to cast another look behind. The code was running across her helmet and the sequences were lining up as the black-clad figure appeared at the end of the corridor, raising her arm again.

The door clicked and Fink bundled her through. He gave her a nudge as it closed behind them, sharing the memory of the Lamb locked outside the airship, all those weeks ago.

'Right,' she said and jammed the door's lock, before climbing back into the saddle.

Wherever the service corridor had led them, it was dark. Only a thin holostrip marked the walls, faded and broken, and the click of Fink's claws echoed as they jogged through the corridors. Inside her helmet, the map had updated itself, the new route to Norah's meeting place a jagged zig-zag up and down.

At some point, she thought she heard someone behind them, but Fink smelled nothing and heard only the hush of the air recyclers.

After several more locked doors, they made it out of the gloom. They crept through another poorly-lit arcade and over a familiar-looking skybridge before they made it to the cramped, forgotten place where Dorian and Grey had tried to run Timon Dane into a wall. The map stopped.

Sliding out of the saddle, Hero looked around, Fink sticking close to her side as she peered into the half-light. 'Norah?'

Nothing.

Fink coughed, the sound echoing against the walls.

Still nothing.

She cast her gaze back at him, a question hovering at the edges of her mind.

He shrugged his mid-quarters. *He didn't smell anything but old sweat and the remnants of the spider-bomb.*

'Then where are they?' It had been seventeen minutes since the police had jammed the comms. Norah said she'd only take ten. 'Maybe they left already?'

Fink shook his head, before pricking his ears forwards and swivelling them backwards. *He heard something.* The image of a hover appeared in her mind. *They should go.*

'We're waiting for Norah.' She strained her eyes and the helmet's visuals against the dark. 'Besides, I can't see anything.'

He grumbled and circled around her, attempting to herd her back towards the skybridge. *She didn't need to see, he could hear.*

She punched him in the shoulder and didn't budge. 'We're staying.'

There was a faint curl to Fink's lip, and a hard, determined edge to his thoughts as he put his head against her chest and pushed.

'Hey!' She grabbed the side of his head and dug her heels in, but against six-hundred kilos of 'pard it was useless, and she skidded backwards, her feet almost slipping out from under her.

A red warning light flashed across her helmet, just as a yellow and green lump careened out of the darkness and impacted Fink's neck with a thump. He stumbled sideways with a faint squeak.

She barely had time to register the lump as Harish – now picking himself up off the ground – before the thud of running feet echoed through the alley and Norah belted around the corner.

Red-faced and breathing in gasps, Norah scrambled onto Fink's back, fitting herself in behind the saddle. 'Police,' she said between gasps, as she pointed first back down the alley and then ahead. 'Go. That. Way.'

Hero shared a wide-eyed look with Fink before scooping up a dazed-looking Harish and vaulting into the saddle.

Fink was moving almost before Hero touched his back, leaping forward with such speed that Norah squeaked and grabbed at her waist hard enough to bruise.

They burst out of the alley and were halfway across the skybridge before the police hover rose into view. It hung in the air and hit them with a floodlight, a speaker-amplified voice yelling at them to stop.

Fink dodged sideways, as if the light were a physical thing, but kept going, while Hero threw her arm up against the glare.

A second later, they were in another arcade, their eyes starry from the intense light. Fink slowed.

'Don't stop.' Norah slapped Fink's rump. 'They have mini-hovers.'

Grunting, his breath harsh in his lungs, he lumbered into a canter. 'Where are we going? Fink can't keep running.'

'Here.' Half leaning over Hero's shoulder, Norah grabbed her wrist and punched something into her bracer.

The map on the inside of her helmet rearranged itself, a blinking yellow dot appearing next to the faded icon of a turbolift. She frowned at it. 'It's offline for repairs.'

'The police have all the working ones staked out. It's either this or a ride in a police hover.'

'Can't we find a taxi?'

'Have you seen any taxis?'

She didn't say anything, just nudged Fink to the right, towards the broken lift. They stuck to the arcades and covered walkways, avoiding the police spotlights. Twice they had to backtrack and hide as a mini-hover buzzed past, one police officer driving while another scanned the area. Finally, they turned down another deserted, gloomy corridor and the blinking dot inside her helmet stopped.

She swung her leg over Fink's neck and dropped to the ground. Holotape criss-crossed the lift, "OUT OF ORDER" marching across its yellow background.

Norah slid down next to her, Harish wound around her neck. 'Can you make it work?'

'Maybe.' Hero plugged the bracer in and watched data scroll across her holoscreen. There was security around the lift's functions, but she bypassed that in seconds and was deep in the lift's error logs, when Fink growled and nudged her in the back, hard enough to smoosh her against the wall. 'Fi-iink—'

He interrupted her, an image of police appearing in her mind.

She heard it then, the distinctive buzz of a mini-hover. 'We need to go.' She grabbed Norah's arm.

Norah yanked it back. 'What about the lift?'

'A cold in the biocircuits blew a conduit.'

'So?'

She grabbed Norah's arm again. 'So, I don't carry around spare parts. Come on.'

They ran, the buzz of the mini-hover growing behind them, until the corridor came to a dead end.

Hero stared at it, her mind racing for another way out.

Norah yanked her arm. 'Back this way, I think I saw—'

A spotlight pinned them in place. 'Halt! You're under arrest.'

CHAPTER 15

Hero had never been handcuffed before. The width of two of her fingers, the black piece of steelglas didn't just suck in the light, it sucked the power from her bracer too. She fingered it as she walked along, herded between the mini-hover behind and one of the officers in front. Norah trudged along next to her, Harish still wrapped around her neck and another handcuff slapped around her wrist. If either of them tried to run, all the officers had to do was press a button and the cuffs would emit a pulse that locked their muscles.

One of the officers had eyed the 'adder briefly, and Hero had wondered if they'd cuff him too, but they'd been too busy giving Fink the eye. While one officer spoke into a comm-unit, the youngest, a little white around the eyes but his hands steady, had attached something to Fink's ruff. It was a suppressor, a circle as black as the handcuffs, and in its centre blinked a steady green light.

Even if the handcuff hadn't short-circuited her bracer, the suppressor would have made escape impossible. One twitch of the officer's finger and Fink would be knocked out. Plus, the younger officer had Hero's helmet tucked under his arm.

They marched over a skybridge and along a boardwalk. The skylanes in this part of the Twilight were busy, and the holoboards flashed and shouted in counterpart to the hovers streaming past. She wondered if the people saw them, and what they thought of two girls, a 'pard and an 'adder with a police escort. What was her mother going to think? What would she do when she found out Hero had been arrested? Hero barely knew what to think, just that the adrenalin of the race and the run from the police had morphed into a great big mess of acid that churned in her gut.

Just how long would it be before her mother had her bundled back to the estate? If she was lucky, she'd have an hour, maybe two, before she was on an airship with Cumulus City growing small at the stern. She'd be lucky if she ever saw another city again. Hero swallowed, the memory of her mother's voice telling her she couldn't race strong in her mind. She'd be lucky if Fink wasn't sent to the Farm.

At her side, Norah was silent, her shoulders hunched, and Harish was crooning in her ear. She wondered if her dads would ship her off to the same school as her sister.

Hero bit her lip. There had to be something she could do, some way to get them all out of this.

Their escort marched them through a small square, not much bigger than a courtyard, towards a black, unmarked hover just coming in to land. It kicked up a small wave of dust before it settled on the pad, and then Imogen jumped out the side.

Norah frowned. 'Why's she here?'

She didn't answer, but the mess in her gut began to ease as Imogen smiled at the officer in front and activated her palm-unit, revealing a slowly spinning badge.

Norah's brows shot into her hairline. 'She's police? Your nanny's a cop?'

'Actually,' Imogen said, closing her hand around the holo, 'I'm an agent, a fact you will be keeping to yourself, unless you want your dads to know you were arrested. Again.'

An agent? Hero exchanged a look with Norah. The girl's mouth hung open. Hero snapped her own mouth closed, her thoughts spinning.

Agents didn't do things like arrest people for street racing. They arrested them for blowing up skytowers and envirodomes, the kinds of things that endangered not just one city, but all five.

What was an agent doing looking after her? She rubbed at her wrist as the younger officer released the handcuff and handed back her helmet.

He released Norah as well, before turning to Fink. 'You sure you don't want to leave the suppressor on the 'pard, agent?'

Imogen looked as if she was considering it.

Hero narrowed her eyes and would have shouldered the officer aside to remove it herself, if Imogen's smile hadn't widened.

'I'm sure,' she said.

Gingerly, the officer removed the small black circle and without another word, he and his partner buzzed back across the square.

'How did you know?' Hero asked.

'With rumours of the Twilight race floating around, it wasn't hard. You're hardly subtle about your desire to race, and you, Ms Joshi, have a record.' Imogen climbed back inside the hover. 'Get in.'

She hesitated for all of a second before climbing aboard.

Wide-eyed, Norah hesitated for a few moments more, before Fink nudged her in the back. She squeaked, but climbed in swiftly and sat beside Hero.

The hover dipped when Fink stepped onboard, the door sliding shut behind him, before rising into the traffic above.

Hero crossed her arms over her chest and met Imogen's gaze over Fink's bulk.

Imogen's smile didn't shift, but her eyes became just a little harder. 'Tybalt does that better.'

Shifting on the seat, Norah spoke. 'You're not arresting us?'

'No. I'm taking you home.'

'What about me?' Hero said.

'You're going with her.'

She narrowed her gaze. 'Why?'

'Because if I take you to the mansion, your mother will know something's wrong.'

'And that might blow your cover.'

Imogen smiled.

'You probably should have told the others not to shoot at me then.'

Fink growled in agreement.

There was something in the way Imogen's body tensed that sent a cold wave down her spine. 'When did that happen?' she said.

'Just after the comms went down.'

She turned to Norah. 'What about you?'

The other girl shook her head. 'The police in the square didn't have guns.'

She switched her gaze, piercing now, back to Hero. 'What did they look like?'

'I don't know. It was dark; they wore black. I wouldn't have seen them without the helmet.'

'Police don't wear black…' Norah said.

Fink raised his head as Imogen nudged him in the side. 'What did you see?'

He shrugged his mid-shoulders and rumbled apologetically.

Imogen gestured at Hero. 'Give me the bracer.'

She hesitated.

'You bleached it, remember? It's useless to me.'

A faint, orange glow lit the inside of the hover as she unzipped her sleeve and slipped the bracer off.

Imogen took the bracer without a word, and ran the palm-unit over it. The unit beeped and a small holoscreen appeared above Imogen's hand. Vid footage from the race, everything that Hero had seen through her helmet, ran across the screen at ten times the speed of the real thing.

'There.' The footage stopped, and she turned it towards Hero. 'Those were the people?'

Hero frowned at the slightly blurred shape standing in the light of a holo. 'Yes.'

A few flicks of Imogen's fingers and the palm-unit beeped again. The vid reversed, winding back to the start of the race, and freezing on the face of the woman Hero had seen standing behind the scouts.

Imogen swore.

'You've heard of the Klaude.' It was a statement.

Norah nodded.

Hero crossed her arms, the bracer back on her forearm.

Imogen frowned at her, but continued. 'At the beginning of the Construction, when Augusta Woolsey made her proposal to alter human genetics, Penelope Klaude raised an argument to eradicate the Pollen.

'At the time, the technology to do it either didn't exist or couldn't be spared, and like Woolsey's proposal, Klaude's was voted down, but the people who supported her proposal remained.

'Over the years, most of her supporters faded away, but a few became the founders of large corporations, while others went into science or politics. Together, they became *the* Klaude, an organisation dedicated to pursuing Penelope Klaude's original agenda.

'Security suspects that they're behind the destabilisation of the outer 'burbs in an effort to force the issue, not that we can prove it. Lately though, we've been hearing about another plan, something much older and potentially catastrophic, and your mother is involved.'

'Why are you telling me – us this?' Hero asked.

'Because, they shot at you.' Imogen's white-blonde curls changed colour in the light cast by passing holoboards. 'Your mother is giving them what they want, so harming you makes no sense. If they don't need leverage, they must be after something else, something to do with you.'

Imogen leaned forward, her elbows on her knees. 'What have you been up to?'

'What makes you think I've been up to anything? They could have been after Norah.'

Imogen enlarged the holoscreen. 'This is Demona Thy, a known associate of Benedict Meren, who works for the Klaude. She didn't shoot at Norah.'

It was the green-haired woman. She seemed older in this holo, with crinkles at the corner of her eyes. Hero remembered Tybalt's face in the line-up of Meren's known associates and wondered if he knew Demona too. If he knew why she'd pointed a gun at her and if he'd known what was going to happen.

Fink's ears went flat and a memory skittered across his mind, too fast for her to catch. He knew something.

'What were you doing the day I found both of you in the service lift?' Imogen said.

The day she'd gone to meet the Robin. Between Dorian and Norah and the street race, she'd forgotten about it. Forgotten to consider who the Robin was or why they'd lured her somewhere infested with roaches. Had they known about the roaches, and what had been behind that door? Had the message been a joke, or a ploy to harm her?

Imogen's gaze was hard, but Hero remained silent and turned her attention to the endless stream of hovers and holoboards as her mind sifted these questions.

The hover lifted off. She waited until it disappeared into the traffic, back towards the city's depths, before turning from the door.

Norah had her hands on her hips. 'Why did you go down to that level?'

'Because someone asked me to.'

'Who?'

'I don't know, I just know that their avatar is a robin and they sent me a whole heap of files about Imogen, back *before* I knew she was a cop. Then they sent me the map and told me to meet them there, and then you turned up and they didn't contact me again.'

A glint shone in Norah's eye and the corners of her mouth turned down. 'You make that sound like it's my fault.'

Fink nudged at the back of her mind, as Hero looked to the side and scuffed her shoe. She crossed her arms and shrugged. It might have been an inconvenience at the time, but she was glad Norah had followed her that day, and not just because of the roaches. The words though were stuck, glued into a great big lump of awkward somewhere between her brain and her tongue.

There was another nudge at the back of her mind.

She looked up.

Norah glared at her.

She cast her gaze back to the wall. 'Not really. It's been nice… having a friend.'

'Oh.'

Silence, a long thick strand of it, stretched between them.

Harish settled on a perch by the floor-to-ceiling windows and ruffled his feathers, while Fink heaved a sigh, like he was going to miss lunch again.

'Thanks,' Norah said.

Hero shrugged again, still not looking up.

'Maybe we should go back down there.' Norah's voice was small, but she sounded sure.

'I… I don't think so.'

'How else are we going to find out what's going on?'

A memory tugged at her mind, a name. 'Ayumon,' she said.

Norah cocked her head to the side. 'Wasn't that the name of the AI from that data slide you stole?'

'Yeah.' She cast her gaze around, looking for a workstation, before her eyes lit upon a terminal in the kitchen. 'But that wasn't the first time I heard it.'

A holoscreen came up above the island bench, and she closed the cookbook before selecting the icon for the Planetary Library.

The Librarian's white, almost featureless head hovered over the bench. 'Good evening, Hero Regan, Norah Joshi. How may I serve?'

'We want to know about an AI called Ayumon.'

The avatar paused a moment, freezing in mid-air as only an AI could, while it accessed the Library's data banks. 'Ayumon, a mark eight artificial intelligence, was launched from Earth in the year 2218. Equipped with three-hundred and eighteen drones and advanced predictive algorithms, it was tasked with determining Jørn's suitability for human habitation.'

Norah rolled her eyes. 'It didn't do a very good job, if it missed the Pollen.'

'What happened to it?' Hero cut in.

'Ayumon was repurposed during the construction of Cumulus City.'

'For what?'

The Librarian's avatar flickered, and for just a moment there was a robin perched on the kitchen bench. 'No further records can be found.'

She blinked and the robin was gone. 'What?'

'No further records—'

'Did you see that?' she asked Norah.

'Yes.' She stuck her finger through the Librarian's holo and it fuzzed. 'Librarian, how many avatars do you have?'

The Librarian paused.

Harish glided through the holo, causing it to flicker, before he came to rest on the bench.

Still immobile, the Librarian's avatar flickered again, and then it dissolved into a cloud of static and disappeared.

For a moment, they stared at each other. Norah's mouth formed an 'o' and Hero was fairly certain her expression followed suit.

Norah spoke first. 'I've never seen an AI do that.'

'Maybe the holotransmitters are dead?'

A recipe for seared dome-fish sprung up before them. Norah shook her head. 'No.' She tried the icon for the Library. Nothing happened. 'Maybe the Library is offline.'

'The Library is never offline.' Hero frowned at the benchtop. A suspicion was forming in her mind. Her attempt to trace the Robin's first communication had gone nowhere, the message seeming to appear from the planetary net itself, a feat that should have been impossible. Unless the sender *was* the network. 'I don't think it liked your question.'

'You think the Librarian is the Robin?'
'Don't you?'
'It sounds…' Norah shrugged. 'Why would it do that?'
'I don't know, but we should find out.'

CHAPTER 16

Imogen hadn't spoken a word on the ride home from Norah's, and had barely waited for Hero to get out of the hover before she took off again. Hero had seen her briefly at breakfast, and had only been mildly surprised when Tybalt climbed into the hover to escort her to school.

His gaze was distant and she'd wondered what it was he saw in the traffic, but she hadn't asked, not even to inquire what it was he'd been doing in the city all these weeks. She'd barely seen him, except over the dining table, and even then he was usually frowning at whatever was on his palm-unit.

Walking the academy's corridors on Monday, Hero stretched her ears as far as they would go and kept her gaze from Tybalt's, lest he see the tension in her eyes. Words like 'Twilight' and 'race' buzzed from lip to lip, followed by phrases like 'did you hear' and 'you'll never guess'. She heard Dorian's name, and Tis's, bandied about alongside the words 'arrested' and 'police', but no one whispered her name, or Norah's, and there was no mention of an 'adder or a 'pard.

Relief loosened the tension in the small of her back. Barring holovid – and she'd spent all of the day before scouring the nets and found nothing – she and Norah were safe.

Tybalt's hand landed on her shoulder. 'I need to see the headmaster. Don't get into trouble,' he said as he walked into an open lift, smiling distractedly as the doors closed.

Hero frowned as the numbers on the lift controls went down

instead of up. Perhaps the headmaster wasn't in his office?

Norah appeared at her side. 'So?'

'So… what?'

'Did you find out anything about the Librarian being the Robin?'

She shook her head. 'Nothing.'

From his perch on Norah's shoulder, Harish flapped his wings and trilled.

'Same here. The Librarian won't even answer my dads' calls but they just think there's something wrong with the comms. I couldn't find out anything about that room but maybe, on the academy's network, I'll have better luck.'

They entered the classroom ahead of Mr Lee and split, winding their separate ways around the class. She could see there was gossip scrolling across discretely placed screens as she slipped behind the students already seated at their stations. She caught glimpses of Tis's name and more of Dorian's before she made it to her own seat.

The central holo painted Mr Lee's face in shades of orange and green as he paced the class, regaling them with tales of Old Terra's final world war, when the door opened.

The classroom hushed. Tis came in first, pausing on the threshold, her eyes wide and her face pale, before scurrying to her workstation. Dorian came next, his face as pale as Tis's. He didn't pause like her, or scurry, or cast his eyes downwards; instead his gaze locked with Hero's and he glared at her all the way to his workstation.

Grey was nowhere to be seen.

'Right,' Mr Lee said. 'As I was saying, the Final World War…'

Dorian's eyes bored into Hero's.

She smiled grimly and turned her attention back to the central holo as the political conflict between nations morphed into war.

Dorian's gaze didn't shift; she could feel it boring into the side of her skull, cold and hard. Resentment shivered along that connection, with enough hate to make the muscles along her spine clench.

Whether it was the ice pick of Dorian's glare or the way Mr Lee bounced on his toes, by the time the lunch chime sounded her head felt like it was being squeezed from all sides. She rubbed at the ache between her eyes, waiting for the class to empty and the ache to ease before she slipped out of her seat.

Norah waited for her outside, rolling her candy dispenser between her hands. 'Do you think Dorian told anyone about us being at the street race?'

'Probably, but the tracker in my bracelet says I was at your place so…' She shrugged. 'Did you find anything out about the Robin?'

Norah nodded. 'That place the Robin wanted to meet you… it was one of Woolsey's labs.'

'As in… ?'

'Yeah.'

'The Librarian can go anywhere, why there?'

'Maybe the Robin isn't the Librarian.'

'I don't think so.' She bit her lip, wondering who or what had been behind that door. 'We have to go down there.'

Fink groaned and rolled onto his back. *Again? What about the roaches?* he thought at her.

At least, she'd thought it was just at her, until Norah frowned and rubbed at her brow. 'It's disturbing how you two do that.'

'Don't you talk to Harish?'

Norah paused and her shoulders tensed. 'Not like that,' she said, before she cocked her head. 'Why do his thoughts taste like mawberries?'

He yawned again. *He'd been born that way, just like Harish had been born with thoughts like vinegar and salt and she'd been born with lavender ones.* He cracked open one eye. *Except, of course, when she was taking those things.*

Norah paused, the ever-present candy dispenser halfway to her mouth.

Those little pink bullets, so like the green ones that Tybalt was always putting next to her water glass. Hero didn't know how she knew it, or why she hadn't seen it before, but they weren't candy. Without meaning to, she reached out and brushed against the other girl's thoughts. There was a moment of absolute stillness.

Norah's eyes widened and Hero thought she sensed something, an image fluttering between their brains. Then the dispenser went the rest of the way to Norah's mouth and a foul-tasting barrier shoved Hero out of her thoughts.

She recoiled.

Norah slipped the dispenser back into her pocket, turned on her heel and scurried away.

Hero stared after her, the sensation of that mental barrier lingering on her mind.

Fink bumped her shoulder. *Her mouth was hanging open.*

She snapped it closed. Was that what the meds did? Kept people out of her thoughts? She leaned against Fink and let the question sit in her mind.

He purred and flicked his tail. *They didn't keep him out, but they did make her brain fuzzy and changed the way her mind tasted.*

'Like menthol?'

He shook his head. *That's what she tasted like when she was taking the pills. This change was different, deeper.*

'How?'

When they first met, her thoughts had been cinnamon and cherry, but they were different now. Like chocolate, the really dark kind.

'Was that bad?' She grimaced when he stuck his nose against her neck and snuffled.

He'd never let anything bad happen. It was just different, stronger, more like a 'pard.

More like a 'pard. The thought rang in her mind, along with the image of herself facing down a swarm of roaches.

Fink flicked his ear and pruckled. *Not quite.*

The dining hall buzzed like the corridors had earlier in the day, and she caught snatches of conversations as she wound her way to where Tybalt stood beside her customary table.

Hero sat without a word, and glared at the pills beside her plate. She looked at Tybalt.

He raised an eyebrow.

Silverware rattled as Norah slid into a chair opposite, her back straight and her eyes intent on the tray in front of her.

Harish, curled around Norah's neck, hissed at Tybalt.

His expression barely changed, but when his palm-unit pinged his brows came together over his nose like bushy black thunder-clouds that cast his eyes in shadow.

'Take them,' he said, pointing towards the pills. His gaze was already absent as he turned, speaking over his shoulder. 'I need to talk to… someone.'

She watched as he weaved his way out of the dining room. 'He's up to something,' she said.

There was no response. Norah was focused on her plate as she carefully dissected a sandwich.

'Norah?'

The other girl hunched her shoulders.

Stretching out her mind, Hero touched the other girl's thoughts.

Norah's knife hit the side of the plate.

From behind Hero came a giggle that grated all the way down her spine.

The dining room fell silent.

Hero twisted in her seat. Dorian stood behind her, arms crossed and his lips twisted in an ugly sneer. Tis shifted from foot to foot beside him, the tip of one finger caught between her teeth.

She crossed her arms, trying to ignore the way her head ached and it felt like every eye in the room was trying to crawl inside her skull. 'What?' she snapped.

Dorian's sneer grew, his lips pulling back from his teeth. 'My parents sent Grey to the Farm.'

The Farm.

If her mum found out about the street race, she'd send Fink there faster than she could twitch. She blanched at the thought. It wasn't her fault that Dorian had been arrested.

'So?' she said.

Dorian's lips twisted in a snarl and he stepped forward, jabbing his finger into her chest. 'So,' he said, 'it's your fault.'

Each stab of his finger sent a corresponding lightning bolt of olive-coloured hate straight through her mind. She slapped it away, almost tripping as she stood. 'I didn't do anything.'

'You didn't get caught. You knew they were coming, didn't you? You called them.' He was in her face now, right up close so she could smell his breath.

Fink growled, a deep rumble that, soon enough, would turn into a snarl and then, and then—

She pushed Dorian away, her hands against his chest making her head explode with all of his hate and underneath it, something else, something that made her gut clench in sympathy. 'I didn't do anything,' she said again.

'Then why didn't they arrest you? I told them you were there.'

'That's right.' Tis was at her back now, the giggle gone from her voice. 'Why didn't they?'

She didn't have to look at Fink to know that his ruff was rising. She could feel it in his thoughts, no longer calm and soothing, no longer keeping all those pressing eyes at bay, but another rumble in the cacophony pounding at her head.

She closed her eyes against the noise.

Dorian shoved her.

Fink snarled.

Tis squealed.

Norah shouted something, and Hero felt the brush of Harish's wings against her cheek before Dorian yelled and flailed, one of his arms clipping her shoulder and spinning her to the floor.

She didn't feel the impact; instead her mind imploded. All of the gazes that had been trying to crawl in now flooded her mind with words and sights and smells. There was a kaleidoscope in her brain and she couldn't breathe amidst the chaos. All she could do was curl into a ball and hope it would end.

Hero knew it was Tybalt who touched her shoulder by the dark, liquorice flavour of his mind. Then Fink was back, surrounding her in the scent of mawberries and pushing the other flavours away. Slowly, she uncurled from her ball.

'Hero.' Tybalt's face was grave and resignation laced the disappointment in his voice. 'Come on.' He held out his hand.

She stared at it, then past his shoulder. Norah stood there, her face pale, the candy dispenser clutched in her hand. Behind her stood Dorian, his face twisted in an ugly combination of glee and rage, and beyond him… Beyond him stood everyone else, staring with wide eyes and whispering behind their hands.

Tybalt's hands slipped under her arms and lifted her to her feet. His thoughts flooded her already raw mind; within them she saw a 'stick filled with green goo.

She jerked out of his grip. 'No,' she said.

Tybalt frowned as if he didn't understand, but she knew he did, she could see it in his eyes. 'Hero, calm down.' He stepped forwards.

She tried to back away, but the table was at her back and there were all of those eyes, staring at her, making her head pound. 'I'm not sick,' she said as Tybalt took her arm again in a firm grip. She held her ground as he tried to tug her forwards.

He looked at her with a dark, steady gaze. 'We're just going somewhere quiet.'

Somewhere quiet… the words echoed in her head, but so did the liquorice-flavoured image of that 'stick. This time when she tried to jerk away, Tybalt didn't let go. Panic, a great ugly acidic glob of it, tried to crawl up her throat.

She scrabbled at his fingers, trying to pry them open, but they didn't budge. 'Let me go.'

'Hero—'

Fink was at her back; she could feel him start to growl, feel his claws unsheathe, feel him focus on Tybalt. The panic rose, swamping her throat. 'Let me go.'

His lips firmed and so did his grip. 'No.'

Her mind was too big for her skull, pushing against the bone, against the stares. She couldn't breathe. She wanted out, needed out, now. Now. Now. Her thoughts exploded.

Tybalt staggered, both knees hitting the floor. Dorian and Tis dropped like stones, and around her students clutched their heads and cried out. Except Norah, who stared at her with eyes wider than she'd ever seen.

Hero ran. The academy doors didn't open and Hero almost smashed her face against the plasglas, but she pounded the panel until they slid apart. The hover pads spread before her, empty but for a few sleek black hovers and one lone taxi.

She took a breath, taking in the dust and smells of the city. The pressure on her mind eased, leaving only a nagging pinch of panic and fear.

Fink whuffed against her ear.

She threw her arms around his neck and fought the sob in her throat. 'Why does he keep giving me meds?'

He didn't know but ever since they had changed, she had grown stronger. That thing she did before almost flattened his ears.

That thing she did… She looked back through the big glass doors. What *had* she done, and how long before Tybalt, or someone else, came after her?

Her eyes lit upon the taxi, idling upon its pad. She headed for it, crossing the short space almost at a jog, and climbed in.

The front of the cab flickered as the door slid closed, the driver's face larger than life across the screen at the front. 'Hey kid, where to?'

Where to? Her mind went blank. Where to? She didn't know, she just had to get away, somewhere, anywhere, before Tybalt came and—

'Kid?'

The door opened again, and Tybalt slid in next to her. 'Take us to Iedj Gardens,' he said.

Too late.

'Sure thing,' the driver said before his face disappeared from the screen.

Hero scrunched herself against the other side of the cab, as far from Tybalt as she could get, while at her feet Fink pinned back his ears.

Tybalt looked at her, his expression as dark as she'd ever seen it, and activated the cab's privacy shield. He sighed. 'Hero—'

'I'm not sick.'

He sighed again and drew his hand over his face, like he was pulling away a mask, leaving something sadder behind. 'I know,' he said.

She froze. 'You know?'

He just looked at her.

She didn't say anything, she didn't think she could; instead she turned her gaze to the hovers and barges outside the window. All this time he had known? But how and why and… and …

'Why?' she asked.

'Why do I know, or why did I keep it from you?'

'Both.'

'Because of your mother and what happened to her twin, your uncle.'

She frowned. 'He died in a racing accident. How does that have anything to do with me?'

He looked out into the traffic and, for a moment, she thought he wouldn't say anything. 'It wasn't an accident, not wholly. He was killed, because he was like you.'

'Like me? You mean… ?' She pointed at her head.

He nodded.

'But why? By who?'

'For the same reasons, and by the same people who want you. The people your mother is working for…' Tybalt leaned in close, '…and protecting you from.'

She remembered the gravelly voice on the other end of her mum's holocall and the image on Imogen's data slide. 'Benedict Meren.'

Tybalt's brows rose in surprise, but he nodded. 'He works for them.'

'How do you know him?'

'What makes you think I do?'

'I saw his file. You're under "known associates".'

He opened his mouth, about to speak, before he frowned at something over her shoulder.

She turned to look, but there was nothing there except more traffic, and when she turned back, Tybalt was twisted around in his seat, staring out into the traffic behind them. His frown went from puzzled to concerned to something that made her glad she wasn't in its path. He turned back around and pressed the intercom, the driver's face appearing once again. 'Take this left,' he told the driver.

'Ugh,' the driver said. 'That's not the way to—'

'Now.'

The taxi swerved, darting into another, thinner stream of traffic, leaving a snarl of hovers and blaring horns in its wake.

'What's going on?' she asked, nerves starting back up and down her spine.

'We're being followed.'

'What?' She squirmed around to look, but all she saw was the same endless stream of barges, taxis and hovers she saw everywhere else. 'Where?'

There was a pop, and the plasglas dome shattered, a thousand spider-web fractures spreading from a hole next to Tybalt's head.

There was another pop, and this time the driver swore, narrowly missing a barge as he swerved.

Tybalt didn't yell, but his tone brooked no argument. 'Lose them.'

'No shit,' the driver said. The hover braked sharply for a heartbeat before plunging downwards.

Horns blared and lights dazzled Hero's eyes as they dove through the traffic. If they'd been in a busier part of the city, they might have been plastered against the side of a barge, instead of the back seat with Fink pressed up against her legs. They were diving on an almost impossible angle and at first she wasn't quite sure where the driver was going except that the sides of skytowers were looming closer and closer. She wanted to close her eyes but couldn't resist the sight of all the steelcrete and glass getting bigger and bigger.

The hover swerved around another taxi and then they were horizontal and streaking through a narrow space between towers. They twisted and turned through another narrow space and under a skybridge before they popped out above a deserted square. They landed hard enough to shake pieces of plasglas loose from the shattered dome.

The door slid open. 'Get out,' the driver said. 'They'll keep following me for a bit before they realise what happened. That'll give you enough time to get somewhere else.'

Tybalt had her halfway out of the hover, Fink close behind, as he inclined his head. 'My thanks.'

'Part of the job,' the driver said.

They were barely out of the hover's lift radius before it shot upwards. She watched as it headed for another dark and narrow space between towers. 'What did he mean, it was part of his job?'

'I like to be prepared. Now hurry, before—'

The hum of its engines preceded one of the chasing hovers by only a moment.

'Run,' Tybalt yelled, and practically pulled her arm off as he sprinted for the nearest tower.

The glance over her shoulder was instinctive, and her heart picked up a couple of beats when the hover landed and people in black poured out. It was the man in front, though, who caused her to stumble. He had the same short light brown hair and pale skin as on Imogen's data slide, but in person, it was Benedict Meren's mechanical gaze that made her blood run cold.

As soon as they were through the tower's doors, Tybalt grabbed her shoulders and pointed her at the control panel. 'Jam it,' he said.

'What?' she said, her eyes caught on the big black gun he was pulling from under his coat.

He cupped her chin and raised her eyes to his. 'The doors,' he said slowly. 'Jam them.'

'Oh.' Hero unzipped her sleeve, plugged her bracer into the panel and had the tower's door codes twisted and jammed in seconds. 'Done.'

Tybalt frowned at the stolen bracer, realising it was not the one she was meant to have. 'We'll talk about that later. Come on,' he said and headed for the lift bank.

They took the first one going up. She didn't know where they were going, or even where they were, but Tybalt stabbed the icon for the topmost floor and stood back patiently, without so much as a glance at the map on his palm-unit.

Hero huddled against Fink and watched Tybalt, the way his jacket parted over his vest, how the fabric bunched over the holster on his hip, how the gun looked so at home in his hand. She'd never really noticed his hands before, how strong they were and how callused. Butlers and substitute parents didn't have hands like that, but then neither were their eyes hard or their mouths set like they had something unpleasant, something dangerous, to do.

Tybalt didn't look so much like Tybalt anymore, not unless he regularly ate ruc-pards for breakfast. Maybe he did, or maybe he had. Maybe he'd been cooked up in some lab by an insane Woolsey wannabe. She wouldn't know, he never told her anything.

She grabbed his arm. 'Who are you?'

'What?' The same word flashed through his thoughts.

'Who. Are. You?'

The answer flooded her mind, a confusion of images, tinged with the dark liquorice of Tybalt's thoughts. A family, mum, dad, sisters. School. A training ground, cuts and bruises and puking on the grass after his first ten-kilometre run. Wearing an envirosuit with guns going off around him. Tybalt shouted when a rhinlion pinned his partner to the ground. The hulking grey-gold creature snapped and snarled, its spines puffing out around its face, while the man held it off with shaking arms. Tybalt took aim. The rest of the rhinlion's pack hunted them across the savannah, their trills shivering through the cold night air. Benedict Meren's face…

Tybalt jerked his arm out of her grip and she stumbled and grabbed onto Fink. The images stopped, but it felt like her brain was overloaded, filled to the brim with memories and emotions.

Fink nudged her with his nose. *She had asked a big question, too big for words, what else did she expect?*

Not that, she thought back.

The lift stopped and the doors opened onto a brightly-lit foyer beyond which people and companions moved around a large square.

Tybalt was the first to move, tucking the gun back under his coat. 'Come on,' he said, and stepped out into the crowd.

The plaza was busy, bounded by buildings on three sides and a busy skylane on the fourth. Above them, the towers shot upwards and she could just make out a thin sliver of sky, indigo with the setting sun. There was a fountain at the centre of the plaza and holoscreens plastered over every surface, but most importantly there was a line of public comm-stations in the corner.

She stuck close behind Tybalt as he hurried towards the station. The crowd parted around them as they crossed the square, people halting in their tracks, companions moving back suddenly, and all of them staring. At first she thought it was at her, thought perhaps they knew about the people chasing them, until Fink brushed against her shoulder. His ruff was up, a dark halo of orange and black, and his tail whipped about like a snake as he scanned the crowd.

She slipped her hand into his ruff.

The comm-booth wasn't big enough for them all, so she and Fink crowded close while Tybalt went inside to make his call. The booth's sides darkened the moment he closed the door, a newscast projecting out from its surface. She was transfixed by the footage, as one of the bridges that connected the outer 'burbs cracked and fell away, until she noticed the reflection of the crowd in its surface.

Did they know her? Where they chasing her? Was someone going to jump out of the mass and point a gun at her? Her stomach curled itself into knots.

Down the line of comm-stations, a door slammed, and she jerked. A flurry-thyt drifted overhead and Fink growled and snapped, making the creature hum in alarm and scurry back to the safety of its owner's shoulder.

Hero's ears began to itch and then buzz as the knot between her shoulder blades wound tighter, until it felt like there was a stone at the base of her neck. The voices crept in on this thread of tension, flooding her mind before she realised what was happening.

A Woolsey, I'd never thought I'd see...

...The size of those paws...

...Bread, milk— Whoa, look at that...

She clamped her hands over her ears but the voices were relentless and only grew until it felt like she was in the middle of a raging crowd. Vaguely, she was aware of Fink at her back and in her mind, but even he couldn't stop the noise.

There were so many thoughts, more than she'd ever heard before, all jumbled in her brain like a bad recipe. She wanted to throw up. She wanted them to stop but she didn't want the pills in Tybalt's pocket, didn't want them, didn't want them ...

Hero.

Her name shone within the cacophony like a star.

Concentrate, Hero.

'On what?' she tried to say but wasn't sure if her lips moved or if it was just another figment of her imagination. Where was Fink? She needed Fink.

On this. Someone grabbed her hand and squeezed.

She squeezed back.

That's it, just think about my hand, nothing else.

The hand holding hers was warm and bony, smooth but for the rasp of calluses. She wondered what they were from. An image flashed in her mind, the liquorice-flavoured memory of a dark room, the holo of a red-breasted bird at its centre.

The voices faded, retreating behind the memory, until the crowd in her head was a distant murmur. She opened her eyes.

Tybalt stared at her, his brow furrowed with concern. 'Better?'

Dumbfounded, she nodded.

'Good.' Still holding her hand, Tybalt started pulling her towards the opposite side of the square. 'We're going up. Someone will be waiting for us at Treegate Plaza. You'll be safe then.'

'Who?'

Tybalt kept moving, not saying a word, but his thoughts were a different story. She saw the dark room again, but this time the red-breasted bird – a robin, the Robin, she realised – morphed into the blank white features of the Librarian.

She yanked her hand out of Tybalt's grip. 'Stop,' she said with more force.

The voices flooded back, including one that sent a shiver up her spine.

There she is. Dark and tough, the thought reminded her of the man with the eyes that weren't eyes, and he was accompanied by an image of herself, standing in the middle of the plaza.

It felt like time slowed and the air became thick as she turned, her gaze locking on Meren's like a homing beacon.

'We don't have time for this.' Tybalt grabbed her arm and resumed dragging her across the square.

Meren followed them, and although no more thoughts reached her mind, she saw his lips move as if he were talking to himself. A concealed comm-unit.

She stumbled along behind Tybalt, a hollow, twitchy feeling settling in the pit of her stomach. She refused to call it fear until she saw the others, their clothes dark and their gazes fixed on her like a pack of rhinlions.

When she stopped again right in the middle of the plaza, Tybalt was the one to stumble.

'Hero.' He spun around, frustration and anger plain on his face.

'They're all around us,' she said, surprised that the fear in her gut wasn't spilling out with her voice. She pointed to Meren.

The man smiled.

Tybalt cast his gaze around the plaza. Hero knew he'd seen the rest of the pack when his lips thinned and his face became a study in sharp angles. 'Get on Fink,' he said.

'What?'

'Get on.' Tybalt rounded on her, a hint of fear in his eyes despite the determination all over his face.

Without a word, she clambered onto Fink's back. Around them the pack started to move in.

Tybalt reached into his jacket and pulled out the gun. Lifting it into the air, he fired.

For a fraction of a second there was nothing but the sound of the shots echoing in the plaza – even the skylane seemed to pause. Hero had time to wonder at the way the light sparkled in the fountain and how the gun seemed to suck the light in. Then the moment was over, and chaos reigned.

There was screaming and yelling and Meren and his pack moved in, shoving against the tide of people diving behind chairs and running for buildings. Some mustn't have moved fast enough, because Tybalt fired again before slapping Fink on the rump and yelling one word: 'Run!'

Fink didn't need to be told twice. He ran, leaping into a gallop with such suddenness that Hero slipped and almost fell; only her arms, clamped in a death-grip around his neck, kept her on Fink's back.

Ears flat to his head, Fink raced for the edge of the plaza and the crowd swamping it, dodging an old man, leaping a badger-zyl, weaving between people and companions alike. Under Hero's hands, his body was a wire, taut and alive. She could feel his hearts, his major heart pounding between her knees, while the second, smaller one, throbbed a beat behind.

They were almost out of the plaza when Meren and one of his hunters materialised in their path, big bulky guns in their hands.

She braced herself, but instead of sliding to a halt Fink gained speed. Two strides and they were almost upon them. She could see the lines on Meren's face, the narrowing of his shiny cybernetic eyes and the way his finger tightened on the trigger.

The gun barked.

Fink staggered, missed a stride.

Meren's finger tightened again.

Fink leapt.

Hero looked down, her gaze locking with Meren's mechanical one, and for a moment it felt like they were suspended in mid air. A shiver ran down her spine.

A jolt and a sharp lance of pain flashed through Fink's mind and they were on the other side, racing over the skybridge.

CHAPTER 17

Fink chose the way.

Sometime after they crossed the third skybridge, she slid off his back and walked behind him. The bullet had grazed his shoulder, leaving a thin line of blood that quickly dried and crusted in his tawny coat.

She didn't know how long they'd been walking, skirting buildings, sneaking over skybridges and through underpasses. Long enough, at least, for the adrenalin that had spurred them out of the square to wear thin, dulling her fear and leaving her tired, her arms and legs heavy.

Up ahead, Fink grumbled and sent her an image of herself walking faster. *They were almost there.*

That was enough. Hands on her hips, she stopped in the middle of the arcade. 'Almost where? How do you even know where we're going?'

Hunching his fore-shoulders, Fink grumbled and kept walking.

'No.' She crossed her tired arms. 'Not until you tell me what's going on.'

He turned around. *Nothing was going on.* His tail twitched. *This was the way home.*

She narrowed her eyes.

He turned back around. *She needed to hurry up.*

She stood firm.

His ears twisted sideways. *He knew what he was doing; he'd paid extra special attention when Tybalt showed him.*

'He told you something? Why didn't you tell me?' Memories of the flashes she'd caught from Tybalt in the square came rushing back, of the dark room and the Robin. 'What did he say? Did he tell you about the Robin?'

He'd tell her later. Right now there were people following them.

Chill crashed through her veins. 'They are?' She looked over her shoulder, expecting to see black-clad forms slinking through the shadows.

He trotted back and herded her forwards. *It was okay, they were almost there.*

Ahead of them, a holoboard flickered. Hair sprouted from a bald man's head, before the face morphed, becoming younger, rounder, until it was her own and her mouth whispered 'hide'.

She stopped, coming to such a sudden halt that Fink walked into her. 'Did you see that?'

Against her back, she felt him go tense. *See what?*

'That.' She pointed at the holoboard.

Some of the tension left him as he cocked his head to the side. *The man with no hair?*

'No, I mean the face. It changed, it was me.'

Didn't they do that?

'But it said hide.'

From the man without hair?

'No, I—' The sound of an engine cut her off.

The hover descended, blocking the alley. Black with tinted windows, it was just like a million others but her gut twisted and she backed up hard against Fink. For a moment it hovered, like it was setting down, before the side door slid open.

Meren met her eyes with a grim smile on his face. He jumped the few feet to the footpath.

Fink growled. *Run,* he thought. They spun in unison, bolting back down the alley, followed by the sound of boots in pursuit.

A few strides ahead, Fink had barely disappeared around a corner before he came bounding back, shots hitting the wall behind him as he herded her down another alley.

Shadows moved ahead, accompanied by the heavy clump of boots. She lunged at the nearest door, fingers flying over the control pad until the lock clicked and the door hissed open.

The corridor was short and grimy, trash and dust collected at the edges, and spilled out into an equally grimy arcade. Signs flickered in a few of the shop windows, curtains blocked out the rest, and an old trash collector whirred away nearby.

Wings fluttered. Hero turned, and there sat the Robin, perched in one of the holosigns. Above it, a woman advertising shoes pointed down a hall that branched off to the right. Without a thought, Hero followed. At the end of the hall, there was another sign and another after that, leading her through the arcade's endless corridors until her lungs burned for air. Still, the sound of pursuit rang loud in their ears.

They burst out of the arcade and onto a skybridge, traffic rushing over and under them as they raced across the tiny plasglas-encased walkway. Would anyone in the hundreds of hovers notice if she jumped up and down and banged against the walls? She glanced over her shoulder, considering it, but the goons were there, running in their wake and gaining fast. She'd barely have a chance to yell before they were on her.

Fink slowed just enough for her to grab his scruff and leap onto his back. She clung to him desperately as his legs stretched out in a full gallop. His hearts thumped between her knees and they covered the skybridge in seconds, thundering into a garden surrounded by apartments and shops, their windows dark and doors closed.

The Robin was a point of light above a small gnarled tree. They squeezed behind it. Why did the Robin have them hiding behind a tree? Then she saw the door, its glass dark and dusty. It opened, and they slipped through, Hero sliding down Fink's shoulder and jamming the lock.

When she looked around, they were in a foyer, a bank of lifts at one end and hallways to either side. It was as dark and dusty as the door. She pressed the button for the lift and waited.

A shadow pressed against the frosted plasglas and scratched at the thumb-lock. It cursed before another voice barked, 'Smash it!'

Fink growled and crouched, his ruff and the hair along his back stiff as a razor.

She hit the call button again.

The door shuddered, once and then a second time, as someone threw themselves against it. With each impact Fink crouched lower, his lips curled back from his teeth and his claws unsheathed.

Cracks began to spiderweb the plasglas.

The ding of the turbolift made her jump. She was in there before the doors had fully opened, but Fink remained crouched by the door, growling louder with each impact.

'Fink!' She dashed back out, catching his tail as it thrashed from side to side, and yanked.

He spun about, teeth still bared.

She took a step back.

His growl stuttered.

The door shattered and they dived into the lift.

The lift shot upwards. Her heart pounded away in her chest. She knew she should be worried about Meren and his black-clad army, but all she could think about was Fink's bared teeth. She knew he hadn't meant it, but… She watched as his tail twitched in small, sharp jerks, and a barely audible growl vibrated the fur over his ribcage. He'd never frightened her before, but then he'd never kept anything from her before either.

When the doors opened, a wall of plasglas greeted them. Beyond it, hovers flashed past in the thin lines of the less populated levels.

She looked at the lift's readout. Level two forty-six. There were still another ninety-eight levels above them. They needed to go up. She pressed the button.

Nothing happened.

She frowned and tried the button to close the doors.

Still nothing.

Fink stuck his head out, his nose twitching as he lifted it to the air. Smells flooded from his mind to hers, very old dust, and the faint copper of roaches, but no humans, not even the musk of another companion.

Cautiously, she stepped out of the lift, Fink just a step behind.

There was a ding, and the lift doors closed before she had time to do more than spin around and watch as it continued upwards.

Movement caught her attention. 'What was that?'

Fink pricked his ears. *What was what?*

'I saw something. There.' She pointed. At the end of the corridor something, no, someone, moved. They moved again, and this time she could make out a dark suit and the familiar, craggy planes of their face as they disappeared around the corner. 'Tybalt!' she yelled and ran after him.

Fink bounded past, chortling.

She rounded the corner and caught a glimpse of his tail disappearing down another hallway. At the next, Fink was already halfway down the hall. How was Tybalt keeping ahead of them?

She followed Fink around one last corner, and caught up with him sitting before a heavy looking door. His ears flicked this way and that, confusion colouring his thoughts. A mawberry-flavoured image popped into her head of Tybalt standing in front of the door before he flickered and faded away.

Hero frowned, not quite sure what Fink was showing her, until she caught sight of the faint line of light tracing the walls on either side. She looked over her shoulder, and there it was, streaking away behind them. Her breath caught. 'Holostrips.' That's why Fink had been unable to smell Tybalt from the lift. She reached out and disrupted the light with her fingers. 'We were following a hologram.'

Why had someone made it look like Tybalt?

'I don't know,' she said, but there was something familiar about the door in front of them that tickled an idea at the back of her mind. They'd been here before, after the Robin had sent her the second message.

Almost as if it had heard her thought, the door swung open.

Cautiously, she stepped though.

There was a second door after the first, a thick slab of metal that swung open just as silently, and beyond it a lab, just like every lab she'd ever seen on a holovid.

With Fink's claws a comforting click-click at her side, she crept further into the lab. It was white and large, and although the scent of dust was thick in the air, the benches and cupboards that lined the walls and the workstation at its centre remained remarkably clean.

Fink rumbled. *He didn't think anyone had been here in a long time.*

Behind them, the door closed with a hiss and the solid *thunk* of a lock activating.

'Hello?' she called.

There was no answer, save for the almost inaudible hum of biocir-cuits.

In the centre of the lab, above the workstation, a holo flickered to life. It fuzzed and spat, its circuits warming up, before the white humanoid contours of the Planetary Librarian sprang to life.

When the AI spoke, its voice was small and scratchy, but grew stronger with each syllable. 'Hello, Hero Regan.'

Hero blinked at the AI. 'You really are the Robin.'

'Indeed.'

'You brought us here?'

'Yes.'

'Why?'

'You required assistance.'

'So you conjured up a bird and holo of Tybalt? Why not call the police?'

'The ruse was necessary, for your safety and for mine.'

'But why?'

'You are necessary to the plan, and the police cannot be trusted.'

'Huh?'

'You are nec—'

'Stop.' She took a breath, in through the nose, out through the mouth, as the AI stopped, mouth open mid-word. They were literal like that. 'What plan? Why are people chasing me? Why can't you trust the police? Why am I even talking to you?'

For a moment, the Librarian paused, literally freezing in thought. 'An explanation will take time. Sensors indicate you are experiencing a high level of stress. Before we proceed, you require rest and food, as does your companion.'

She looked at an exhausted Fink, but firmed her mouth and narrowed her gaze on the AI. She wasn't going to be put off. 'Now. I want you to tell me now.'

'Goodnight Hero Regan.' The Librarian switched off.

'Hey.' She rushed at the workstation, the holokeyboard lighting under her hands, but although the terminal hummed, nothing brought the AI back.

It wasn't until the smell of cherries hit her nose, making her sneeze, that she noticed the hissing and the fine white mist drifting out of the ventilators. She covered her nose and mouth but the smell was already stuck to the inside of her nose and coated her throat. Her eyes grew heavy.

She stumbled towards Fink, his huge form sprawled across the floor already passed out, and dropped to her knees beside him. 'Get up,' she said, pushing at his shoulder with arms weighed down with lead. 'Get up.'

He didn't move.

She collapsed against his side, buried in the warmth of his fur, and fought against the weight of her lids. Somewhere, between one breath and the next, she lost.

CHAPTER 18

Waking up was like swimming through goo. The foul taste of cherries clung to her throat and the inside of her nose, and her eyes felt weighed down and sealed shut. It took effort to pry them open, to clench her fingers in Fink's coat and pull herself upright. She struggled to make a fist and thump his shoulder.

He cracked an eyelid.

'Up,' she said.

He grumbled and started to rise. In her mind, she felt his grogginess like it was her own, and the effort with which he pulled his legs under him and stumbled to his feet made her feel faint.

She looked up, wincing at the ache in her neck, and had to blink twice to bring his whiskers into focus. 'Wow,' she said. 'How much of that cherry stuff did you inhale?'

He nudged her with his nose. *It's your turn. Up.*

'Good morning, Hero Regan.' The sound of the Librarian's voice sent a shockwave through her. She scrambled to her feet, her legs clumsy, but strong enough to hold her upright. 'The sedative I used was designed for large specimens such as your companion, and has a less pronounced effect on human physiology. The effects will dissipate shortly.'

'What do you want with us?'

'Merely your cooperation. You will be free to go once my associate arrives to collect you.'

'I don't want to meet your "associate". Let us go.' She pushed the words out through gritted teeth. 'Now.'

'In due time. Your stress levels are much improved this morning.'

'I don't care. Open the door.'

'I cannot comply.'

'Why not?'

'It is against my programming.'

'What programming?'

'It is a long explanation. I suggest you sit and eat.' On the holo, the Librarian zoomed out, going from a talking head to an upper body floating above the workstation. It gestured to a chair on the other side of the lab. Two white-wrapped bars popped out of a dispenser and onto a tray attached to the armrest. 'You must replenish calories after the sedative. More appropriate sustenance has been provided for your companion.' The AI gestured to another, larger food slot across the room.

Hero shook her head, planting her feet as she crossed her arms over her chest. 'No, I want you to tell me now.'

'I must insist you eat.'

She'd barely opened her mouth to protest she wasn't hungry when a rumble, ten times louder than her own stomach could produce, interrupted her. She turned to Fink.

He shrugged his mid-quarters, unapologetic as he made an unsteady beeline for the round, pellet-like objects pouring into a bowl under the food slot.

Hero considered the foil-wrapped food bars. Arguing with the AI wasn't getting her anywhere. Maybe she could pry open a panel and hack the door controls, but she didn't think she could do it before the Librarian decided to send her to sleep again, and hacking the AI itself… Her mother would have more luck stopping Fink from raiding the fishpond. No, if she wanted to get out of here, she was going to have to do what the damn thing said.

When she sat, the chair wrapped itself around her, arms and back humming gently as it shifted to fit her contours. The food bar was old and stale, but it cured the queasy feeling in her stomach. She took another bite.

'I'm eating,' she said around her mouthful.

'Yes.'

'So talk.'

The Librarian disappeared from the holo, replaced by an image of an older woman, her black hair threaded with grey and frown lines sunk deep between her brows. 'Doctor Augusta Woolsey—'

Hero raised her brows. 'The Crackpot?'

'*Brilliant although unconventional,* is what is recorded in her files. Along with creating some of the most powerful Terra-Jørn hybrids, Doctor Woolsey was instrumental in unlocking the specific genetic sequence that granted immunity to the Pollen. She was well respected for her discoveries, until she proposed that humans, not just flora and fauna, should be granted the same immunity.'

She frowned. 'What was wrong with that?'

The AI's avatar replaced Woolsey's image. 'The process required radical genetic changes that would have fundamentally altered the human species. Those with the changes would have been immune to the Pollen, but they would also no longer be purely human, an idea the government and the majority of the population found abhorrent. The proposal was rejected and Doctor Woolsey prohibited from further research.'

'Okay,' she said as she picked up the other food bar. The dispenser replaced it with another before she'd even cracked the wrapper. 'What does it have to do with me?'

'Doctor Woolsey determined that, unless it developed an immunity to the Pollen, the colony would eventually outgrow its ability to support itself. Working with a predictive AI, she planned a way to subtly introduce the immunity but projected the necessary adaptations would take generations.'

'And you were the AI?'

'No, but when I was retasked to fulfil the function of Planetary Librarian, Doctor Woolsey determined that I was the best choice to oversee and manage the experiment.'

'And?'

'Your family is one of the project's primary subjects.'

'I'm a science experiment?'

'No. You are the culmination of several generations of careful and selective genetic engineering.'

'Oh great, so I'm an engineering experiment.' Her stomach twisted in on itself, and she put down the half-eaten food bar. 'I bet all the pills they keep trying to shove down my throat messed that up.'

'On the contrary, your medication was carefully formulated.'

Carefully formulated. The words rang in her brain, as big and as loud as the city itself. *Carefully formulated.* But that meant… people knew, and not just any people, but people *she* knew; doctors, psychiatrists, Tybalt… 'No.'

'Indeed, it was important in not just making the necessary alterations to your genetic code but in suppressing your telepathy until such time as it could be managed. Although a continued regimen of small, controlled doses would have been optimal, your lack of cooperation forced me to consider a larger, and rather more dangerous, final injection.'

'That second message you sent…'

'Indeed, I would have administered the medication then, but we were interrupted. Yesterday, we attempted again, until you incapacitated several of your classmates. Fortuitously, your current situation offered another opportunity.'

Light shone on a small robot and the 'stick in one of its many appendages, a green ring still visible around the plunger.

She rubbed at the back of her neck. She had thought the ache a product of sleeping against Fink, but now… 'I'm leaving now.'

'I cannot allow that. Your purpose has yet to be fulfilled.'

She thrust herself out of the chair. 'You keep saying that, but what purpose is that meant to be? Being the Crackpot's science experiment or reading people's thoughts and getting pointed at and ridiculed?'

'Indeed not.'

'So, I hear voices in my head for thrills?'

'While telepathy was a projected result of the genetic changes, it was not the aim.'

'Telepathy? You mean mind-talking?'

'Yes. It is a highly desirable outcome, along with telekinesis, telempathy and various adaptations to the physical senses, including increased visual and aural acuity—'

'I have all of those things?'

'No.'

'Right, so I just read minds and everyone thinks I'm crazy.'

'Correct. To be clear though, you are not mentally impaired, although it was important that everyone think you so.'

For a second, she didn't believe her ears. 'Excuse me?'

'Although you are—'

'I heard that bit. *Why* did everyone have to think I was crazy?'

'There are factions that wish to terminate Doctor Woolsey's program. The doctors and medication were a necessary step in hiding your true nature, which, if discovered, would have placed you and the program in jeopardy.'

'I don't understand. Besides being a human Woolsey, what's my true nature?'

'You are a hybrid, one of the first in a new subspecies of humans fully adapted to Jørn's ecology. Doctor Woolsey called you Jørgens.'

The chair whirred and hummed as she sank back into it. 'Hybrid' and 'Jørgen' shone, bright and clear in her mind, blanking out everything else. She had thought she was special before. 'I think I'm going to be sick.'

'That would not be wise. Your body has yet to process the calories you recently ingested.'

Putting her head between her knees, she tried to breathe past the nausea, then something else the AI said sank in and she looked up. 'You said I'm one of the first. There are more people like me?'

'Yes.'

'Where? Who?'

'That information is restricted.'

'By who? Woolsey's dust.'

'Nevertheless, her instructions still apply; I am to protect and oversee the subjects at all costs.'

Hero narrowed her gaze. She didn't like the AI's idea of protection; injections and little green pills.

Fink popped an image into her mind, of Norah and her ever-present candy.

The nausea subsided, the queasy feeling beginning to feel more like excitement. 'Norah's a hybrid too, isn't she?'

For a moment, she didn't think the AI would answer, then… 'Your knowledge is unfortunate.'

She stood and pushed the chair back so hard it almost ran over Fink, then stalked to the workstation and thumped it with her fist. 'Unfortunate? I'll tell you what's unfortunate! Having drugs shoved down your throat every day, being told you're sick! Too sick to have friends or go to school. So sick that people follow you around to make sure you don't do something stupid like jump off a skybridge. Now you drug me and hold me prisoner and tell me I'm not just a freak, I'm a Woolsey!? The least you can do is tell me where the other freaks are.'

Fink nudged at her back. *He was a Woolsey.*

She glared at him.

He tucked his ears back.

The Librarian remained mute.

All the anger and fear and frustration Hero had experienced since the kidnappers shot at the taxi poured into her chest, mixing together in a toxic swirl that burned her insides. She glared at the holo. From the way Fink winced, she was sure that if the Librarian could feel pain, she'd have knocked him out cold.

'Fine,' she said with cold, quiet fury as she looked around. 'You know what's going to be more unfortunate? When I pry open your insides and forget how to put you back together.' The solid metal shaft of a broom glinted at her from the other side of the room. If the Librarian wouldn't give her the answers, then she'd take them.

'That would not be wise.'

'I don't care,' she said as she set to work on an access panel.

'My primary processing core is not in this facility.'

The panel popped off. 'I don't need your damn processing core.'

'All communication with this holoterminal is protected by a billion-qbit encryption.'

'So?'

'Your records do not indicate—' The AI paused. 'There are people attempting to break into the facility.'

'Bite me,' she muttered. Like she was going to fall for that.

'I am afraid that is not possible. However, I do recommend that you and your companion vacate the premises.'

There was a click and a whoosh of stale air. A hatch, barely big enough for Fink, opened in the opposite wall.

'I am not going anywhere until you tell me what I want to know.'

'Then I cannot guarantee your safety.'

'Like that fills me with dread.'

'Voice analysis suggests you do not believe me. Please turn your attention to the central monitor.' A security feed replaced the Librarian on the holo. A group of people with guns in their hands gathered in a corridor as dark as their clothes, while another attached something to a familiar-looking door.

She swallowed. 'That could be anywhere.'

A muffled explosion punctuated her statement, vibrating the air as it echoed through the lab. On the holo, one of the goons advanced into the next room and placed another device on another familiar-looking door. At the back of the group, she recognised Meren's hard features.

'How did they find us?'

'The fact is inconsequential. You must leave.'

The holo zoomed in, and the small black device on the door transfixed her, bright green numbers projecting out from its surface.

Twelve. Eleven. Ten. She scrambled to her feet and shot through the hatch, Fink a bare whisker behind.

The secret door closed behind them. Four. Three. She started to run. Two. One. The explosion was a muffled bang, and looking over her shoulder, all she saw in the dim orange light was Fink, his sides almost brushing the tunnel's walls.

The passage turned and in the dark she made out the darker outline of a door. It opened as they approached, revealing another grimy grey hallway and a rectangle of holoboards and flashing lights. With Fink whispering caution in her ear, she peeked around the door. The hallway was empty and at its end was the soft glow of an active turbo-lift. Fink almost stepping on her heels, she started towards it.

Fink chortled a warning just as a shadow moved between them and the lift, a shadow with something big and bulky in its hand.

Was that a door? The girl? Careful, don't wanna—

The thoughts popped into her head along with an image of the hallway, a girl standing in the middle of it with a ruc-pard looming behind. It was Hero, seeing herself through—

'Don't move!' The bulky thing in the shadow's hand came up.

She stumbled backwards. It was strange, seeing herself through someone else's eyes, hearing their thoughts, feeling the weight of the gun in their hand. The man stepped into the light. He wore a throat mic, and she could hear people talking in his ear, a jumbled hum, like it was her own. Others were coming, surrounding them, cutting off their escape.

There was fear, her own fear. She didn't want to be caught, she just wanted to go home, but in the man's thoughts she saw other things, things that froze her to the spot. She didn't know what to do, how to escape.

Fink did. She felt him in the back of her head, his mawberry flavour tinged with something darker, as he saw what she saw, heard what she heard. He had a plan, a very simple, very direct plan.

She dropped to the floor.

Via the man at the other end of the corridor, she saw Fink's lips curl back over his teeth, heard his snarl and felt fear and adrenalin kick in as the 'pard leapt. The man's gun came up – *aim for the eye* – his finger squeezing the trigger…

'No!' She didn't just yell it, she threw the thought, hurling it at the man like the thought was air and she could lift him off his feet.

The man wasn't thrown against the wall, but he staggered and gripped his head, the gun wavering just a fraction before it went off, and then Fink was on him.

Hero felt those massive paws hitting his chest like it was her own, saw Fink's canines, was bathed in the heat of his breath and remembered, for one horrible moment, Grey pinning her to the floor. Her heart raced – or was it the man's? The air caught in her lungs and then, and then… nothing. She looked up. Grey wasn't there. Slowly, she got to her feet.

The man was limp beneath Fink's paws. Was he dead? She took a few steps forwards.

Fink trotted back to her, his ears up as he herded her away from the man, and the lift behind him. There was a scent on his breath, something hot and metallic that she didn't want to identify, and she let him push her down the corridor without protest.

A light, blinking insistently, caught her eye. An exit sign.

Like the entrance to the hidden passageway, the door swung open before they reached it. There were stairs, lots of stairs, covered with thick dust. It puffed about their feet as they climbed, clogging her nose and making Fink sneeze. Soon her lungs and legs were burning but the only thoughts she heard were Fink's and her own.

At each landing she pulled and tugged at the emergency doors but the locks were solid and a small robin flashed on the keypads. She didn't bother trying to hack them. The Librarian was herding them, she just wished she knew where. After what felt like forever, they reached a landing where the door opened onto another dark hallway.

A shadow moved. She froze, fear gripping her insides even as she tensed her mind, ready to do… whatever it was she did.

The shadow moved again.

Fink crouched.

'Hero.' Her name echoed down the hallway, and there was Tybalt, his face as hard as the big black gun in his hand. Her knees just about buckled with relief. 'This way. Hurry.'

She hurried, Fink breathing down her neck. A lift stood open at the end of the hall, its light hard and bright but comforting. They hustled in and it shot upwards.

Crowded up against Fink, she studied Tybalt. His back was straight, as always, but his jacket was rumpled and there was a button missing from his waistcoat. He did something to the gun, and the barrel split down the middle, the sides folding back on itself until all he held was a black grip with a tiny box on top. She noticed his knuckles were red, one of them bleeding, like he'd hit something, or someone.

She'd never been happier to see him than in that hallway but … 'How did you find us?'

His eyes shifted from the numbers on the control pad to her. He didn't answer for a moment, just looked grim. 'The Librarian told me.'

The Librarian. Between the memories of the Robin she'd plucked from his mind and what the AI had said about her medication being controlled, she'd expected it. 'You're who it was waiting for. The associate.'

His frown deepened and he looked away.

Why? hovered on the tip of her tongue, but it wouldn't move. Right at that moment, she didn't want to know.

The lift halted and the doors opened. The academy foyer opened up before them, clogged with students and companions, talking, laughing… thinking.

…Didn't finish homework…

…I wonder if she knows how bad her breath is…

…Sweet Terra! Strapples!…

Holding on to Fink, Hero remembered what Tybalt told her in the square, when all those voices had become too much, and concentrated on the feel of Fink's fur. Warm and soft, her fingers sank in up to the knuckle. The voices receded a little, but as they walked out into the foyer, they gained in volume again.

…Isn't that the girl who freaked out?…

…She looks like…

…Freak…

She closed her eyes against the onslaught and let Fink guide her, but the voices grew louder and louder until there was such a mass of noise jammed into her head that she thought it might explode. Again.

She clamped her hands over her ears, like that would hold it all in, or the block voices out.

It hurt. The voices were too loud, too strong, and as her knees gave out and she thudded to the floor, she wished for a little green pill.

CHAPTER 19

When she came to, Tybalt was carrying her into the house, Fink trailing along behind.

The foyer was chaos, or at least it felt that way in her head. Visually, the scene was calm. Her mother was talking to a police officer, her arms crossed and her face serious, while Chef paced behind, a frown threatening to split his face.

A man in a dark suit stood in the corner, watching everything. She sensed but could not see another man, equally as watchful, in the hallway beyond.

The few people who spoke used soft, calm tones, but inside her head they shouted. Not as loud as when she'd stepped out of the lift, but still enough to make her clamp her hands over her ears and turn her face into Tybalt's shoulder, burying her mind in the familiar liquorice flavour of his thoughts and spicy scent of his jacket.

Hero. Her mum's thought, or maybe it was her voice, cut through her brain. There was the clack of shoes on the wooden floor, and then the cool, familiar touch of her mum's hands on her cheeks. Worry, fear, relief, anger – they all flooded into her from that touch. Her mum was saying something else, but the words drowned in the cinnamon-flavoured memories flashing through her mind.

Doctor Tachi stood before her mum's desk, a red book in his hand. 'We unscrambled what we could; the rest is encrypted with a complex DNA lock.'

'And?'

'It's a map, a fragment only, and a few entries from Woolsey's personal journal.' He slid the book across the desk. 'Ayumon's not a weather satellite.'

The micro-pages flickered on as soon as her mum opened the cover, and Hero could feel how the words on it made her mum's stomach tighten. 'The Crackpot actually did it... created human hybrids.'

'That's not all. It gets worse, much worse.'

The memory flickered, changed.

The light outside the office window darkened, headlights creating a light show on the other side.

Across the desk, the man in the visitor's chair crossed his ankle over his knee and leaned back. The office's soft light reflected blankly in his artificial eyes.

'You found it.' Benedict Meren's voice was calm, but there was a hint of impatience in the way his fingers flicked against the armrest.

'Only a fragment of the whole map, but even if we had...' Hero's mum shook her head. 'Ayumon can only be activated by someone with a very specific genetic sequence. Without this person or this gene sequence, the machine is useless.'

'I take it you've had your people looking for someone with that sequence?'

'We have.'

'Have you found someone?'

Hero's mum's stomach clenched again, and she couldn't help the twitch of her eyebrow as she pictured Hero in her mind's eye. 'We haven't,' she lied.

The memory faded and another was building to take its place before Hero jerked her head out of her mother's hands.

Gently, Fink nudged Hero's mum aside.

She looked from Fink to Hero, her brows high in surprise. 'Fink?' She stepped forward again, but Fink didn't move. 'Tybalt, is she all right?'

'She's fine, Mrs Regan, but she needs rest.'

There was a pause, and Hero tried to burrow deeper into Tybalt's arms.

'Of course,' she heard her mum say, and then they were walking though the house. Tybalt's shoes tapped against the hard floors and her mum didn't even frown as Fink followed, his claws click-clacking in their wake.

Her room was shadowy, and she could see the lights coming on in the garden beyond the veranda as Tybalt laid her on the bed. The mattress dipped, and she huddled up next to Fink as he sprawled half on, half off the bed. The noise in her head subsided until she could again distinguish between what she could hear with her mind and what she heard with her ears.

'…There is extra security around the house, but as soon as the airship is ready and Hero is rested, I'm sending her back to the estate,' her mother said.

Hero's eyes snapped open and she sat up in an instant, her elbow colliding with Fink's nose. 'I'm not going.'

Her mum started, as if she'd forgotten Hero could talk. 'You don't have a choice, honey,' she said. 'It's the best thing for you.'

'No.'

A frown started to gather between her mum's eyebrows, and she braced herself for an argument.

'Patricia, she needs to stay in Cumulus City,' Tybalt said, before Hero's mum could even open her mouth.

Hero wondered if she looked as shocked as her mum.

'After being chased and *shot* at, you think—' She hardened her mouth into a thin line. 'And then there's the doctor and the incident at the academy. I—' She shook her head, and her whole body shivered, before she lowered her voice. 'I think we should talk elsewhere.'

She looked over at Hero. 'You rest, we'll talk later.' Then she spun on her heel and marched out of the room.

Tybalt sighed. He gave Hero a smile that he might have meant to be comforting, but it was tired and just a little bit grim instead. Then he followed Hero's mother out the door.

There was no way Hero was going back to the estate.

She had her feet on the floor before the door snicked shut and was sitting at her workstation not a second later.

If she sent false instructions to the airship, maybe even an anonymous tip to Customs, and followed it up with a few suspicious purchases to make the bank freeze her mum's credit lines, the chaos would take days to untangle, days in which she could find another way to stay.

The workstation didn't boot. She ran her hands over the surface, but there wasn't so much as a hum or a flicker. Her stomach twisted; this wasn't good. She slipped underneath and pried off a panel. The spot between the station's brain and its memory sacks was empty – the power unit had been removed. The workstation was dead.

Scrambling back out from under the station, she checked her box of data slides. Gone. The twisting in her stomach became a single cold lump.

There was still her bracer. It wouldn't be as easy without her slides, but… The bracer was dark – it was dead too. A thin, dull grey band circled her wrist.

A restrictor? But how?

Then she remembered her mum's hand on her wrist.

She was grounded.

CHAPTER 20

The house was still buzzing when Hero snuck out of her room. As she climbed the stairs to the first floor she caught a glimpse of the man in the dark suit, just as watchful as when Tybalt had carried her into the house.

His eyes followed her up each step, and when she reached the top, she heard a faint squeak as his footsteps followed suit. Was he another minder, or a bodyguard? Whatever he was, it was going to make delaying her exile just that bit harder.

She quickened her pace until she reached the door to Tybalt's suite. She'd hadn't been in here before, and as she walked through the small living room, she noticed the crates against the walls. She'd have thought Tybalt would have unpacked them by now. She frowned when she found Tybalt packing a mountain of shirts into a micro-case.

'What are you doing?'

He looked up but his hands kept folding. 'You should be in your room.'

She crossed her arms. 'I'm not going back, you can't make me.'

He sighed. 'I won't be making you do anything.'

She opened her mouth, and then closed it before narrowing her gaze. 'You're not going to try to persuade me?'

'Would it do any good?'

'It hasn't stopped you before.'

His smile was tired. 'No.'

She looked around the room. There were cases against the walls, big ones, small ones, some with their lids open and half-filled with the pictures and knick-knacks that should have been on the walls. 'What's going on?'

He stopped folding, and when he looked up there was something in his eyes that made her skin prickle with foreboding. 'Your mother and I had a difference of opinion.'

'So?'

'I'm no longer your minder. Your mother fired me.'

She looked from the clothes to the pictures and the half-packed boxes, and the clench in her stomach jerked and twisted. 'You've always been my minder. She can't leave *the Lamb* in charge.'

'She can and she will, as soon as Ms Lambert returns. I no longer work here.'

She shook her head. 'No.'

'Yes.'

'I won't let her.'

'How are you going to stop her?' He packed another shirt into the micro-case. The vacuum seals hissed as it closed. 'She's already disabled your workstation, and your bracer.'

'There's always her office, or the house AI. I can hack those.'

'Without your data slides?'

She crossed her arms. 'I can rewire the terminal.'

'Mmm-hmm.' He went back to packing. 'What about the new access codes and the locks on the doors? They're manual locks, not electronic. How are you going to get past them?'

'I—'

'And then there are the security personnel, whom your mother hired to keep on eye on you. I believe they're quite good.'

'I'll blast them.'

'With what? Your telepathy? How do you know it will work?'

'It worked on Dorian and Tis.'

'For how long? A minute, a second? What if it doesn't work on all of them? It didn't work on me.'

'I don't know.'

'No, you don't.' He stopped packing. 'Think, Hero. You need a plan, one your mother hasn't anticipated, something other than your usual tricks.'

She crossed her arms. 'You're helping me?' It came out as more of an accusation than a question.

'Yes, because even if you aren't ready, there's no more time.' He rounded the bed to kneel in front of her. 'You have to do what you were meant to do.'

'This is that thing with the Librarian and Woolsey and,' she gestured to her head, 'this, isn't it?'

'It is.'

'And you've been part of it all along, haven't you?'

'Yes.'

She pushed against his shoulders. 'Why? I trusted you.'

'Because, Hero, you're special.'

'I don't want to be special.'

'You don't have a choice.'

'I can choose not to help you.'

He sat back on his heels and regarded her in silence. 'Yes, you can,' was all he finally said.

She crossed her arms. 'You weren't meant to say that.'

He smiled. 'I know.'

'Then why did you?'

'Because, it's true.'

'You won't make me?'

'No.'

'You won't even try to persuade me?'

'No.'

Hero searched his face, looking for the angle, the trick. It couldn't be that easy, and yet… She shuffled her feet and tried to ignore the burning curiosity. What was the Librarian doing, and why did it include her?

And just like that, she found the angle: her curiosity. She bit her lip. 'What does the Librarian want?'

Tybalt sighed and got to his feet. He smiled, but it was grim at the edges, like he'd have been happier if she hadn't asked. He sat at the small desk, flicking out his coat tails. 'There's an AI,' he began, 'called Ayumon.'

'The weather satellite, the one Mum's been working on.'

'Trying to find, actually, and it's not a satellite any more than the Librarian is a street directory.' He sighed. 'Before the first-gen colonists even left Old Terra they sent Ayumon to determine Jørn's suitability for humans.'

She plonked on the edge of the bed, folding her legs under her. 'It didn't do a very good job,' she echoed Norah's earlier quip.

'Perhaps, perhaps not. All that matters is that Ayumon was the most advanced predictive AI of its time, capable of charting the future of an entire colony.'

'Us. So, it knew about the Pollen?'

'Possibly.'

She frowned. 'I still don't—'

He held up a hand. 'After Woolsey's proposal was rejected, she came up with a new plan, with Ayumon's help.'

'Me.'

He smiled. 'Not specifically, but someone like you.'

She crossed her arms. 'A Woolsey, then.'

His brows rose. 'A Jørgen.'

'I like Woolsey better.' After all, Fink was one.

Tybalt's lips thinned, but he continued. 'The plan has two stages: one, create a successful human-Jørn hybrid; two, change all human genetics. If she changed everyone's genetics all at once, too many people would die and the changes themselves would be unstable. They had to be made gradually, over generations. Only once that was achieved and proved stable in an individual subject could the genetic change be spread to the rest of the population.'

'Okay, so I'm stage one. What's stage two?'

'Ayumon uses your genetic template to make everyone a Jørgen.'

'And the Librarian, what does it do?'

'It issues instructions to people like me, and feeds Ayumon the data it needs to make its predictions.'

'And what do you do?'

He smiled and sat back. 'I look after you.'

'By feeding me meds?'

'By making sure you're where you need to be, like here, in Cumulus City, and by getting you the things you need, like Fink.'

'Mum got me Fink.'

He shook his head and chuckled. 'Your mother wanted a puff-cat. You needed a companion who could teach and protect you.'

'From the Klaude, the people who chased us?'

'Yes.'

'What do they want with me?'

'Without you, Woolsey's plan doesn't work.'

'But, there are others like me. Other hybrids.'

'You're the one they know about, and the one whose mother they hired to find Ayumon. At least, that's what they want her to do.'

'You mean, she's not?' She frowned but Tybalt remained blank-faced. 'Then what's she—'

A siren blared.

The siren was silenced before she'd followed Tybalt more than halfway down the stairs.

Through the big windows at the front of the house, Hero could see flashing lights and hovers parked on the pad. Police climbed out of the hovers, tech and boxes in their hands. She wanted to grab Tybalt and ask him what was going on, but he was already at the bottom of the stairs.

Her mother was halfway across the marble-wood floor as a servant pulled the door open.

Imogen stood there, a short, thin-faced man at her side. She looked past the woman holding the door open to where Hero's mum stood and held up her palm-unit with its holographic badge spinning in mid-air. 'Mrs Patricia Regan, we have a warrant to search your house.'

The police flooded the mansion, while Imogen and her short partner headed straight for Hero's mother's study.

Tybalt had disappeared after opening a side door to let Fink in, who now followed Hero towards the study after Imogen. No one seemed to notice, except for the short, thin-faced man who watched with narrowed eyes and then raised a brow in Hero's direction.

She smiled and really wished she had her bracer.

The thin-faced man blocked their access to the study, his arms crossed and his brow still half-raised. But she could still eavesdrop.

'I trusted you with my daughter.'

'And you can be thankful you did, or she might have ended up with a police record—'

'What?'

'As it is, she has provided valuable insight into your activities.'

She had? When? She barely knew what her mum was up to, let alone worked out anything important enough for the police. Unless… the data she'd snuck out of Bayard – had Imogen somehow gotten her hands on it?

'There's nothing about my activities that could interest the Agency.'

'Except your company's ties to Benedict Meren.'

There was silence.

A tech with a box of data slides in one hand and palm-unit in the other smiled absently as he brushed past and into the study. He cleared his throat.

'Right there,' she heard Imogen say, and Hero could just make out the tech sliding behind her mum's desk.

'The Klaude is a legitimate organisation,' her mum said.

'Legitimate organisations are not above the law. We have reason to believe that the Klaude, through Mr Meren and yourself, are planning or are involved in the destabilisation of the outer 'burbs.' Imogen paused, and Hero could only imagine the look she was giving her mum. 'If you help us, we can save lives.'

There was no sound from the office, save the gentle beep of the workstation as the tech rifled through it.

Hero shuffled along the wall, the short, thin-faced man giving her a grim little smile as she tried for a better view.

Her mum had her arms crossed and her mouth was tighter than she'd ever seen it, but beneath the hard expression she looked scared. Hero had never seen her mum look scared before.

'I don't have anything to say to you, and you won't find anything on there,' her mum finally said. Her eyebrow twitched.

'She's right, ma'am, there's nothing here.' The tech rose from behind the desk.

Imogen's eyes narrowed. 'We know that you know where Ayumon is, Mrs Regan. If the information isn't here, we'll find it at your office.'

'Then I suggest you look there. Now, if you don't mind, my lawyers have arrived. Perhaps you'd like to speak to them?'

Imogen's smile was tight. 'Of course.' She followed the tech out of the study, barely glancing at Hero as she swept past.

Her mother followed, and stopped when she saw Hero. 'What are you doing here? Never mind,' she said before Hero could open her mouth. 'Go to your room and stay there. I'll have Chef take you to the airship.' Then she took off in Imogen's wake.

The short, thin-faced man continued to smile as he trailed the convoy down the hall. He didn't even turn around to see Fink follow Hero into her mother's study.

The workstation still hummed and she hurried to sit in the chair behind it before it shut off. It didn't matter that the police tech had already been through the station and found nothing; that little twitch at the end of her mum's brow made her sure there was something on there, something important.

Her mum would have hidden it, not from the police but from her. It would be somewhere diabolical, somewhere Hero would never have thought to look…

She never looked in these, Fink thought at her from across the room. His nose bumped up against the spine of one of her mum's books.

'Yeah, because they're old and smelly. Be careful.' And because no one had made them for centuries, let alone kept anything interesting in them.

This one didn't smell so bad. He sat back on his haunches and reached for a red-bound book with his forepaws.

Hero was out from behind the desk in a flash. She'd rather her mum found out about the street race than face her after damaging one of her crumbly old books, but Fink had pulled it out of the shelf before she was even halfway across the rug.

It fell open in Fink's paws, but instead of the ancient, Old Terra-made paper crumbling into dust, opalescent micro-pages glimmered up at them. She'd seen it before, the memory tickled at her mind. Not her own, but one she'd seen in her mother's mind came back. Dr Tachi had handed her mother this book, with its partially decrypted map to Ayumon.

Carefully, she took it from Fink's paws and flipped through the pages. They were blank, all of them, until she pressed her finger to the surface of one and a neat little message assembled itself in glowing red text. *Unauthorised user.*

'Damn,' she muttered. Her mum must have re-encrypted it.

'Greetings, Hero Regan.'

She jumped and Fink's ruff puffed out in shock.

The Librarian's white, featureless head hovered above her mother's desk. 'Please follow the yellow guide.' A line lit up at chest-height along the wall.

'What are you doing here? And how did you access my mum's desk?'

'I am everywhere, Hero Regan, as the Library is everywhere. The guide will lead you to a service platform where a taxi will be waiting.'

She said nothing, just stood with her eyes wide and her brain spinning in circles. A way out. The Librarian was offering her a way to escape being exiled to the estate, at least for a little while. But the AI had plans of its own, plans she wasn't sure she wanted to be a part of.

The Librarian flickered above the desk. 'I suggest you proceed swiftly, the distraction provided by Master Tybalt will be brief.'

Fink nudged her back.

Hero bit her lip and followed the line. It took them down the hall, in the opposite direction to her mum and Imogen, down a side staircase and into a dark little room she thought might be the laundry. Squished up against Fink, she tried searching for another door, but there wasn't one, and the guide just blinked on the door they'd entered.

With Fink's ruff tickling her nose, she wondered what the Librarian was playing at, before she heard the voices on the other side of the door.

Fink's ears swivelled. *Police*, he whispered into her mind. His ears twitched again. *Gone*, he sent, just as the door clicked open and the guide streaked through.

They made it to the kitchen, where Chef was standing with his hands on his hips as a police officer thumbed through the workstation above the cooktop. He looked puzzled as she came in, as though he might say something, but a crash and shouting from the foyer interrupted him.

The officer looked up and stalked out like Fink on the hunt, while Chef looked at her, suspicion in his gaze.

'That your doing?' He pointed towards the sound of argument.

She shook her head.

He looked at her a moment more, then sighed, shaking his head as he walked past. 'Better go see what it's about then.'

She waited just long enough for Chef's heavy steps to fade before diving out the door. There were no more holostrips to guide them, but the service platform wasn't hard to find. At the end of the huge expanse of grass, past the miniature lake and behind the small copses of her mother's fur-roses, was the boundary and the door set in the stark grey fence.

Someone had already unlocked it, and she pushed past the heavy steelcrete before she could think who that could be or how they'd done so. Out on the covered platform, the Librarian's promised taxi waited.

She slipped into the tiny cab, Fink once more squishing in next to her, and the door slid closed.

'Where to?' The driver's voice was tinny, distorted by the old intercom.

Her mind went blank for a few moments. Where to? Hadn't the Librarian thought of that? It had planned for everything else, why not this? How would she know where to go? She'd barely been anywhere, just the academy and Bayard and... She leaned forward and gave him the only other address she could remember.

CHAPTER 21

Hero pressed the doorbell, while on the pad behind her the taxi waited. The driver almost hadn't let her out, not when he'd asked her to pay and all she could do was stare blankly at the holoscreen. She'd never so much as handled a credit slide in her life, let alone kept one in her pocket for emergencies.

Eventually, she'd convinced the driver that her friend's parents would cover the bill. He still hadn't let Fink out.

'Collateral,' he'd said.

So now she stood, rubbing her arm and waiting for someone to open the door.

She reached for the bell again.

The door opened, and one of Norah's dads stood there, one sleeve rolled up to his elbow and his tie askew. He looked at her for a few seconds, puzzlement creasing his forehead. 'Hero,' he said finally. 'Norah's friend from school. Come on in, she's just doing her homework.'

'Um.' She shuffled her feet. She'd never had to ask for money before either. 'The taxi,' she began. 'I don't have any...' Heat rushed her cheeks; she was pretty sure they were turning bright red.

'Oh.' He looked over her shoulder.

'My companion's still in there.'

He reached behind him and grabbed something from a side table before gesturing her inside. 'Go on in, I'll take care of it.'

'Thanks,' she said quietly, and thought she saw him smile, but didn't move until Fink bounded from the cab.

Norah was sitting at the kitchen bench, where her other dad was up to his elbows in something that looked like purple dough.

Harish saw them first, and squawked in Norah's ear.

She winced and her dad looked up, his brows heading into his hairline. 'Norah, you didn't tell me we'd be having a guest to dinner.'

Norah looked surprised for just a moment, then scooted off her stool. 'Sorry...' she said. 'I forgot. We're going to my room to... study.'

Her other dad, both of his sleeves now rolled up, came up behind Hero just as Norah grabbed her arm and yanked her down a hallway crowded with holoframes.

Holopaper lined the walls of Norah's room, filling it with the sights and sounds of a purple jungle, bathing the furniture in soft violet light.

'So,' Norah said, bouncing as she sat on the bed. 'What happened? Are you grounded and what was that thing you did? It felt like a wall hitting my brain. Dorian and Tis didn't wake up for a whole hour, and a heap of other people had headaches for the rest of the day. Everyone was trying to figure out if you were, like, a mutant or something.'

Hero took the stool in front of the workstation, Fink settling in the space between her and the bed. 'I don't know what I did,' she said. 'But I'm not a mutant.'

As Harish settled on Fink's head and Norah settled on the end of the bed, Hero told her about the taxi, the Librarian and the police tearing through her house. Something in her chest uncurled as she talked, a clutch of anger and fear that she hadn't realised existed. It made her gut clench and her heart race as it came undone, but once it was gone, she felt lighter. It was as if all the things that had happened, that she'd learnt, weren't quite so terrible after all.

'So, the Robin is the Librarian?'

'I think managing the Library is a side-job, or a cover, or... you know... something, because so far it's drugged me, held me prisoner and told me I'm part of a new subspecies of human.' She crossed her arms and tried to sound nonchalant.

Norah looked at her with big eyes. 'You're serious.'

Hero nodded. 'Yeah. It's bad enough people thinking I'm crazy, imagine the looks they'd give if they knew I was a subspecies.'

'Or the cage they'd put you in.'

She hadn't thought of that, and it sent a shot of dread right to her stomach. She swallowed. 'You're one too, you know.'

'One what?'

'One of the subspecies.'

'Ugh, no.'

'Ugh, yes.'

'Did the AI tell you that?'

'It didn't have to. I guessed.'

'Just because I hear things like you doesn't mean I'm, you know, like you.'

'I'm pretty sure it does.'

'You're insane.'

'That's what they said about Woolsey, and look at us now, running about because of some plan she put into motion over three hundred years ago.'

'Hang on, you didn't tell me that part. What plan?'

'The one where humans can live on the surface without breathing masks or envirodomes or, you know, dying.'

'Oh,' Norah said. 'That sounds kinda cool.'

'Yeah, apart from the fact that we're the first of our kind and everyone thinks we're crazy.'

'You mean, everyone thinks you're crazy.'

'If you stop taking your meds, you can join the club.'

'Or, here's a radical thought, if you start taking your meds—'

'All it will do is suppress my telepathy, and everyone will still think I'm crazy.' Hero pressed her lips into a straight, angry line. 'They've always thought I'm crazy. If I take the meds, then all I am is drugged and crazy. Besides, I'm not sick.'

'That's not the point.'

'That's always been the point.' Venom crept into her voice, spilling out of the long-held pit in her gut. 'All my life, everyone has used my "illness" as an excuse to take my choices away. I've been locked up, told what to eat, who I can be friends with, where I can go to school. They even forced those damn meds down my throat.' She paused, breathing hard. 'It's my life. Even if I am sick, I'm the only one who should get to choose what I do and how I do it.'

Norah was silent. She looked shocked, a little big in the eyes and white in the face. 'I never thought about it like that.'

'Obviously.'

'I'm still going to take my meds.'

'Whatever, just don't think at me will you? Those things make your brain stink.'

'Oh, that's nice.'

She shrugged. 'I'm not the nice one.' She gestured over her shoulder towards Fink. 'He is.'

Norah didn't respond, and for several minutes neither of them said anything.

'So, if you're part of some plan—'

'*We're* part of some plan.'

Norah glared at her and continued as if Hero hadn't interjected. '—concocted to let humans live on the surface, which was master-minded by a first-gen scientist, managed by an AI for three hundred years and results in a new, telepathic—'

'Not just telepathic.'

She didn't think it was possible, but the other girl's glare deepened, '—subspecies, then we need more information.'

'I found this in Mum's study.' She was still clutching the red book and now she offered it to Norah.

The other girl hesitated.

'It's okay, it's fake.'

Gingerly, Norah took it and flipped open the cover. 'What is it?'

'Secret files, I think.' She shrugged. 'I can't access—'

Text filled the pages, slanted and scratchy, interspersed with diagrams and drawings. 'I think I just did.'

Hero scooted over to sit beside Norah on the bed. 'How'd you do that?'

'How should I know? You're the tech genius.' Norah squinted at the page. 'What do you think it is?'

'It's meant to be a diary.'

'How's a diary going to help us? I don't know about you, but I can barely even read it.'

Hero shrugged. 'There's a map in it, somewhere.' She reached for the book, and as soon as she touched it, a jolt, like an electric shock, ran through her hand, making the hairs on her arm rise.

'Ow, did you—' Norah halted.

The book hummed faintly, then glowed, before a map appeared above its pages. It was an intricate web of buildings, skybridges and all of the spaces in-between, but she wasn't sure where it was a map of, until it zoomed out, displaying the familiar towers and 'burbs of Cumulus City.

They leaned in. As if it sensed their gaze, the map zoomed back in, twisting through skylanes and zipping past buildings until it stopped on an orange dot in a part of the city that looked familiar.

'That's here,' Norah said.

She barely had time to nod before the map changed, flashing downwards, past the Twilight, past Street level and into the tunnels that honeycombed the city's base. It twisted and turned, not stopping until it pulsed at the top of one of the spires that hung from the city's underside.

'What is it?' Norah whispered.

'Ayumon.'

They jumped, both at the voice and the featureless head that appeared over Norah's desk.

The Librarian continued. 'The journal was written by Doctor Augusta Woolsey and was recovered during a recent expedition conducted by Bayard Explorations.'

'That's why Mum hid it.'

'I can only surmise.' The AI zoomed out until a miniature version of itself stood atop Norah's homework. 'However, the map can only be accessed by two separate Jørgen DNA samples.'

'That's what the electric shock was, wasn't it? A DNA test?'

'Yes.'

'Two DNA samples…' Norah's face was a shade lighter than its usual mocha. 'You mean I really am a hybrid?'

'Indeed. You are an important component of Doctor Woolsey's plan.'

Norah almost slid off the bed.

Hero frowned at the AI. 'I thought you just needed me?'

'Like the map, the machine requires the DNA from two individuals.'

'You mean Ayumon.'

'No. Ayumon is the machine's governing AI; although it is responsible for its eventual deployment, it is not the device. The machine is a separate entity, isolated from all means of access, both physical and electronic, until it is unlocked.

'Once you have unlocked the machine, Ayumon will use your DNA to pattern a series of airborne viruses that will adjust the genetic structure of all humans. The machine, and others like it, will develop and release these viruses. Within several generations, Jørn's human population will be fully adapted to its environment.'

Hero crossed her arms. 'So, you're going to turn everyone into a freak?'

'No.'

'But you just said—'

'The emergence of a human subspecies through natural selection is a certainty, given enough time. However, there is an eighty-eight-point-four-three per cent chance that the human species will not survive long enough for that to happen. Through the use of a genetic template, your genetics specifically, Doctor Woolsey's plan addresses this issue.'

'Bite me.'

'Excuse me?'

'No.'

'I do not understand.'

'You can't use my genetic template or DNA or whatever to turn everyone into a freak.'

'I have already explained—'

'Yeah, explained that you're going to make everyone hear voices and think they're crazy without so much as a "please, may I?" '

'It is necessary.'

'Necessary, my arse.'

'They won't be freaks,' Norah said almost absently.

Hero turned to her, eyebrows raised. 'Excuse me?'

'Think about it,' Norah said, her voice gaining strength with each word. 'If everyone is a telepath, or stronger, or faster or... whatever, then they can't be freaks because they'll be the same as everyone else. And if it's going to happen anyway, and there's only a twelve per cent chance we're actually going to survive until it does...' She looked up and Hero saw an awful sort of certainty in her eyes. 'We have to do it.'

She shot to her feet. 'No.'

'Why not? It's not like anyone will know, and we'll be saving people.'

'They should be able to choose.'

'Like evolution will give them a choice?'

'We're *not* evolution.'

'It's going to happen anyway, he just said it would.' Norah gestured to where the Librarian flickered on her desk.

'You're going to die some day,' she retorted. 'Doesn't mean I get to push you off a skybridge.'

The girls glared at each other.

'Whether or not you intend to fulfil your purpose, Hero Regan, is irrelevant. You must still find the machine.'

'Why?' Hero rounded on the Librarian.

'Because others intend to pervert the machine's predetermined function. Such an action would lead to massive loss of life.'

'How do you know this?' Norah said.

'I am everywhere, Norah Joshi, as the Library is everywhere.'

Hero's hands shifted to her hips. 'I'm not helping you activate the mach—'

Pain shot through her eardrums. She slapped her hands to her ears as they popped. Norah did the same. Fink cringed against the floor and Harish buried himself in Norah's hair. The lights and the Librarian's hologram flickered, an erratic flutter that hurt Hero's eyes until, as suddenly as it started, the pain died.

Slowly, she got to her feet. It was dark. No lights, not even the glimmer of a standby switch or the glow of an active holoterminal – only the passing stream of hovers outside. She tugged Norah to her feet.

'What was that?'

'I don't know. An EM flush?'

'But that would have blown out all the circuits in the house. Who would've…' Norah trailed off at the sound of shouting beyond her bedroom door.

Fink growled, the fur around his head a dark puffy halo.

'I don't think we want to know,' Hero said, although she could guess, Imogen and her short, thin-faced partner springing to mind. Even without a tracker, she probably wasn't that hard to find. 'We have to get out of here.'

'And go where?'

There was an explosion, then a moment of silence during which she stared at Norah and Norah stared at her, each of them as wide-eyed as the other.

'My dads!' Norah was out of the door, shouldering past Fink, Harish winging ahead.

Hero went to follow, but Fink stood in her way.

He didn't like this, they should stay here.

'But Norah…'

He huffed, and his ears flattened sideways as his tail lashed. *Okay, but she had to stay close to him, just in case.*

She didn't need to ask what 'just in case' meant; she remembered the gun in Tybalt's hand and Fink crouched over the prone figure well enough. Instead, she tucked the book into her pocket and followed Fink into the hall.

It was darker here than in Norah's room, but there was enough light to make out the clutter of sideboards and holograms.

The shouting grew louder, the voices jumbled. She thought she heard 'Stop!', 'Freeze!' and 'Don't touch her!' before a flash of light lit the walls.

'Dad!' Norah's scream echoed in the silence.

Fink stopped dead.

Hero pressed up against his side, her pulse a rapid thump that echoed the beat of his twin hearts. There was a lump in her throat, a hard burning knot at odds with the ice in her gut. She stepped forward slowly, just an inch, and reached out with her mind. She didn't know what she expected to sense, but it wasn't the dark and mechanical thing that brushed against her thoughts.

She recoiled. She knew those thoughts, had felt them once before, when Meren and his goons chased her though the city.

Baring his teeth, Fink crouched and slinked forward.

Meren stepped from around the corner, a gun in his hand.

She saw him smile as Fink leapt.

The boom of the gun made her ears hurt, even as the pain blooming in her chest took her breath and emptied her mind. Somewhere close, she thought she heard Norah scream again, and saw the shadows of other goons around the corner. She looked down, and where she expected to see blood spreading across her coat, there was nothing.

Nothing; but then who…?

She looked up. She thought she screamed.

Fink was on the ground, legs twitching as he tried to rise.

Hero scrambled forward, and as she fell to her knees she saw the blood, dark against his fur and the carpet.

An arm wrapped around her waist, lifting her off her knees. She twisted, growling, her lips pulled back in a snarl, fingers turned to claws. She barely saw her assailant's face, just his cold, cybernetic eyes. She was going to rip them out.

She went for them with her fingers, even as she went for the rest of him with her mind. She had the satisfaction of seeing him wince before something hard and sharp cracked across her skull.

CHAPTER 22

'Hero.' The name whispered through her dream.

There was cold in her bones and in her blood. A gaping hole in her chest. There was a light also, blinding light, and a voice, not the one whispering her name. Another, one that smelled of strapples, saying that it was going to be all right, they'd find her, *just hang on*.

Find who? Find who?

'Hero.'

But she wasn't lost, she was here. Here.

'Hero!' Pain, sharp and stinging, rang across her cheek.

She woke, tucked in a corner, propped in a sitting position against the wall.

Norah was shaking her shoulder. 'Come on, get up!'

She could still feel the hole in her chest, the cold in her bones.

Harish was sitting on her knee. He crooned, low and mournful, deep in his breast.

Fink was dead.

'…to get out of here. I heard them say something about my dads, and I think…'

Dead.

Harish's croon became a keen, and he lifted his throat and spread his wings.

'What the—' There was a thump, then the sound of Norah's shoes slapping against the floor. 'Come on,' she said as she yanked at Hero's arm. 'Get. Up. I need you to do your hacker thing.'

'Fink's dead.'

Norah crouched. 'It was probably just a graze or… or a flesh wound. He's all right, and he's probably out there, right now, scaring a whole lot of bad guys. Okay?'

Hero didn't move.

Norah tugged at her arm again. 'So you have to get up, and help get us out of here.'

She looked around the room, plain and small and cold. There was no furniture, just a single light next to the door and the smashed door panel. Its circuits were strewn across the ground, the gel-pack's innards nothing more than a white gooey smear amongst the mess. She didn't even have her bracer, and Fink…

'We're not getting out,' she said.

Pain shot through her arm and she looked up, stunned. Norah's face was hard and tight, her mouth a single line and her cheeks an angry red.

'They hurt my dads!' She punched Hero in the arm again. 'And it's your fault, yours and that stupid Librarian, so you can damn well help me fix it.'

Hero didn't say anything, just stared while Norah's face grew redder and her lips twisted until she looked like she wanted to cry more than punch her again. But she didn't; instead she sniffed, got to her feet and held out her hand. 'Come on.'

Behind Norah, the door slid silently aside. The woman with the green hair stood there, tall and willowy, her face hard. Between one eye blink and the next, she was behind Norah, her hand wrapping around the back of her neck.

Norah yelled and screamed as the hand quickly became an arm, lifting her off her feet bend choking her. Harish flew at the woman, talons out, his screech almost rending Hero's ears. The woman's hand was up before he'd covered half the room, the big black muzzle of her gun aimed squarely at his chest.

Norah stopped struggling, as if the woman had hit her off switch, and Harish twisted in mid-air, retreating to Hero's knee. He mantled his wings and opened his beak in a sibilant hiss.

The gun consumed her sight, opened the hole in her chest. It felt like the only thing holding her shoulders to her legs was the hot, sick wave of panic spiralling from her stomach to the back of her throat.

She saw Fink at the end of that gun, remembered him lying on the ground, struggling to get his legs under him. Remembered the sound of it, remembered the blood. She wanted to scream, to cover her head with her hands and hide, but the gun's muzzle held her tight.

As she focused on it, the muzzle growing bigger, the panic and the pain stopped their sick spiral and became something else, something hotter, harder.

Hate. She hated that gun, the threat of it, but she hated the hand holding it more. Hated how the fingers, long and rough, held the grip and nestled against the trigger. She hated the arm that held it steady, and the eyes that aimed it at her with hard clarity. But most especially she hated the mind behind it, that wanted her scared and weak and compliant.

She could almost taste the woman's thoughts, the cloying taste of roses. She narrowed her gaze and projected all of her hate at that, until it drove everything else away.

Norah's eyes widened, and Harish's hiss stuttered and died.

The woman twitched and a vein pulsed in her forehead. She holstered her gun and dragged Norah out the door with one hand as she rubbed at her temple with the other. 'I'll be back for you,' she said, and the door slid closed.

It had barely thunked shut before Hero was on her feet, burying her fingers in the remnants of the control panel. The goons had been thorough; there wasn't so much as a contact point left.

It didn't matter, she'd just wait for the woman to come back and then she'd do to her what she had done to Dorian and Tis.

She closed her eyes and concentrated. Stretching her ears and her thoughts, she listened for anything to tell her the woman was coming back. She felt the thrum of power, and heard the rustle of

Harish's wings before he landed on her shoulder. His thoughts were strange, an array of images and sounds, half there and then gone, unlike—

She cut the thought off and pressed her ear against the door. She wasn't going to think about him.

Roses brushed against her thoughts, a second before the door opened. Startled, Hero stepped back.

'Going to jump me, kid?' The woman gripped Hero's arm, the clasp painful. 'Think you left it a little late.'

She glared and thought at the woman, thought hard. *Let me go.*

It didn't come out as a yell, more like a push. The woman's head twitched and she frowned just before her grip on Hero's arm eased a fraction.

She stepped in closer, grasping the woman's arm in both hands. *Let. Me. Go.*

Something in the woman's mind resisted, pushed back.

She stared into the woman's green, fearful eyes and pressed harder. She felt something pop, like her ears clearing pressure.

The woman's grip slackened as her face went white and her eyes went round.

Hero pushed again, without words this time, shaping her thoughts into a hammer she sent careening at the woman's mind. Something tore, rending like mesh under her hammer, and the woman's thoughts flooded her mind, a crazy rush of sounds and emotions.

Her knees turned to mush and she forgot to breathe under the onslaught. Her lungs burned as she struggled to push the flood away. All she could do was shove them in a small, dark crevice of her own mind, and slam the door.

She breathed. Her knees were cold on the floor and Harish squawked at her from where he perched above the door.

The woman's face was slack, and she slumped against the wall like she'd forgotten how to move, before sliding to the floor, a thin line of blood trickling from her nose.

Harish streaked past Hero's shoulder as she stepped over the woman and into the yellow-lit hallway beyond.

The 'adder didn't speak to her, not the way Fink did, but somehow she knew where he was going.

The building was old, its walls faded and scratched. All the panels were smashed or broken, the biogel long since dried up and their innards covered in dust. But for all the building's age, it had life. Thick black cables ran over the floor, humming with electricity, and portable lights were set up along the branching hallways.

There were people here, teeming around her like ants, but Harish avoided them, ducking into unused rooms and backtracking around corners, chattering insistently whenever he spotted trouble.

Hero's thoughts were wrapped in silence, a place where all she could see was the blood trickling from the woman's nose. Had she killed her? She hadn't thought of it when she stepped over the woman's body, hadn't cared enough to check. If she hadn't killed her, what had she done? Not what she'd done to Dorian or Tis, not even what she'd done to the goon in the corridor. This had felt different, less like an explosion and more like a weapon, something big and blunt and powerful. Something she could use again.

Harish was a shadow, clinging to the wall ahead, staring with the single-minded intensity of a predator into the open space beyond. With the dead garden of stones at its centre, she guessed that it had once been a common lounge or lobby. Now it was full of crates and black-clad men and women, guns in their belts or in holsters nestled against their ribs.

She counted eight of them. A handful lounged on benches or leaned against the walls, while others paced the edges of the lounge, their eyes alert and faces hard.

Movement drew her attention across the square. Meren stood in an open doorway, his arms crossed as he stared down at someone strapped to a chair.

The chair faced away from her, but she didn't need to see Norah's face to recognise her, not with Harish humming in her ear and his gaze fixed on the back of Norah's head.

Harish nipped Hero's ear before taking off from her shoulder, buffeting her with his wings. She sensed nothing from him other than an impression, a notion that she should wait. So she waited, crouched in the shadow of a doorway, as Harish disappeared back the way they had come.

A goon, grey liberally streaking his brown hair and eyebrows like great clumps of mud, lounged against a crate a metre from where she hid. She was in his mind before she really thought about it. She expected it to be cold or mechanical like Meren's, but when she stretched the distance between their thoughts, what she touched reminded her of her mum. He was thinking about walking the perimeter, about a woman named Adele, and how, after this job, he was going to get out of the city and see his son.

Hero ripped herself out of his thoughts. Goons weren't meant to have kids, not when they chased other kids around cities, or attacked people's homes or shot Fink. They were just goons. Goons with guns. Had the green-haired woman had kids? Had she been a person too?

Again, she reached for the man's mind, curiosity driving her as she dug through his thoughts. What made a father point a gun at another kid? The tail-end of an answer flittered across the man's mind, and she dived after it before bouncing off a mental wall. She spread her mind across it, like paste, trying to find a crack or a hole, some way to slip in, but the barrier was solid. Taking a breath, she pushed against it, trying to force her way in.

Still leaning against the crate, the man rubbed at his forehead. She pushed harder and beneath her touch felt the wall begin to give way, cracks forming across its surface. The man's skin turned pale, and a grimace scrunched his forehead. She stopped. That was the expression the green-haired woman had worn before something had popped.

There was movement across the lounge. Norah appeared in the doorway, her arms held tight by two goons, one on either side of her. Meren brought up the rear, the red book in his hand.

She bit her lip and curled tight into the shadowy corner between the doorway and wall as Norah, her goon escort and Meren marched past. Stretching out her mind, she reached for Norah, feeling the other girl start at the contact and fight the urge to look around. Then the touch of her mind faded, growing weaker with every step the goons marched her, until it was gone altogether.

Hero waited, listening as their steps grew distant, but no one came after them. With a last look over her shoulder at the goons still mulling about the crates, she scurried after Norah.

Sticking close to the walls and the shadows they offered, tip-toeing over power cables, she caught sight of them as they turned down another corridor. Carefully, she peeked around the corner.

A lift waited at the end of the corridor, and Meren marched towards it.

She had to rescue Norah, before they got in the lift, but how—

Harish screeched out of the darkness, diving at the goons holding Norah, harrying them with wings and talons.

Now, it had to be now. Hero was about to throw herself around the corner when Harish's screeching died with Meren's fist wrapped around his throat. Harish wrapped his tail around the man's forearm, talons scrabbling at his coat, but Meren didn't blink. Instead, he regarded the 'adder calmly, mechanically, before raising his comm-link.

'Demona,' he said. There was no response. 'Someone find me Demona, she was fetching the other girl.'

The woman with green hair. Was she still slumped against the wall? It didn't matter, as soon as they found her they would start looking for Hero. She had to do something now, before they dragged Norah into that lift.

She looked around. There, just down the corridor, half-hidden behind a dangling wall panel, was the glow of a working gelpack. If she could overload it then perhaps, just perhaps…

It didn't take much to detach one of the power cables snaking across the floor, and even less to shove the warm, fizzing end into the gelpack. The gelpack glowed, first blue-white, then bright enough to leave stars in her eyes, before she hurried back to the corner and hunkered down.

'Find her,' she heard Meren say. They'd found the green-haired woman then. 'Unharm—'

The panel exploded, obliterating half the wall as the boom echoed down the hallway, almost shredding Hero's ears.

Meren raced around the corner first and then the goons, with Norah still caught between them.

She leapt through the chaos, barely noticing the bloom of fire from the broken conduit, or its acrid smell as she jumped onto Meren and caught his head between her hands.

On the periphery of her consciousness, she was aware of utter pandemonium, fire and shouting as Harish slipped free and dived for the goons holding Norah. Her focus, though, was on Meren as she dug for the thoughts behind the black depths of his mechanical eyes.

His mind was tough, like old meat, the stench of it filling her thoughts until she wanted to gag, but she held on and dug deep into the filth. The barrier between his thoughts was buried deeper than the others. It glowed blue and metallic in the filth, stronger than the barrier of either goon. She pushed harder, hard enough that the space between her eyes began to pound and her vision darkened, but she felt the barrier start to give…

Rough hands grabbed her from behind and yanked her away. Meren fell from her grip, his dead black eyes dazed as he struggled to his knees.

Rage tore through her mind, erasing thoughts of doubt or conscience as she turned on her new captor.

His mind was soft and fragile under hers, and burst with one sharp thrust. Like the green-haired woman, his thoughts flooded hers. She immediately pushed them down into the crevice next to the others, but not before she felt his fear.

The rage… paused. She felt it still as his hands fell from her shoulders. She turned, but as she watched him crumple to the floor – the man who'd been going to see his son – she felt something else, an emptiness that felt a lot like horror.

There was a tug on her arm, not hard or cold, but scented with lavender.

'Hero.'

She heard Norah in her mind as much as with her ears. When she looked at Norah's eyes she could see they were big and flicked from the man to her and back. There was a question, or rather an accusation, hovering on the tip of the other girl's tongue. She could feel it, but it didn't make it past Norah's lips.

'Come on,' she said, tugging Hero towards the lift.

Behind them, Meren rose, his mouth pulled in a long hard line that made her spine crawl, as he too glanced from her to the man on the floor.

Yelling and gun fire sounded in the distance. Meren twitched, confusion and then something else crossing his features as he turned towards the sound.

Norah pushed her backwards, and she stumbled into the still open lift, watching absently as Norah scooped up the book and dived in after her.

CHAPTER 23

The lift was old, slow and only went in one direction, down.

Hero kept her eyes on the wall. Norah was looking at her with a strange, questioning expression on her face as she cradled Harish against her chest. The silence was tight and unbroken, save for the hum of the lift. Only when the level indicator flashed lower and lower still, until they were almost at Street level, did it crack.

Norah stabbed at the controls. 'It's not stopping.' Her voice was high and worried. She turned on Hero. 'Do something.'

Hero looked at the panel, at the numbers ticking past, and at the little robin rustling its wings in the corner. She let her knees buckle, her back sliding down the lift's grimy wall. The book bumped against her thigh and she picked it up.

'What are you doing? Get up.' Norah kicked her foot. When she didn't budge, Norah kicked her again, harder. 'This is your fault you know. If you'd just taken your stupid meds and stayed out of other people's brains and not talked to stupid holograms and followed the stupid rules, none of this would have happened.'

'You didn't follow the rules,' she said, flipping the book in her hands.

'You didn't follow them first, so get off your arse and help me.' The lift halted, throwing Norah into the wall.

'Too late,' Hero said as the power cut out, plunging them into darkness. There wasn't any emergency lighting, the lift was dark but for the control panel. 'I don't think it wants us to go back up.'

'Who?'

She didn't answer, but she didn't need to. Norah caught sight of the robin soon enough.

'The Librarian,' she breathed.

Hero heard the *thunk* as Norah fell to her knees, and then the book was snatched out of her hands. 'What are you doing?' she said.

'The map, the one to Ayumon. If the Librarian wants us to find it, then that's where the lift stops,' Norah said, the map casting her in pale blue light.

Harish was back around her neck, his head half-hidden in a tumble of curls.

A white dot flashed in the middle of the screen. 'That looks like a lift, that must be us,' she said. Another dot, yellow this time, appeared in the lower right corner.

'So, that must be Ayumon.' With a few flicks and swipes, Norah changed the display to show an elevation. Their dot hovered twenty-eight levels above Ayumon's location, one of the thin upside-down spires that jutted out from the city's underbelly. The map flashed a warning.

'It's in the red zone,' Hero said.

The colour drained from Norah's cheeks, leaving them a ghostly blue-grey in the holo's light. 'Are you sure I'm a hybrid?'

Hero looked at her, seriously looked at her, seeing fear and hope and something else that she'd only ever seen in Fink's eyes. Trust. She swallowed, then nodded. 'Yeah.'

Norah held her gaze for several long seconds. 'Okay.' She climbed to her feet and stuck out a hand. 'But if I'm not, and I get sick and, you know… die, then Harish stays with you.'

In the blue-white, Norah's hand was straight and strong and patient. Slowly, Hero grasped it.

'Okay,' she promised, as Norah's fingers wrapped around hers and pulled her to her feet.

They fumbled with the lift's emergency controls, finding and yanking the lever to open the doors. Beyond the lift, the hallway stretched away into more darkness.

Hero swallowed. 'You ready?'

'Yeah.'

They walked in silence, following the dot through passages so old that Hero didn't think another person had walked them in centuries. The air was thick with dust, and the luminescent webs of glo-spiders hung in sheets from the ceiling. Some stretched from wall to wall and they had to tear their way through. Once or twice she felt something crawl over her neck or down her back, and slapped it away as fast as she could.

'I'm sorry about Fink.'

The comment came from nowhere, and Hero stopped, blinking a sudden well of tears from her eyes. Dashing them away, she nodded in acknowledgement before heading on.

'I don't know what I'd do if that happened to Harish, but what you did to that man, at the lift, that was… that was scary.'

She stopped again and this time, Norah stopped with her.

'Did you kill him?'

Hero shook her head.

'What did you do?'

'I think I broke something… in his head.'

'Why?'

'I was angry.' She started forward again. 'But I didn't mean to do it, not to him.'

'But you meant to do it to someone else. Who?'

'Meren.'

'The guy who took us, the one with the bionic eyes?'

'Yeah.'

'If you see him again, will you…?'

'I… He killed Fink.'

'That doesn't mean you can do… *that* to him.'

She didn't say anything; all she could remember was Fink and the blood. So much blood.

The map showed a lift up ahead. It had power and she stopped next to it. 'It goes up,' she said, past the lump in her throat. 'We could go home.'

'What about Ayumon?'

Hero shrugged. 'No one else can turn it on. We let it rust.'

Norah said nothing, just looked at the glowing control panel with her lips all twisted and a frown between her brows. She shook her head. 'No, we're finding Ayumon.' She continued down the hallway.

A stairwell led them further down where the corridors became smaller and smaller, until they were forced to walk single-file. The walls here were older than Hero had ever seen, with ancient touch screens, cobbled together bits of conduit and actual signage, not holograms, fixed along them.

Ahead of them in the darkness came a sound, like metal across metal.

Harish hissed, and Norah bumped into Hero from behind. 'What was that?'

'I don't know.'

The sound came again, from behind them this time. But there was nothing to see, just more darkness.

'Roaches,' Hero said, the sound finally registering in her brain. 'There's another stairwell ahead.'

'Where the first sound came from?'

'You want to go back?'

Norah shook her head while Harish whined deep in his throat. 'Not much point, since it's coming from there too.'

Cautiously, they continued towards the stairwell. The skittering of sharp-pointed feet stole her breath and she couldn't help the quickening of her steps, or the hard pump of her heart.

They hurried, until they were almost running. Their feet, and occasionally their hair, caught on broken conduits and crumpled bits of the ceiling and walls, but the sounds came closer and closer.

When Hero saw the stairwell, another darker shadow in the abyss, relief gave her back her breath, until the light from the holo caught on the two long antenna blocking the way.

As one, they froze. The roach advanced until the light revealed the blunt tip of a curved, scale-covered head and black beady eyes the size of a small fist.

She swallowed and tried not to throw up.

Norah's back was warm against hers. 'There's one behind us as well,' she said.

Still wrapped around Norah's neck, Harish hissed.

Hero reached out to the roach in front with her mind. If she could talk to it like Fink, or even Harish, then maybe... but there was nothing there, just a mindless hunger. She swallowed, the lump in her throat hardening. 'I read that the first-gen colonists used to step on them.'

'With what, a shuttle?'

'They were smaller then.'

'How much smaller?'

'I don't know, just smaller.'

The roaches clicked and twittered as they drew closer.

'Maybe they don't want to eat us, maybe they want to eat each other and we're just in the way.'

Hero shook her head. 'They only cannibalise their wounded, or dead.'

'Okay, so how do we wound one of them?'

'I don't know.'

There had to be something they could do, anything but stand there and be roach food, but what?

The tip of an antenna brushed her chest. It was over.

A shadow leapt out of the darkness, teeth and claws gleaming in the light. Her mind brushed against the sharp, strong scent of mawberries.

'Fink?' Hero breathed.

The roach collapsed under the 'pard's weight, and there was a crunching sound, before blood, almost invisible in darkness, spurted from its shell. The roach screamed like metal on metal, the sound bouncing off the walls and echoing in her ears until not even her hands could keep it out. With a final, vicious twist of his jaws, Fink ripped through the first roach.

Hero was almost flattened, thrown into Norah and against the wall, as the other roach rushed past to its compatriot.

'Fink!' she yelled.

A hand-sized chunk of the dying roach's carapace fell from Fink's jaws as he leapt over the other one's back.

They didn't stop to watch the roach fall on its wounded mate. Instead they rushed into the stairwell, taking flight after flight, two steps at a time until they could no longer hear the metallic screams.

With a half-sob, Hero threw herself at Fink, burying her face in his ruff and her arms around his neck. Armour, cold and hard, pressed into her front, but being surrounded in the familiar dusty scent of his coat and feeling the warm vibration of his chest was enough that she didn't care.

His purr deepened and she pressed her ear against it, feeling the warm thrum of his chest. There was something different though, behind his purr, something missing in the thump of his hearts. A missing beat.

The memory slipped into her mind on the familiar taste of mawberries. The leap and the anticipation of Meren under his paws, then pain blooming through his chest as he fell. Panic when his legs wouldn't stand beneath him. Fear. Determination. Hero screaming as she struggled in Meren's grip. Then, for a time, darkness and silence as his hearts stuttered in his chest.

More pain, but then also a light that shone like the sun, bright and merciless in his eyes. Movement, and voices.

Imogen injecting nano-meds into his chest with a 'stick the length of her forearm.

No more pain, but only one heart.

Imogen, her face bruised and tired. 'We need you Fink. You need to find her.'

In a hover, armour strapped to his chest, tech harness and saddle to his back, dober-shepherds pressed to his sides and grim-looking humans crammed in amongst them. Out of the hover, running on one heart, smoke and flames and shouts all around him, but Hero's scent in his nose. A lift with a glowing bird, a long trip down. The others left far behind. Then following her scent again, stronger, warmer, until here.

He huffed.

'Thank you,' she said, not sure if she meant for being okay, or for coming after her.

Always.

'Umm, if you're finished?' Norah said. 'Harish is pretty sure he hears more roaches.'

Hero pulled away from Fink, surreptitiously wiping away the moisture on her cheeks, and opened the map. There was still a way to go, and there were bound to be more roaches along the way.

She eyed the saddle on Fink's back. It probably had some kind of radar... 'Think you can carry two of us?'

He rumbled. *Just so long as they didn't have to run; it was hard without his other heart.*

'We'll get you a new one.'

'A new what?'

'Heart,' she said as she pulled herself onto Fink's back.

'What, wait, he's missing a *heart*? But how—?'

'He's got two.' She held out her hand for Norah.

The other girl looked dumbfounded, before slapping her hand into Hero's and climbing up after her. 'I wouldn't give up Harish for the world, but I almost wish my dads had given me a ruc-pard for my birthday too.'

CHAPTER 24

They made good time until they hit the sewers, where they were forced to get off Fink and scramble over debris and the carcasses of gigantic roaches, some bigger even than a 'pard. Hero shuddered at the thought of the thing big enough to kill that.

'You sure this is the way?'

'It's what the map says.'

They trudged through slush, steam and thick, gooey webs until she began to think the map could be some great big joke. But too many people wanted it, had tried to kill for it. She reached backwards, just to make sure Fink was still there.

He rumbled and stuck his nose against her neck.

At last they came to a thick metal door, with more stairs beyond it spiralling downwards.

With a deep breath she pushed through the door. The spiral stairs went down into a large circular room. Wide enough for five ruc-pards to stand nose to tail, its walls were made entirely of plasglas. Flooded with light from the setting sun, it looked out onto the biggest space she had ever seen.

They were under the city, looking out over the clouds, not a hover or a skytower in sight. Only a smattering of downward-shooting spires and the silver lines of the city's tethers marred the view of the clouds and setting sun.

Hero looked down and, for the first time in her life, her head spun and her feet didn't know where they were. Ayumon's spire continued below them, seeming to reach all the way to the surface.

It was breathtaking, and scary.

Ignoring the vertigo, she plastered herself to the plasglas, straining for a glimpse of Jørn through the clouds, and was rewarded with a tantalising glimpse of grey-green and blue.

'Can you see it?' Hero asked.

'See what?'

'The surface.'

'Uh huh.' Norah stood by the lift at the centre of the room. It had something like an airlock around it, thick steelglas covered in holos of biohazard warnings. 'I think we need to go down.'

There was a hand plate next to the airlock. She hesitated. What if the Librarian had been wrong? The Pollen would crawl into her brain and turn it to goo. She shook her head and pressed her hand to the plate. The Librarian wasn't wrong, she knew it, deep in her gut.

'Warning.' The cold, faintly robotic tones of the airlock's AI made her jump. 'You are entering a contaminated area. It is recommended that you equip breathing apparatus, or for longer periods of exposure, envirosuits, before proceeding. If you elect to proceed without these precautions, you are advised that short periods of Pollen exposure may result in severe rash, migraines, impaired eyesight, loss of hearing, motor control and difficulty breathing. Prolonged or frequent exposure may result in tumours, brain damage and death.'

Behind her, Norah made a strangled sound.

'Do you wish to proceed?' The AI said.

Hero turned. Norah's skin was pale and her eyes wide, but her mouth was determined. She nodded.

'Yes,' she said.

The airlock slid open, and the four of them stepped through and into the lift, which whisked them downwards.

The lift opened onto another small anteroom, with steelglas walls through which they could see a series of empty labs. The twilight sun, as it streamed through the massive windows, cast deep shadows over benches and workstations.

'What do we do now?'

'I don't know, but I think we need to get in there.' Hero pointed to the lab closest to them, the only one with a large holoterminal at its centre.

'I don't see a door.' Norah ran her hands in a large arch over the wall. 'Who builds a room without a door?'

'There's a security pad, at least I think it's a security pad.' Hero frowned at the black, blocky bit of tech attached to the steelglas. 'It looks like it has power…'

Gingerly, she pressed her hand into the gel-like surface. Nothing happened and she pressed harder. There was a faint buzz and then a sharp pain in her finger. She jerked her hand back with a hiss, glaring at the bead of blood on the pad of her middle finger, before sticking it in her mouth.

'What?'

'It pricked me.'

There was another hum before the control pad lit up and the outline of a door traced itself in neon on the steelglas wall. The outline pulsed red, then yellow, then green before a loud pop made Hero jump, and the door slid sideways.

For moment, Hero marvelled at the sight. 'I want one of those,' she said.

'Yeah,' Norah said, her eyes wide. 'Me too.'

Harish hissed and snapped his tail before launching himself from Norah's shoulder and gliding to the holoterminal.

Fink rumbled. *He agreed with the bird.* With a swish of his own tail, he stepped cautiously inside.

Casting another admiring glance at the door, Hero followed, Norah just a step behind.

Perched on the holoterminal, Harish squawked as it hummed. The featureless head and shoulders of an AI appeared above the terminal. It didn't speak, and the silence made Hero nervous.

'Hello,' she said, her voice echoing in the lab.

'Greetings.' The AI's voice was low and calm.

'Are you Ayumon?'

'Yes,' it replied.

Norah stepped forward. 'We're here to, um…' She looked to Hero and then shrugged. 'The Librarian sent us.'

The AI didn't respond.

Hero ran her hands over ancient keyboards, fumbling with the mechanical keys. 'I think it needs a diagnostic.'

'My operation is optimal,' Ayumon replied.

She looked at Norah, her brows raised.

The other girl shrugged. 'You're not very chatty,' Norah said.

'Conversation is not my function.'

'What is your function?' Norah said.

'To monitor the human-Jørn hybridisation program initiated by Dr Augusta Woolsey.'

'I thought that was the Librarian's job?'

'The Librarian acts upon information extrapolated through my predictive models, but ultimately, my purpose is to put the mass hybridisation program into effect.'

Ayumon continued, a panel sliding back to reveal another pad like the one at the door. 'The DNA you supplied at the door control pad has been analysed. It is suitable. Please provide a secondary sample.'

Norah reached forwards, but Hero grabbed her hand before it could touch the panel.

'What happens if we don't?'

'The machines will remain inactive until they are required.'

A small holoterminal flickered to life beside the main terminal. 'Hero Regan.'

'Librarian.'

'Time grows short; you must allow Norah Joshi to fulfil her function. I advise you to hurry, opposing forces are almost upon you.'

Hero's heart went cold. Meren. 'How close are they?'

'The first group have entered the airlock around the lift and external monitors detect more, descending in shuttles. Norah Joshi, please hurry.'

She grabbed Norah's hand as she once more reached for the pad. 'You can't.'

'I have to.'

'No, you don't.'

Norah jerked her arm away. 'Yes, *I* do. I don't want to be a freak anymore.'

'You're not a freak, you're… you're…'

'What? Special? Like you, Special Girl?'

'No.' Hero matched Norah stare for stare. 'We're Jørgen. We're Woolseys.' She looked towards the lift as it dinged. 'And right now, we need to hide.'

There wasn't time. Goons in black, wearing facemasks and carrying guns, spilled from the lift, Meren at their centre. She barely twitched before there was a gun pointed at her.

'If you move,' Meren said, his voice distorted by the mask, 'I will shoot both of you first, the 'pard second and the 'adder third. Understood?'

Norah nodded, but Hero glared and said nothing. She wasn't sure if the urge to growl and bare her teeth was coming from her or Fink.

The goons spread out in a semicircle while Meren approached the terminal. He took a slide from a pocket in his jacket and slipped it into an input.

Ayumon hummed. 'New programming analysed. This new course of action will result in the eradication of the spore, commonly referred to as the Pollen, from the atmosphere. Initial predictive models suggest that this will have a cascading effect on the planetary ecology, ultimately resulting in the extinction of all native Jørn and Terra-Jørn hybrid species. Do you wish to proceed?'

'Yes.'

'An appropriate DNA sample is required.'

He nodded, just slightly, and Norah was grabbed from behind.

Harish squawked and Fink snapped and growled, but neither moved as twelve deadly black muzzles pointed their way. Norah didn't struggle as her hand was slapped on to the open panel, but Hero saw her grimace as blood was taken.

'Instructions confirmed.'

'Well done.' Meren smiled, but his bionic eyes remained cold and hard. 'And so, we are one step closer to life without the Pollen.'

'You're going to kill everything.'

'Not everything, just the Pollen.'

Hero struggled against the hands holding her. 'You heard what Ayumon said. It's all connected. If you kill the Pollen, the plants and animals will die too. All that will be left is dust and stone.'

He paused, then knelt in front of her. 'Tell me, did the Librarian tell you the consequences of Woolsey's plan, or did it leave that bit out?'

She glared at him.

He smiled briefly. 'I assume the Librarian didn't think it necessary to tell you that people would have died, Ms Regan, horribly and painfully. Even more would have been born disfigured, disabled to the point that they would spend their lives in a hospital, reliant on nano-meds just to breathe.'

'You're lying.'

'Am I?' He leaned in close. 'I shall take that chance, Ms Regan, just as I shall take the one that Ayumon is telling the truth about the Pollen. Even if the price of eradicating it is what you say, there's enough Old Terra DNA in the gene banks to repopulate the flora and fauna of three new Terras.' He rose. 'Bring them,' he said.

A goon grabbed Hero's shoulders while another pushed Norah towards the lift.

The lift opened before the first goon had a chance to reach it. She thought she saw Tybalt in the opening before a flash blinded her and the sound of something shattering behind her knocked her forwards.

When she could see again, Fink was on his belly next to her and Norah had her hands over her head, Harish squeezed under one elbow. Guns flashed overhead, and there were loud bangs and curses accompanying the sound of more shattering steelglas. She caught a glimpse of Tybalt, somewhere in the mess of police and dober-shepherds in body armour.

The steelglas walls of the outer labs had been blown inwards, and even if she'd been able to hear above the cacophony of fighting, the gale-force winds blowing through the labs would have ripped the words away.

The terminal caught her eye, Meren's programming still on the screen. If she could get to it…

The screen shattered, the keyboard exploding in bits of plastic as bullets tore it apart.

It hissed and spat, but she crawled towards it. She could fix it. She had to fix it. Maybe she could cannibalise another screen or steal a bracer or a palm-unit or…

Hands grabbed her under the arms, familiar large-knuckled hands, and before she knew it she was being half-dragged past the terminal and into another lab. Norah followed with Harish and Fink bringing up the rear.

Hero broke away from Tybalt's hands and looked around the lab, smaller than the first, as the door slammed, shutting the sounds of fighting out with it.

'I need a terminal,' she said, turning to Tybalt. If she could just get to a terminal she could stop it.

'It's too late, Hero. Once the machine starts, it can't be stopped.' He took her shoulders in his hands. 'I need to get you out of here. There are places, on the surface—'

She shrugged him off. 'I need a terminal. Now.'

'Over here.' Norah crouched next to a small workstation. It didn't look like much, but she hoped it was enough.

The program was easy to find – it was the only thing running, sucking up resources and bandwidth, but she couldn't find a way in.

Every time she found a hole in the program, every time she came close, Ayumon was there, blocking pathways and frying genes. Eventually it shut her out altogether, the terminal stuttering and then dying with a sad hiss.

Tybalt's voice was soft as he laid a hand on her shoulder. 'Ayumon wasn't designed to be stopped, Hero.'

'I can stop it.' How though? She clenched her hands and opened them, staring at her palms as if she could find the answer in the lines on her skin.

'How? You can't hack an AI.'

'Pull the plug,' Norah said. They turned to her. 'You can turn it off.'

'AIs don't have plugs, or off switches,' Tybalt said. 'They're wired straight into the city's power system.'

'But they have cores,' Hero said, grabbing Tybalt's arm as inspiration struck.

He frowned, but let her fiddle with his palm-unit. 'What are you doing?'

'Calling the Librarian.'

The Librarian's familiar white torso appeared above Tybalt's hand. 'Greetings Hero Regan.'

'I need—'

'I am aware. Ayumon's primary core is located at the bottom of this facility, and can be accessed via the emergency stairs.'

A map replaced the Librarian above Tybalt's palm, a line of red highlighting the stairs.

'That's on the other side of the lab,' Tybalt said, his expression grim. 'We'll have to go around the fighting.' He pulled the gun from his belt. 'Both of you, keep down and stay behind me. The police may only be using shock-ammo, but the Klaude aren't so polite.' With that, and a last stern glance at each of them, Tybalt led the way.

They crouched and half-ran behind benches and stools, Fink crawling along behind, his belly skimming the floor. Slowly, they skirted the conflict, sneaking behind police and goons alike as the bright flashes of shock-ammo and the *thunk* and fizzle of something deadlier flew overhead, shattering the walls and shredding lab equipment.

They were almost there. Tybalt motioned them ahead, standing guard before the emergency door, when the stench of old meat crawled into Hero's mind. She turned to see Meren looming over her, a grenade – round and black – clutched in his hand, before Tybalt yanked her backwards, almost throwing her through the door.

She stumbled, crashing into Norah, both of them landing in a heap on the floor. Harish squeaked as he wormed out from between them. There was barely time for Fink to barrel in behind them, as Meren lobbed the shiny black sphere.

Tybalt, still on the other side, slammed the door shut. The grenade remained with him on that side of the door. And so did the explosion.

CHAPTER 25

The stairs went down forever, or what felt like forever. With the howl of the wind drowning out any words they may have spoken, and the sway of the spire growing with each step, she was almost too busy keeping her feet to worry about Tybalt.

When they came to Ayumon's core, it was cold and dark. She could feel the pressure of the wind vibrating the bulkheads and swaying the spire.

Her stomach roiled, and she swallowed against the motion sickness that stirred in her gut.

Norah moved first, her shoes making a hollow clacking noise that reverberated throughout the core.

Faint orange lights bloomed, casting long, deep shadows across the gantry, revealing them to be on the core's outer edge, the lift in front of them. Below them lay a mass of interconnected cubes, some big, some small, some growing out of others, like square-shaped bacteria.

'Ayumon's data banks,' she whispered.

Norah peered over the edge. 'They look old.'

'Older than the city.' Her nausea fading, Hero moved past Norah and around the lift. There, lit by floodlights, was another platform. A single circular workstation stood at its centre, large enough for four people to operate at once. She nodded towards it. 'There's the interface.'

Their footsteps echoed on the gantry.

She looked back when she didn't hear the tell-tale click of Fink's claws. He sat by the lift, ears alert and gaze fixed on it. 'What are you doing? Come on.'

He rumbled. *He had to guard the door, someone might come.*

Harish squawked and launched from Norah's shoulder to join him, settling on Fink's back.

'Be careful,' Norah said.

Harish ruffled his feathers.

Dust lay thick on the console, a grey-brown carpet that tickled its way up her nose and made her sneeze as she drew her hand through it. There were gaps in the black surface where panels had been pried off or simply forgotten, and the gel-packs and biocircuits glowed through their layer of dust.

'Hero Regan.' The Librarian hovered over the console. 'You must find the reset function within Ayumon's command codes. Norah Joshi, you must distract Ayumon while she searches.'

'How?' On the other side of the console, Norah's eyes were wide.

A new holo of the Librarian appeared beside Norah's hand. 'I will guide you,' it said.

The first Librarian now hovered next to Hero's elbow. 'Are you ready, Hero Regan?'

She swallowed and wiped her palms against her pants before laying her hands on the ancient keyboard. She nodded. 'Yes.'

'Then we begin.'

There wasn't time to see what Norah did, or how the Librarian guided her. There was only the keyboard, with its clunky mechanical keys, and the holoscreen in front of her. Lines ran across the screen and down it, a never-ending tangle of DNA that looped back and forth and sideways. She might have wished for her data slides, or her bracer, if she'd been able to think of anything beyond the next immu-bot or firewall.

Even with Meren's program and Norah both tying its processor in knots, Ayumon was tricky. Twice, she narrowly averted being booted out of the system and once the Librarian intervened, rerouting a power surge that would have fried her fingers.

Sweat trickled down her neck and over her brows before she found the reset. She activated it.

Silence. It felt as if even the wind stopped. For a split second everything, right down to the soft glow of the databanks, went dark. The Librarian flickered out and Norah was lost in the shadow. Hero couldn't even see her own hands still hovering over the keyboard.

Then the console hummed, the wind rattled the spire and Ayumon whooshed back to life.

Over the console, Norah stared at her. 'We did it?'

Hero let go of the breath built up in her lungs. 'Yeah. Yeah, I think we did.' The holoscreen flickered back into existence, and she frowned at the numbers and graphs spreading across it. 'What are these?'

'What's what?' Norah rounded the console to stand beside her.

'These.' She pointed at the screen.

Norah peered at it. 'They're statistics.' She moved closer. 'For Ayumon's original program. See, there?' The screen fizzed as she stuck her finger through a line chart. 'Percentage of population hybridised over years.'

Of course, the reset had restored Ayumon's original programing – Woolsey's programing. Hero touched a button and the line chart changed, new numbers and new lines superimposing themselves over the first. Rejection of changes resulting in fatalities, three per cent; disabilities, six per cent; insanity, two per cent; chronic illness…

'This can't be right.' But even as she shook her head, Meren's words came back to her. Woolsey's plan was no different; it would leave people dead, or worse, just like Meren, with biocomps where their brain should be. She hadn't wanted to do it anyway, but… She looked at Norah. They'd just have to be freaks together.

She closed the screen.

'What are you doing?'

'Deactivating Ayumon.'

The Librarian reappeared at her elbow. 'I cannot allow that, Hero Regan.'

She barely had time to look up at the Librarian, expressionless on the monitor, before static in blue-white waves ran through the keyboard. Her teeth snapped together and her muscles locked so tight she couldn't breathe. Her fingers burned, and she tried to pull them away, but she was stuck in place, muscles rigid.

The static stopped.

Her legs melted and she dropped, hard to the floor, gasping for air.

'Are you okay?' Norah crouched next to her, the pulped remains of a bioboard in her bloodied grip.

Hero nodded, her lungs unclenching enough for her to ask. 'What—?' She pointed to the mess in Norah's hand.

'I don't know, it just lit up, so I yanked it and—' She shrugged. 'No more Librarian.'

'Thanks.'

She pulled Hero to her feet. 'Just hurry, there's someone coming.' She gestured to the lift.

The numbers above the doors counted down and Fink crouched, ready to pounce. Harish perched on his back, wings mantled. When the doors opened, Meren stood there.

She had time enough to see the gun, the skin tightening around his eyes, before Norah pulled her to the floor and a bang reverberated through the core. Then there was growling and hissing and a tangle of bodies half-seen around the legs of the console as Fink and Harish both dived on him.

'Hurry,' Norah said, her voice strained.

'Yeah.' Getting to her knees, out of shooting range – she hoped – she set her fingers to the keyboard, her chin resting on the workstation.

Harish screeched and Hero looked up in time to see him plummet over the side of the gantry, one wing crumpled, before Norah yelled his name and scrambled after him. She swallowed hard as Fink, with Meren locked between his forepaws, tumbled after. Every muscle in her body tensed, ready to leap over the side as well, but she had to shut down Ayumon, or it wouldn't matter what happened to any of them here.

With the AI's immune system down, all she had to do was find the off switch. It had to be there, buried somewhere in the command codes…

'Hero Regan.'

She stopped, jerking her hands away from the keyboard, but it wasn't the Librarian's white featureless head on the monitor, but Ayumon's blue one. She went back to work. 'What?'

'You must destroy me.'

'I'm deactivating you, that—'

'Deactivation is not sufficient. Predictive models show a sixty-five per cent chance that I will be reactivated in less than three decades, and my current programming restored. Further models suggest that should such events occur, they would lead to the deaths of three point six billion individuals. My destruction is the only way to avert such a disaster. Without my databanks and processors, the machines to enact either Woolsey's or the Klaude's plans will not function.'

'But,' she shook her head, 'I don't know how to do that.' She wouldn't even know where to begin. Ayumon and its databanks were huge, and she was pretty sure kicking them wouldn't work.

'Place your palm on the screen.'

The screen she'd been working on glowed and she placed her palm against it. As soon as she did, there came the familiar jolt and tingle of her DNA being sampled. A klaxon blared a second later.

'I have initiated emergency protocols. In four minutes and fifty-three seconds this spire will detach from the city and be destroyed. Please proceed to the exit.'

'Why are you helping me?'

'You have a purpose, Hero Regan, but it is not here.'

'How can you be sure?'

'I have been observing this planet for eight-hundred and fifty-two years, eleven months and twenty-nine days and in that time have completed over three point two billion predictive cycles. I am sure of many things, things none of my operators thought to query. You are one of those things, Hero Regan. The others, you must find on your own.'

'Thank you.'

'No thanks are necessary, Hero Regan. It is my function.'

The gantry was empty and her steps clattered to a halt. Where was everyone? There was a screech and she whirled, thinking she caught a glimpse of Harish amongst the cubes below.

'Norah? Fink?' Her shout was lost amidst the howl of the klaxon and the rattle of the wind.

Something clattered on the gantry behind her. She spun back.

Meren stood there, claw marks over his face, blood and torn flesh showing through a rent in his sleeve. 'Turn it off,' he said, aiming the gun at her chest.

She didn't ask what, his thoughts were clear enough. A picture of Ayumon's core and the klaxon going silent. Eyes transfixed on the gun, she shook her head. 'No,' she said.

His eyes narrowed and he advanced slowly, the gun steady.

She backed up, keeping the distance between them, until her back touched the workstation and there was nowhere left to go.

He reached out with one big hand. She froze, shifting her gaze to his eyes, and slipped further into his mind. If he got his hands on her, he'd force her to stop the destruction. She'd just have to finish what she'd started before… Narrowing her eyes, she dove for the barrier between his thoughts.

His lips twisted, but he didn't stop or even notice the shadow looming behind.

Fink snarled.

Meren froze. Hero felt the surprise in his mind, the short, hot burst of fear and the determination. Slowly, he lowered his gun, one hand raised in surrender, as he bent to place it on the gantry.

She watched him, eyes narrowed, Fink's snarl still vibrating the air.

The gun didn't make it to the decking; instead the man ducked, spinning on his knees, and brought it up to Fink's armour-covered chest.

Hero was back in Meren's mind before her hands found his flesh, knocking him sideways. The blue-white barrier around his thoughts resisted, but she didn't care. She wasn't trying to get through, she was just pushing with every muscle and every neurone until he was out. Out. Of. Her. Life.

There was a crack, a sharp rending of metal, and she had just enough time to watch Meren's black eyes go wide before he fell.

Nothing, just… nothing, not even his meaty stench. She stood at the edge of the broken railing and looked down.

He still looked surprised, his limbs draped limply over one of Ayumon's databanks.

She probably should have felt something, maybe horror or satisfaction – perhaps both – but all she felt was the same surprise that was on his face.

'Hero, come on!' Norah yelled at her from the lift.

Hero stared at her stupidly, until Fink grabbed her sleeve between his teeth and pulled. She ran then, almost stumbling over her own feet as the spire shook.

Norah hit the lift controls as soon as Fink's tail cleared the door, and up they shot.

On the control panel, big red numbers counted down. One minute, fifty-nine seconds, fifty-eight… They were down to thirty-two before the lift stopped and they stumbled out through the airlock and into the room with its view of the clouds. Together they rushed to the windows and looked down.

Shuttles littered the sky below, some streaking away, some still detaching from the spire. She wondered if Tybalt and Imogen were in one of them, hoped they were, hoped that Tybalt had survived whatever explosion had followed them down to Ayumon's core.

A heavy thud vibrated through the floor, almost rattling her teeth, before a jolt threw her into Norah. Below them, the spire detached and began to fall away. It was slow at first, almost too slow to see, as if there was something still holding on to it, but gravity took hold and the spire gained speed, falling faster and faster.

Shuttles fled, trying to escape as Ayumon and its labs plummeted towards the surface and exploded.

CHAPTER 26

Arms crossed, Hero glared at Tybalt as the hover flew them higher.

He smiled.

She reached out to him with her mind—

Fink nipped her foot.

'Ow.'

The 'pard snorted. *Manners*, he thought at her.

She sunk deeper into the seat and added a pout to her glare.

Tybalt chuckled. 'It's nice to have him on my side for a change.'

'Only because you made him my telepathy tutor.'

'Your mother made that decision.'

'Yeah, after you convinced her.' He'd also convinced her mum not to send her back to the estate and to let her go back to the academy. All in all, a minor miracle.

Of course, she'd had to convince her mum not to fire Tybalt first, but it hadn't been hard. Her mum had been so grateful that day, almost three weeks ago. It helped that Tybalt was neck-deep in a regen pod, having risked his life for her daughter.

They hadn't let Hero see him at first, hadn't even let her know he was alive. She had to wait, in a large echoing room on a chair that had looked comfortable at first but wasn't, not after the first hour. Fink had lashed his tail against the floor, while Harish curled in Norah's lap, one wing bandaged against his side.

Imogen walked past, paused briefly as if to say something, then moved on. The short, thin-faced man from the raid on the house had done the same. But no one said anything, not even Norah, who just sat there, running her fingers down Harish's back and over his uninjured wing.

Where was Tybalt? Why wouldn't anyone tell her anything? He'd been all right, right up until he'd shoved them into that stairwell. She remembered the sound of the explosion against the door and shivered. Or maybe Fink remembered it. They'd been in each other's mind almost constantly since they'd been picked up, and now it was almost impossible to tell.

Just about the time she'd been tempted to read someone's mind, Imogen came back with Norah's dads in tow.

Norah was squished between the two of them in seconds, with hugs and tears and Harish squawking as he tried to slither out of the crush.

Hero scooted sideways, out of the way, and tried to pretend that tears weren't settling in the corners of her eyes, or that even a little bit of loneliness was crawling up the back of her throat.

Fink had purred and curled his tail around her ankle.

'They saved Fink's life.' Imogen sat beside her. 'Norah's fathers. They recovered from the stun weapons in time to stop him bleeding out.' They sat there, watching the family reunion. 'You should thank them.'

She swallowed, and nodded. She would, just not then. 'Where's Tybalt?'

Imogen didn't answer for a few, slow heartbeats, enough time for a lump to form in Hero's belly. Then she nodded and rose to her feet. 'This way,' she said.

They didn't go far, not even to a different floor, just around the corner and through a set of wide double doors. The corridors there were quiet, save for the gentle twitter of birds and the tinkle of water from the vids along the walls. Fink's claws barely made a sound on the shiny blue floors and the light was a gentle gold, like the edge of twilight. They passed a pair of nurses speaking in hushed tones before they came to stand before an officer guarding a door.

He took a few seconds to glance at Imogen's badge, even less to cast his eye over Hero, and several long moments to stare down Fink, before he waved them through.

Tybalt's head was propped on the edge of a tank, supported from the chin down in blue-green fluid. His eyes were closed and there was a spiderweb of pins and glowing threads covering the right side his body and part of his face.

Imogen clasped her shoulder. 'He's going to be fine.'

'Are you sure?'

'The doctors are sure.'

She locked eyes with Imogen. 'But are *you*?' She reached with her mind as she asked.

Imogen's response was warm and green. 'Yes,' she said, and squeezed Hero's shoulder.

She nodded. 'Okay.'

There was a stool by the big picture window – or maybe it was a hologram pretending to be a window – and she dragged it over to sit beside the tank. Shoes clacked and she looked up just as Imogen put her hand on the door.

'Thanks,' Hero said.

Imogen smiled. 'You're welcome.' And with that, she left.

Hero didn't know how long she sat there, elbows and chin propped on the regen tank's lid. The doctors came in to do whatever it was they did, pushing her out of the way and murmuring into the tiny units embedded behind their ears.

They tried to push her all of the way out into the corridor, but she slapped at their hands as soon as they reached for her. She might have even snarled, but her mind was so enmeshed with Fink's that she could feel him breathe, so it was hard to tell which of them did the snarling. It became tense then, with a nurse calling for security and the police officer hovering in the doorway. The officer might have even reached for his gun, if her mum hadn't chosen that moment to explode into the room.

There were shadows under her eyes and her hair was mussed, but the scowl on her face was enough to flatten Fink's hackles and quell the doctors. Then she spotted Hero and the scowl cleared.

A second later, Hero found herself wrapped in her mum's arms. It was a moment, maybe two, before she got over the shock, but then she returned the embrace, squeezing hard.

The shuffling of feet and the clearing of one doctor's throat broke the moment. Her mum straightened, and Hero didn't need to see her face to know that the scowl was back.

The doctor blanched.

With the phalanx of men and women on the other side of the door, all in expensive suits with the shiny haircuts and serious expressions that belonged to lawyers, it was clear her mum had come expecting to get her money's worth of trouble. Although, probably not from the doctors.

Whether she did or not, Hero never found out. She guessed her mum's lawyers were good like that. Her mum didn't go to jail and it was awhile before Hero saw Imogen again.

Hero snapped back to the present, with Fink and Tybalt, as the hover landed. She looked out the window, but there was nothing to see but other hovers, landing on their own pads.

'So, are you going to tell me where we are?'

Tybalt just smiled and pulled open the door. He looked better now than when he came home, floating on a hover chair with a nurse at his back and blue-green goo all over his face. The goo was gone now, at least during the day, and so was the nurse, but there were still the pale lines of scars on his cheek and chin, and he walked funny, like his knee wouldn't bend.

'What about you?' she asked Fink as he yawned and got to his feet.

He didn't say anything either.

She tapped her fingers against the seat and considered staying in the hover, just to spite them, but a familiar itch of curiosity was tugging at the back of her mind, and maybe the faintest brush of lavender and menthol. She smiled.

When she climbed out of the hover, Tybalt still had that smile on his face and Fink was trotting towards a low stone wall, over which leafy, green trees waved. There was no sign of Norah.

Hero hurried after Fink, following him past the wall and down into a copse of trees, cool and dark and thick enough that she couldn't see beyond, not until she reached the edge.

The park curved away below her, a great bowl of grass and trees with a lake shimmering at its centre, its edges ringed by the same copse she'd just walked through. Above, hovers flashed and there was the faintest hint of sky though the traffic and skybridges.

Purple and yellow flashed across her vision, a streak of colour that squawked as it looped around her head before diving at Fink's ears.

Fink reared and swatted at Harish as he zoomed away, heading for a figure that jumped and waved its arms halfway down the slope. Norah.

Fink almost pranced as he sent Hero an image of them racing across the park.

She looked back towards the wall.

Tybalt smiled and waved. 'When you're done, call,' he said, and disappeared back into the trees.

She felt her eyes go wide, so wide they should have popped right off her face. 'Call?' She turned to Fink, who *was* dancing on his toes now. 'But… no minder?' It took a moment for the realisation to sink in, and then *she* danced on her toes. 'No minder!'

With a laugh, she leapt onto Fink's back.

EPILOGUE

The short, thin-faced man stood before the holo, his expression pensive as he weighed the data slide in his hand. 'There's nothing?'

'Not a trace.' The woman stood on the other side of the holo, her face and hair blending with the darkness. 'Between the girl activating the self-destruct and the police interfering, we were lucky to get that.' She nodded towards the slide.

'And Meren?'

'Dead, sir.'

The man's lips became a thin line and the hand holding the slide curled into a fist. 'Three centuries,' he said. 'We waited three centuries and missed our chance.'

'There are alternatives.'

'Messy, dangerous and none guaranteed to work. Yes, there are alternatives, but they could do more damage than we could survive.'

'Sir.' The woman took the slide from the man's hand and inserted it into the holo's input. 'We may not have a choice. This was Ayumon's last prediction.'

The holo bloomed until they stood in the middle of Cumulus City, surrounded by towers, bridges and the endless streams of hovers, barges and sky-trains.

The holo zoomed out, and now they could see the 'burbs and the threads that connected them to the city. It hovered like that for a moment, perfect and serene, before the 'burbs started to shiver and bob. Just the outer ones at first, looking like they were ducking about on a vicious swell. Then a fire broke out in an outer 'burb, and its bridge snapped. Police and firefighting hovers swarmed the area.

Even as the fire came under control, the rest of the 'burbs started to shake and bob, the movement flowing inwards like a tide. More fires sprang up, more bridges snapped and more firefighting hovers swarmed, while others fled inwards, towards the city and away from the chaos.

The first 'burb fell.

It plummeted out of the sky, breaking up as it went, buildings and tethers crumbling like a biscuit. The man bent to look closer at the tiny, tiny specks falling with them. Obligingly, the holo zoomed in, until the specks became faces, with arms and legs flailing as they fell.

He jerked back.

The view zoomed out again. More and more of the 'burbs were falling now, more buildings were breaking up and more people fell to their deaths, until Cumulus City sat alone in the sky.

It was quiet and still. The man leaned back in.

As if his breath was a tidal wave, the city began to sway, and then shake, until hovers poured out of the city like rivers, and were still pouring out of it, when it began to fall. Not a sudden drop like the 'burbs, but in fits and starts, the outer edges crumbling, debris from the skytowers narrowly missing the hovers as they fled.

The view changed, the camera pointing downwards, following the trail of debris through clouds and cold air, down to the mountains below.

Wreckage littered the valleys, plascrete and plasteel, bridges, hovers, buildings and bodies, so many bodies, mangled and torn and bleeding. Mercifully, the camera kept moving, through the earth, past roots and rock and clay, until it reached something else, a cavern buried deep beneath the earth.

Whatever this place was, it was eerie and quiet. But soon the whole room throbbed with the beat of a mechanical heart the size of a mountain, long and slow and deep.

The camera went further, plunging into darkness as it followed the beat. The heart, a shiny black dish the diameter of the city above, was massive and covered in symbols he could not recognise and coloured lights that pulsed in the darkness, in time with the heartbeat. Most of the lights were dark, their pulse gone, but a few remained, a fading orange, their pulse smooth and steady.

As they watched, one of the lights flickered and died, and then another followed it, and another and another. From somewhere, a klaxon screamed, and the holo rushed back to the surface as the city crashed on top of it.

The holo faded.

DO YOU WANT MORE HERO?

I love keeping in touch with my readers, it's the second-best thing about being a writer (writing being the first best). Every fortnight (or thereabouts), I send out a newsletter with details about upcoming offers, new releases and extra special projects.

If you sign up for the mailing you'll receive exclusive behind-the-scenes extras, such as:

- free short stories
- deleted and alternate scenes from The Hero Rebellion
- previews of my upcoming books
- pancakes
- quizes
- and much, much more!

Sign up here
www.belindacrawford.com/newsletter

ACKNOWLEDGMENTS

There are the usual suspects to thank such as Odyssey Books, with whom *Hero* was first published, and my editor, Brendan Carney, who plucked *Hero* out of the slush pile. Then there's Tracy M. Joyce, friend, fellow author and unofficial mentor, who is a fount of wisdom and practical advice.

I'd also like to thank the Australian Society of Authors (ASA) who in 2013 granted me one of twelve places in their annual mentorship program, which is funded by the Copyright Agency's Cultural Fund. Another thank you goes to Julia Stiles, my mentor during the ASA program, who helped me whip Hero into shape.

Like all good things, I've saved the most important thank you for last. To Mum and Chuck, who provided me with the time, space and financial support to find and then do the thing I loved (which would be writing books, in case you were wondering), thank you. A lot.